THE TROUBLE
WITH
RED LIPSTICK

K.J. DIXON

Booktrope Editions
Seattle, WA 2015

COPYRIGHT 2015 K.J.DIXON

This work is licensed under a Creative Commons Attribution-Noncommercial-No Derivative Works 3.0 Unported License.

Attribution — You must attribute the work in the manner specified by the author or licensor (but not in any way that suggests that they endorse you or your use of the work).

Noncommercial — You may not use this work for commercial purposes.

No Derivative Works — You may not alter, transform, or build upon this work.

Inquiries about additional permissions
should be directed to: info@booktrope.com

Cover Design by Michelle Fairbanks
Edited by Andie Gibson

This is a work of fiction. Names, characters, places, brands, media, and incidents are either the product of the author's imagination or are used fictitiously. Any resemblance to similarly named places or to persons living or deceased is unintentional.

PRINT ISBN: 978-1-5137-0456-2
EPUB ISBN: 978-1-5137-0506-4
Library of Congress Control Number: 2015917610

Acknowledgments

This book would never have been written and produced without the support of many—for whom I'm eternally grateful.

Jay Schaefer, you're an awesome book consultant, editor and friend. You've been one of my loudest cheerleaders, even when I was being stubborn and throwing adult temper tantrums. Your patience is endless, and your encouragement has kept me writing. Booktrope family members Andie Gibson and Samantha March, you've saved me from burying this manuscript under a tree in my back yard next to my puppy's leftover milk bones. Thank you for your keen observations and for digging the characters in this story. It's a wonder that I ever passed any of my Language Arts classes in high school without the two of you. The lovely Michelle Fairbanks has allowed me to worry the hell out of her for months without end about the placement of alphabet letters and tubes of lipstick on the book cover. Thank you for being a brilliant artist and for not strangling me when I couldn't make up my mind! And to my supportive friend and trusted advisor G.E. Johnson—I don't think we could have pulled it together without you.

My family and friends have provided an amazing support system for me and have served as my beta readers, unpaid personal assistants, unlicensed therapists, voluntold public relations consultants and soundboards. I'm forever indebted to them all, but I owe a special thanks to Adonness and Chiquita for always reading everything I've ever written and for giving me their honest feedback seasoned with plenty of encouragement. For holding on to me real tight and making me feel loved throughout this process, I appreciate all, but especially Mama and John, Daddy, Kim, Gina, Terry, Shawn, Simone, TC, Nina, Teresa, Taqua, Robert, Cherie, Charna, Barbie, Keisha J., Keisha C., Tonya, Annette,

Cherrie, Lashea, Ebony, and Sid P. Much love to each of you in a very special way.

Bree, I can't thank you enough for saying "You can do it Mommy" each time you caught me looking frustrated in front of my computer. Keep reading everything you can (but you'd better not pick up this book until you're at least twenty-five years old). I love you more than words could ever begin to explain.

And Lord, thank you for blessing me with a gift and for ordering each step of my path. I'll never take any of this for granted.

xoxo

For Mama and Bree

Emily

Help the Bear

DIABETES CAN KISS my black ass.

Who's to say when I will leave this earth, or for what reason, except for sweet Jesus? It damn sure isn't these people, and I have no intention of living like I'm already dead. Every week they wheel somebody else out of here on a stretcher, but more often than that, I've seen the residents around this place waste their last few days away by eating meals that taste like crackers and never being able to drink any real juice that contains real sugar. Most of them probably die from an artificial sweetener overdose. Or from loneliness, or worse—they start believing that they are as invalid as everyone treats them. That's half of the reason why I'd rather live here than with one of my know-it-all children. They talk about me like I've already gone on to glory, or sometimes worse, like I am a child incapable of thinking with good sense. I managed to raise their asses without causing any visible damage and I do not appreciate having those nappy-headed crumb snatchers I birthed try to think up all my thoughts for me.

Hell to the naw. I need a boss about as much as I need another asshole.

What I could really use is one of those power wheelchairs like the ones the commercial says to order from the "Scooter Store," and for somebody to teach me sign language so I can have some better conversations. Besides, all my children ever understood in the past were curse words anyway and, unfortunately, now that seems to be all they understand. I think it's a very sad thing when you can't just tell your children to sit down, but instead, you have to turn up your volume and yell "sit your ass down!" They were born with thick skulls. That's a paternal gene.

And speaking of Frog, Mr. Paternity himself, it was only a hot minute after I got him in the ground (and was looking forward to spending his check) that I had my own stroke. Everybody knows that God don't like ugly, but I couldn't help being mad at the timing. I think even our kids knew Frog and I were waiting to see who would die first. Now he's gone and I can't even talk or move well. It feels like he and Jesus have played a mean trick on me.

Hold on.

Shit.

I'm sorry for thinking that.

But as much as I love the Lord, I do not profess to completely understand His ways. My Big Mama forced me to go to church every Sunday and made me sit through all those hours of choir practice during the week and there are still a lot of questions I can't answer about Jesus. I was a teenager before I realized that church hours were the time for her to get a free babysitter and do all of her screwing when I walked home early because I started my period and caught her on top of the insurance man with her face down and her behind up in the air. Besides, on Monday through Saturday, I couldn't ever tell any difference between the ones that went to church and the ones that didn't.

Speaking of church, Antioch Atlanta Baptist is where I believe my middle child can be found at the moment. I'm looking forward to Karen bringing me some Sunday dinner today. And she better not step her dumb blonde-on-the-inside behind in here without something good, and, hopefully, some new shoes for me. The sneakers I'm wearing are turning brown on the toe part. For her to be a doctor, she doesn't seem to express enough concern for the well-being of her mother. You would think that my having a stroke would be enough, but I have to damn near pretend to be blind and deaf in order for her to give me some real attention, like buying me some new glasses or taking me to get my hair trimmed and curled. I sometimes pray the Lord will allow me to have an intelligent conversation with her, but when you have had a Texas-sized stroke like the one that I had, then it's like somebody removes the antennae from your TV set and leaves you with nothing but static coming out and there's absolutely nothing that you can do about it.

A sound I wasn't expecting to hear makes me jump.

"Emily!" calls out a woman's voice that I don't recognize.

I squeeze my eyes shut for a full second, then turn around to see who called my name. When I do, I find a nurse with a nasty-looking neck looking down at me. I wanted to finish my damn nap in peace, and I am trying so hard, too hard, not to let my aggravation show on my face. The nurses here are getting to be a bit ridiculous. It should have been clear to anybody with a half a brain that I'm staring out of this window in order to think in peace. Alone. But I don't say that out loud. In fact, I don't say anything at all. I just raise my eyebrows at her to give her permission to speak.

She doesn't open her mouth quickly enough so I stomp my good foot.

"You didn't finish your applesauce, yet, Emily," the nurse with the nasty neck finally says. She's speaking too loudly, as though she's talking to a deaf person.

I look down at the Mott's container and spoon in my lap before shaking my head "no" back and forth at her. "My daughter brings me my dinner on Sundays."

"What did you say?" she asks, even more loudly this time.

"She said that her daughter, Karen, always brings her Sunday dinner," says a voice from another corner. "She should be here any minute now." I recognize the voice of Denise, my favorite nurse and probably the only real nurse who works here, who I hadn't even realized was listening, before I actually see her. "Besides," Denise continues, "Ms. Turnipseed doesn't like that sugar-free stuff."

I could kiss her for speaking up for me. There is a God! I've been missing Denise ever since she was transferred to the North Tower. I hadn't even noticed her standing over there in the other back corner of the dining room.

"But her diet plan says otherwise," says the nurse with the nasty neck.

"Give her family a few more minutes to show up, Gladys. I'm floating today. I'll make sure she gets her medicine with her meals. You can skip this patient," Denise says while squeezing me on the knee. I nod my head in agreement, as if someone asked me my opinion.

I want to return to my thoughts when Nasty Neck and Denise both leave me in peace, but it's nearly impossible after having been interrupted. I wheel myself back to my room, and it looks as though I arrived just in time to catch some new drama going on with Alice, my neighbor across the hall. Watching her drama is better than watching daytime soap operas, or maybe even the movies. And actually, the West wing of the Derbyshire Manor assisted living facility has been nothing short of a live comedy show all day long. I often feel like I'm in the middle of a Tyler Perry play instead of living as a resident here. And the only thing I'm missing today is popcorn and a Coke. Except I can no longer eat popcorn because it exceeds the amount of allowable salt in my diet plan. Nor can I drink Coke without fear of slipping into a diabetic coma.

    Right this minute, Alice is pretending not to recognize her husband. She keeps asking him, "Who you?" I know she's putting on this little show because he forgot their anniversary she kept bragging about last week, but he doesn't know this is the cruel game she plays in order to get revenge. Alice had spent the whole day waiting for her flowers to be delivered. Every time the front door opened she looked to see if it was a delivery man. Unfortunately, he's dabbing at his eyes with a handkerchief he keeps stuffing in his pocket and fishing right back out, which lets me know she's winning this game today. She and I both are looking at him hard, trying to determine if the tears in his eye sockets are real. I look past his eyes and onto the rest of him. He has a head full of gray hair and walks with a little bit of a limp, but even so, I find him to be a very handsome gentleman. Shoot, now he's speaking to her so softly that I can hardly hear. I scoot closer to the door. It's a shame that I can't see well enough to read lips. I used to be good at that. If I put on my regular glasses then I can't see close up. If I put on my reading glasses then I can't see my damn toes. My cheap-ass bifocals just give me a headache.

    Most residents of Derbyshire's West wing are still very active, and some even date one another. Who would have thought you could find yourself a boyfriend in a place for senior citizens? Some men will even spend their whole Social Security check by messing around trying to pay for trips to the in-house barber shop or on cards and teddy bears during Valentine's Day or on chocolate bunnies for Easter—all in the name of trying to entertain some company up in here. I wouldn't put it past some of the women too, if they're stupid enough to do it. Dating is an expensive business, even in the nursing home.

    Alice is actually one of the few women on this hallway with a husband who still lives at home. Most couples come here together, after their children get tired of trying to please them and ship them both off. But not Alice's family. And the more I watch her, the less I can blame them because Alice is mean as a snake. That much I, and everybody else around this place, know very well. And boy is she jealous! I don't take it personally when she bothers me because I know the reason she doesn't like me is because I'm pretty. I keep hearing I don't look a day over sixty. My hair is still long and thick (and would still be jet black if my daughters would get with the program and get me to the hair salon on a halfway regular basis so Betty can finally put some Clairol on these roots), and you have to look real hard to find wrinkles on my face. I'd be willing to bet that Alice's husband would think so too if he had the time enough in between managing his wife and his girlfriend to stop and take a good look at me. I once planned to drop my glasses in the hallway in front of his feet to give me an opportunity to start a conversation with him, but I couldn't get the damn wheelchair over the hump in my doorway fast enough. Before I knew it, he was out of the front door. I did, however, follow him to the window (wheels can move faster than legs in our ages and conditions) and peek out just in time to see him jump in the car with a red-headed lady that sure as hell wasn't his daughter (I know this because Alice loves to brag about her two boys and what a good job she did raising them both into lawyers, plus the woman didn't look anything like those boys). Her youngest son—the one who always wears tight pants—is usually here by this time on Sunday. The other son likes to wear tight shirts instead but he hardly visits his mother at all.

I caught my youngest daughter Tessa flirting with one of Alice's boys for a brief moment before she realized he wasn't into women. I believe she was looking too closely at his wallet to pay attention to his walk. Tessa has always been my favorite child even though I would never admit it out loud and everybody knows that a mother isn't supposed to have a favorite, but she's also the one who concerns me the most. I'm convinced she is the prettiest girl in the state of Georgia, and I'm not just saying that because she's my child. Her skin is the most beautiful shade of brown and it's smooth and flawless—reminds me coffee with two or three little cups of cream in it, and she has eyes so big and black she can make anybody's heart melt. She got this from me, of course. I would never say this out loud either, but Tessa is a real-life beauty queen without even trying. As far as I know, she doesn't even wear any make-up, except for occasionally some mascara. She inherited my dimples and long, thick black hair that she keeps trying to cut off. She knows how to play a man like a board game—Candy Land comes to mind because she licks them dry like suckers—but her only problem is that she will open up her legs to them faster than greased lightning.

On second thought, that's not her only problem.

You would think that a person who can be that tricky and conniving should be book smart too and be able to pass a teaching test on the first or at least the second time they try, but she's either too lazy or just afraid of failing to put some real effort into much of anything. She can be as mean as her daddy's mama too—and selfish! But no sir-ee Bob, that piece of DNA did not come from my side of the family. When she's in a good mood she is so much fun to be around. She got that part from me, too. It's amazing how you can look at your children and pick apart what they got from who.

I have spent many a day praying that Tessa will put her pretty head to good use and get herself a real teaching degree or certificate or whatever piece of paper you're supposed to have in order to teach mathematics to people's children before she suffocates all her brain cells to death with marijuana smoke. She has screwed somebody to get every real job she's had and has the nerve to think I can't figure it out. I think her daddy spoiled her into being stupid. Either that or all that television she watches is starting to rot her mind.

My thoughts are interrupted by a chocolate woman with blonde hair who pokes her head in the door and introduces herself as Mary. She explains she's been assigned to provide my care today. I swear these people who are in charge of our home can't keep people working here for longer than a week.

"Are you finished eating, Ms. Emily?" asks Mary.

I nod.

She pushes the medication cart into my room and props the door open with the kickstand. Mary then hands me a tiny cup that is fit only for mouthwash and pours in just enough water that it rises to fill the baby cup only half way. She carefully slides three pills over to me on the table and begins writing on her chart. I run out of water after the first damn pill. This is ridiculous—and feels like it's on the verge of being abuse. I wonder if I should call the lawyer from that television commercial that comes on every day during *One Life to Live* who always asks, "Are your loved ones being abused?" I wish I could remember the phone number to dial, but I don't. So I just pop myself on the lips and cough. Mary catches the hint.

"Still thirsty, Emily?" she asks. "Let me pour you a little more water."

I frown up my face when I see that she pours my "a little more water" into another medicine cup. And instead of swallowing the second pill, I silently protest by putting it under my tongue and take a second to consider my next move. I can also see Alice peeking at me from across the hall. Now I'm the one being watched like television. I narrow my eyes into slits and poke my tongue out at her. Mary stops writing on the chart. "Ms. Emily, I need for you to take your medicine, sweetie," she sings in her island-accent. I look at her and point to the pitcher of water. I should knock it onto the floor, as thirsty as I am. If I die from malnutrition or thirst or exhaustion, my family—no, make that my girls—hell, probably just Tessa—she's the one who's most need of some lawsuit money—will surely to goodness sue her Jamaican ass, or whatever she is. I look at Mary from head to toe and squint so that I can more closely examine that cheap jewelry that takes up every one of her fingers and half of her neck and ears and quickly decide that suing my nursing assistant will not likely win Tessa enough money to even buy new pantyhose. Hell, I'm the one who needs to think up a good reason to file a lawsuit on the nursing home so I can finally get a power wheelchair.

I try to speak. The word thirsty comes out of my mouth sounding more like "tata!"

For a moment, Mary looks confused. Her beautiful ebony skin wrinkles up into a single crease across her forehead. She's very pretty to me, but I think she thinks too slowly and appears to suffer from anxiety like half of the residents here because she's waving her hand back and forth as if to suggest she can take no more. So I keep going. I touch the water pitcher and try to pretend like I want to pour my own kiddie cup but I can't get my fingers to stretch around the handle. Instead, I push it enough to spill a splash of water out and onto the table. She looks pissed. I am halfway amused.

Across the hall, Alice's nosy ass jerks her foot to scratch her ankle and accidently lets her door fall shut. She's going to have to wait for Mary to make it to her side of the hallway before it is opened again. I smile. Mary frowns.

"Emily, you've already had two glasses of water and a Powerade this evening. You shouldn't be this thirsty after only sitting up in your room for two hours. My Lord, you act like you've run a marathon. I wonder if your diabetes medicine is working. I'm going to punch your finger to check your sugar. I'll be right back."

I try to open my mouth and convince her that really it's not necessary, that she should just pour me a glass of damn juice and skip the hard thinking, but nothing comes out except a grunt and she wastes no time leaving my room. I immediately push myself back on the bed and lie down on my left side. I feel a fart brewing and instead of holding my butt muscles together like a good little resident, I push out as hard as I can. At first, nothing comes out except for air. With another push, I feel the warm shit hit my Depends. Perfect. As if on cue, Mary steps back into the room. I lift my left leg and drag the right one open as best as I can. I throw back the sheet to make sure that she catches a good whiff. And right as according to plan, Mary drops the Gluco-pen on the floor and runs for another assistant and some cleaning supplies. My left toe kicks the Gluco-pen underneath the bed on the first try. Mary re-enters the room with a new girl whose name I cannot remember, but I always recognize those finger waves. She is sweet as pie and follows instructions well as she brings me a glass of Kool-aid the very first time I point at the water cup and raise my eyebrows up as high as I possibly can. It's red flavored and ice cold. God is good.

As I chomp down on the red ice, my mind quickly goes back to thinking about my middle daughter. Karen is only thirty-eight years old but she has accomplished so much professionally, and, according to *Atlanta Magazine*, is one of the best doctors in the city. She makes me proud in that way, but I wish she could let some of her common sense borrow from her smart pot, just a little bit. And wouldn't you know that as much as that girl has it going on, she carries a jealous streak in her! I still can't figure out where she got that from, because if I had to name my own faults the biggest one would have to be that I was absolutely conceited and hell on wheels at her damn age (and probably would still have been up until now except for the fact that saggy breasts and hair that is beginning to have more gray than black in it has a peculiar way of bringing a reality check along with it). I try to tell her she would feel better about herself if she tried losing a little weight but she gets mad every time I poke on her hips. She went to Florida A&M University on a full academic scholarship—thank you, Lord—and then had her way paid through medical school at Morehouse School of Medicine with one of those programs that makes you promise to work in a country town for four years and then you get to walk away debt free, but she doesn't seem any happier to me than regular folks with regular jobs and regular bills. All she talks about is how bad she is wanting a man, needing a man, wanting a man, needing a man, repeat and then repeat again. If you ask me, she should have gone to school to learn how to fix penises instead of vaginas and then maybe she could keep somebody. Karen is starving for attention and I pray to the Lord that she doesn't get herself in any trouble. If she really knew what I knew then she would take all that doctor money and make her own damn self happy. She could start by buying herself some real clothes and maybe some cute shoes and get rid of the ones with the heels that are worn down with the wire showing at the bottom. It wouldn't hurt for her to invest in some real makeup which she absolutely does need, because eating all of that bullshit as a teenager gave her bad skin and acne scars that make her forehead look like Swiss cheese. Can't no prescription for antibiotics stop bumps faster than Noxzema can, but she won't listen. And no I did not need to go to medical school in order to figure that out, but I'm her mama and I just know. But instead of listening to me when I offer her suggestions on how she can improve herself, she runs around with plain-looking white folks with no sense of style whatsoever and cries about being fat to whoever will listen and is trying to grow out her perm and go natural which I think could be okay except she keeps alternating back and forth between natural styles and weave and the textures just don't match. She dresses cheap and then tries to cover it up by carrying expensive pocket books. She also makes me sick but I love her in spite of herself even though she probably is the one who gave me the damn diabetes when she called herself taking care of me after my stroke. I think they teach doctors how to give people that shit in medical school.

 Now Patricia has more common sense than Karen and Tessa put together, but lacks the very-necessary self-confidence to go with it and has no excuse for the lack of judgment she demonstrates in her day-to-day life. She's the only one of my girls who is married but her sex life might just be the most boring. She sincerely believes she's hiding the fact that she's outgrown her husband from me and the rest of the world, but as far as I'm concerned, the only person who is unaware of that fact is Gary, and that's only because he's too busy out in the streets to notice. I'm still waiting to get a good return on my investment in her because she's the one I put the most effort into raising. She already makes six figures by playing with the government's computers and claiming she's fixing them, but then she wants to reinvent herself by starting and stopping a catering business every other month. What I know that she can't seem to figure out is that feeding people won't make them love you, and she's dying on the inside from sheer boredom. Her husband is a good man overall but he's controlling and he's also a whore. A major problem in my mind is that he always thought he was prettier than her. I don't like that. I used to call him Mr. Too-Cool but he doesn't look so cool anymore ever since one of his front teeth got knocked out in what he claims was a motorcycle accident. (The new tooth is too big for his mouth and never looked natural.) And whether he is a real cool daddy or not, she was the one that chose to get married in her senior year of high school before she had a chance to figure out who she is and what she likes. I believe her when she says she was a virgin until the day she got married. She was too busy feeling sorry for herself because she had a different daddy from the other two and swears she got short-changed somewhere down the line. She can go to all the sorority meetings she wants to and cook up enough chicken to put Colonel Sanders out of business, but she hasn't anything to prove to anybody except herself. What she doesn't know is that she has had life better than anybody else who ever grew out of one of Frog's sperm, and that the younger version of me was probably a lot more patient and careful as a mother than what the other two experienced. She needs to stop telling the people at work all of her personal business and just work on making peace with her own identity and then maybe her family. Patricia depresses her damn self and could stand to take one of the happy pills that they push down my throat in here.

 As smart as all three of my girls are and could be, I can't help but wonder why the Lord didn't bless them with much of my common sense. They all have such special potential, and their talents vary widely, but it's almost all for not because they waste it with their poor-ass decisions. I no longer judge parents when their children grow up to be non-productive members of society. I'm starting to really believe mine chose to get dumb by their damn selves. I haven't been to anybody's college but I know I have way more sense than all of them and their degrees put together. And while I may not have ever been a contender for the Mother-of-the-Year Award, I did not teach them neither by direct instruction nor by example to do half of the stupid shit I see them get involved in. Matter of fact, I raised them to be strong. I can remember plenty of days when I covered up my lips, which I had chewed up because of bad nerves, with red lipstick, just to make a point to them that you can never show the world that you're weak. If you do, then it'll eat you up alive.

Keeping a marriage and family together while facing impossible odds like having a husband who strays and too many mouths and not enough food will shorten anybody's patience. Sometimes--most of the time—the best answer I could give them when they started asking questions was "because I fucking said so," or "stay out of grown folks' business." Patricia, especially, had a knack for asking dumb questions that I either didn't have the answer to, or even if I did, I couldn't figure out how in the world to explain it to a child. Karen would have rather talked to her imaginary friends in her books than to spend a lot of time up under me, and Tessa never seemed to give a damn about much of anything, including the beatings and good cussings I gave her for being so damn fast.

I raised my children the way I was taught, by example. Isn't that what we all do? Do unto others what was done unto us? Well, that's how I operated, at least. I gave out more orders than I did hugs, and when everything else failed, I beat the hell out of them. One time, I locked Tessa in the closet for six hours. The first two were because I found out she had tried to change all the F's on her report card into A's (she used a black pen to make another line down the right-hand side of the first two F's, then switched to blue ink to finish the last two letters after the black had run out) and it was all I could do not to kill her. The last four hours were because I'd forgotten that I'd put her narrow ass in there.

These are the things my children will never forget. They won't, however, remember the times I sacrificed sleep for an entire month so I could clean houses during the day and clean office buildings at night, just so they could have enough lunch money to take to school and to be able to participate in all those extracurricular activities they wanted to do in order to try to keep up with the other kids. How unfortunate they won't remember the times when they all had colds and nobody could breathe, that I stayed up watching them sleep and rubbing Vicks VapoRub on their necks just to make sure their little chests continued to rise and fall all night. Too bad and so sad if they didn't notice that I had to patch up my own raggedy-ass pantyhose with clear nail polish so I could take what little money we had left to make sure they all had a fresh pair for church each Sunday. I did the best I could, and I really didn't care if anybody thought otherwise. I'd rather my children see me as being crazy and mean than soft and vulnerable.

A knock on the metal door frame makes me jump. I look up and see my sister, who comes into my bedroom just as Mary and Finger Waves are exiting stage left with plastic bags that are filled with soiled towels and Depends that are courtesy of yours truly. I am happy to see Camilla—the one person in this world I can talk to without getting tired.

Camilla sits down on my bed and frowns up her face, letting me know that the smell of my shit has not yet drifted out of the room. She smells sweet—like an orange blossom.

"What are you doing, Emily? Giving these people a hard time, as usual?"

I shrug my good shoulder.

She sniffs the air. "Did you shit your bed?"

I do my best to give her an even smile—I'm trying really hard to make both corners of my mouth turn up in equal amounts.

"You ought to be ashamed of yourself," she says. "Karen's money won't stop them from putting your old trifling behind out of here," she says, then laughs before adding, "You know, Emily, you never have given a damn what people think about you."

"These people should have figured out by now who they're dealing with," I say as clearly as I possibly can. "I may have some troubles here and there, but I'm a strong woman, not some puny ass weakling."

My sister, one of the few people who can understand my muffled sounds, always knows what's going to come out of my mouth next. She's just waiting for me to form the words and roll them off my tongue because she loves to hear me say them, even if I can barely shape the phrases. I choose not to deny her the pleasure, so I continue.

"If you ever come upon me and a bear having a fight in the woods, you don't need to help me. You'd better help the bear."

Contessa

Fifty Dollars

PUSSY IS NOT FREE. Period. No, fuck that. Exclamation point.
It's for this very reason that I'm wondering what I should tell Mr. Turner that I want from him for Christmas when he shows up here in a few minutes. I could go easy on him and just let him place a few one-hundred dollar bills into a card. But then again, the Honda could use some new brakes and tires. And let's also not forget that the little pink and brown Louis Vuitton bag with the tiny LVs all over it has recently gone on sale! No wait. These fumes must be getting to me. I'd better get some more damn brakes on that car.

    I've been cleaning and thinking about shit like this for the past couple hours—cleaning and thinking hard has become a Saturday morning ritual. First I start by using the vacuum cleaner with which I symbolically suck up all my bills, then comes the Fabuloso that I pour into a bucket of hot water for mopping, which for some reason makes me think about squeezing test answers out of my brain and earning the teaching certificate that the county says I need to have earned by the end of next school year. Next comes the Febreeze spray all over the cloth furniture which makes me wonder how long this wet weather will last. I swear this has been the warmest, rainiest November I've ever seen. I keep looking out of windows to see if animals are getting ready to start lining up, two by two. Dusting, mopping, vacuuming and straightening are always on my list of things to do every Saturday morning, but today, I'm paying extra special attention to the dusty cracks and corners in my apartment. Like Mama always says—no man likes a nasty ass woman. Not even the old ones. And as much as I hate to admit it, I can think my best when I'm slinging some bleach and a mop. Maybe the fumes help me to think. Inhalation tends to be a very effective method of relaxation. For me anyway.

I light some Vanilla Musk incense and stand still by the front door of my condo to take a look around. Everything looks sparkly clean and smells like bleach. This will be the first time I've allowed him in my home. This also will be the first time, I'm sure, his old butt is expecting to get some booty from me. The past few weeks have been filled with some really nice dinner dates to Ray's on a River, Oceanaire, Ocean Prime, and probably a few other places I'm sure I've forgotten. We've talked on the phone a few times in the evenings when he can get free to call me, but mostly, we text. And to be a mature gentleman (I have never asked him his age but I'm guessing somewhere between sixty and sixty-five) he seems to know how to work his smartphone better than me, but I realize that isn't saying much. The phones these days are smarter than we are, but I like that he's cool and stays current. And he didn't seem to mind buying me another one when I threw mine out the window because I couldn't figure out how to turn off the voice recognition feature and make the phone just dial a damn number. He had it mailed to my P.O. Box at work.

Hiring me for a real teaching position at Cedarview was the first thing he did that landed him in my good graces. I had done about two or three months of substitute teaching after I was let go from my ten-year job at the state following a bad case of the governmental budget reduction let-gos. Administrative assistants just didn't make the final cut, no matter how smart you were and how many words you could type per minute. Although I wasn't exactly qualified to teach full time by Fulton County standards (even though I hold an associate degree in Criminal Justice from Atlanta Metropolitan College and I can speak better English and add numbers better than ninety-nine percent of the teacher's I've met lately) I had heard I could still do some substitute teaching. I have always loved children, although the grown-ass adolescents with developing breasts and dicks that disguise themselves as high-schoolers no longer qualify in my mind as children and I was happy to start working at Cedarview after a very short interview with Principal Mark Turner.

I could tell right away he was interested in hiring me for more than teaching math. In fact, he had all the dead-ringer giveaways: gray hair, eyes glued to my behind and a wedding ring on his left hand. I'm not sure he even heard me recite a bit of the qualifications I had rehearsed after Karen had written them for me, but I left his office that day thanking God and heaven above for blessing me with a nice, firm behind and a trial run at team-teaching. Three months into laughing at those kids in between shouting at them to shut their damn mouths during the fifty-five minutes that each class is required to sit in the classroom, Mrs. Brown decided she was going to make her maternity leave her full time job and *voila*! I was absolutely ecstatic and easily ignored the whispers of the other teachers' aides with whom I had already had conversations divulging my teaching credentials, or lack of, depending on how you looked at it.

The congratulatory bouquet that he sent to my house was a nice touch. I had been rushing out of the house to try to make it to the post office in time to mail off some bills because they close early on Saturdays. When I opened the door and saw an assortment of tulips and lilies bound together in a purple glass vase, I didn't even stop to think about who they might have been from. It had been such a long time since I had received a professional bouquet of flowers, and I don't count the ones that Kenny, my last boyfriend, used to like to pick up from Publix. When I read the card, signed "A gentleman admirer," the only thing I could really think was this man has some class.

I don't know why, but I have never been the type of woman to do a whole lot of falling in love, and the idea of it has never been that appealing to me. The closest thing I can really think of to having ever experienced it was my boyfriend right after high school, Randy. I don't think I would have had to have him so much if he wasn't such a successful street salesman and was damn near a neighborhood celebrity. And even with him, after the parties and nights I couldn't remember were over, and after the baby mamas finally stopped calling my phone to curse me and hang up, the romance was over within a good eighteen months. What I can say about that relationship was that it taught me a valuable lesson: Every man you date or marry will give you some bullshit in varying degrees, so the least you can do is have a man who is able to compensate you some for your pain and suffering. At this point in my life, I don't even have the desire to get married. Most of my girlfriends who are married are miserable.

My mama was stupid when it came to Frog but at least we had a daddy. That's more than what a lot of kids who grew up in our neighborhood could say. And regardless of what my sisters think about him, I know he loved me the most. He always did. He even told me. I was his favorite daughter because I kept his secrets. For example, I remember the time I was walking home from the corner store one afternoon after Mama had given me some money to buy her some baking powder. She had told me to keep the change and buy whatever I wanted. My best friend, Ashley, and I were headed back home when I saw Frog's car zoom past me then slow down before pulling over on the side of the road into a brush, next to a fence full of kudzu and ivy. The back of a woman's head in the front seat was visible all the way through the rear window from behind the car, which is where I was standing and staring with my mouth hanging open. I knew this was not the back of my mama's head. I heard my dill pickle-flavored potato chips and red Faygo soda leave my fingers and fall into the grass beside my feet.

Frog rolled the passenger side window down after exchanging a few brief words with Jessica Rabbit. When it let down, I still had to wait a second or two for the cigarette smoke to clear out of the car before I could see their faces clearly. She was a thick, curvy woman wearing a light green dress that reminded me of springtime, even though the winter cold had barely broken. Her dress had a plunging neckline and showed her buxom breasts without her even having to lean down. Her greasy hair was long and thick, and the color was a cross between dirty red and brown. It had looked awkward to me, because the curls were too tight at the end, sort of like she had been rolling it up at night with pink sponge rollers. Her eyes were light gray and reminded me of a cat.

"Why are we stopping?" Ashley had wanted to know.

I ignored her question and instead turned to Frog and posed my own. "Daddy, who is this?"

He ignored my question, and asked me one right back. "What are you two gals doing walking down this street today?"

That was a stupid question, because I always walked to the store with Ashley whenever we finished doing our chores and our mamas let us out of the house. Jessica Rabbit looked town at the floor mats in daddy's Crown Victoria. It was then that I noticed that her red lipstick was smudged. To me, she looked like her mouth was bleeding.

He didn't wait for me to answer. "Y'all come on and get in this car. It's too hot to be walking around out here like you're two throwaways."

But it couldn't have been any warmer than sixty, maybe seventy degrees that day at the most. I remember because I still had on my favorite blue and red polka dot sweater. I stood still, but Ashley grabbed the door handle closest to us and tried to get in.

"Tessa, show your friend how to go around and get in on the other side of the car and stop staring like you're stupid. You know I still haven't gotten around to fixing the door back there on the right. And be careful while you're doing it—these other cars ride so fast down this street that they won't know they hit you until you're already gone to see Jesus."

And that was typical. Something was always broken on Frog's car. The reason for that was because all his cars had always belonged to someone else before they came into his car shop needing to be fixed. Much later on I realized that all of his women had belonged to someone else before they came to see him for a fixing, too, but I kept that information to myself.

I blink the memories of my deceased daddy out of my mind so that I can concentrate on lighting this display of what feels like a million more tiny candles, all for the sake of creating the ambiance of a real romance. I am actually looking forward to seeing Mr. Turner's face when he sees the Victoria's Secret slip I'm wearing. I also hope he has taken his Viagra or Cialis or Levitra or whatever because I refuse to work hard just to get him to stand up. I also hope he doesn't take a long time to get there because I want to get him out and cleaned up for a good night's rest so that I can meet Eulinda to study for the teacher's certificate tomorrow. Still, there is something very enticing to me about a man who really wants me. I love the way he looks at my body. Maybe before his forty-fifth birthday he could have been called a five or six out of a scale of ten, but now, he'd be lucky if anybody scored him a three. The older I get, the more I like who likes me. And something about his five-foot-seven, maybe two-hundred-pound frame and glasses and creamy skin, not-old-looking-yet body really turns me on. He looks smart. But not school-boyish-all-the-girls-are-after-me-because-I'm-handsome–and-educated-and-would-make-some-pretty-children-smart. I hate those. That's the kind Karen wishes she had. She doesn't know what kind of headaches she's really in for when she gets one.

Where in the world is my R. Kelly mixed CD? Maybe this is a sign I should put on some other type of music or maybe none at all. I hope he's not expecting to hear any Al Green or Marvin Gaye because the farthest back I will go is to Keith Sweat. Mood is just as important as the action but I don't want him to think I'm setting up a porn scene. If it's your first time doing it, I think a woman should make it appear subtle. Like the sex "just happens." Ten minutes later, I am in my bedroom thinking to hell with subtleties but this time looking for my jazz instrumental, the one that I got at the local concert that Eulinda hosted in her backyard, when the doorbell rings. I glance at the clock. As usual, he's very prompt.

I open the door to find him standing in a gray pin-striped suit with a tie around his neck and a huge grin. He also has what looks like about five or six red roses in his hands. I wonder how he managed to leave the house with that suit on without his wife suspecting anything. I look down to try and see if he's wearing his wedding band but the flowers are covering the skin on his left ring finger. "Hey, Mr. Turner," I say, while tightening my robe. I can feel a mild breeze in the air that rushes past my open door.

"Tessa, you're even gorgeous in a bathrobe." He gives me a quick kiss on the cheek before almost stepping on my toe trying to get into my house. I look around just to see if my nosy neighbors have noticed that I have a visitor.

I smile before taking the flowers out of his hand and lead him through the foyer and toward the kitchen. I can feel his eyeballs burning a hole through the back of my robe. He doesn't even have to be standing close to me for me to smell and recognize his Old Spice.

"Anything good cooking?" He looks around for signs of baking, broiling or even microwaving. I start to feel guilty for not offering to feed him, or for not even thinking about this ahead of time. Then I change my mind. I am not his wife. He should have eaten before he left his damn house. I can't be responsible for everything.

"No, but let me pour you some wine."

"Okay, but give me something nice and easy. I'm not much of a drinker, you know."

Yes, I did know. He had only sipped sweet tea while watching me enjoy margaritas with my seafood on the two occasions that we had eaten together. I pour him a little taste of pinot noir from my glass. Then I take a tiny sip from his glass before pressing my mouth against his to share the taste with him. "How do you like?" I ask.

He doesn't need to answer—I feel a small bulge begin to press against me through his pants. Watching him in his state of arousal turns me on a little bit. Seeing the way he looks at me, I figure this is the right time to discuss a few things that have been on my mind. Square a few pieces of business away before we become too distracted.

I move his hand from my behind up to my head and direct him to stroke my hair. "Do you like the way I look for you tonight?"

"Of course I do, Ms. Tessa. You are such a sexy breath of fresh air." I now can see his bare ring finger. The print of a wedding band is still there, of course.

"You don't mind helping me to keep staying nice for you, right?"

"No, baby, of course I don't." He pets my hair as if he's trying to keep from messing it up, sort of stroking the hairs back in place. I don't think he understands.

"Then I'm sure you won't mind giving me what I need to keep everything nice for you."

"I sure don't," he says and begins to unzip his pants.

"I think about five-hundred every two weeks should do it then," I say, before pecking him on the lips. "We can start with maybe Wednesday afternoon getaways, and every now and then on the weekends if you think that you can get away from the house without her noticing."

"Five-hundred? Dollars, you mean?"

"Yes, sugar. That's all," I say, before helping him to remove the buttons from his shirt.

"Every two weeks, did you say?"

I sit up straight but keep my fingers on his shirt buttons. "Yes," I say, while making firm eye contact.

"You mean just give it to you?"

I feel him stiffen. Now I stop with the buttons. I wonder what the fuck there is not to understand. "Yes, I do mean give it to me. You can just leave it around the house when you come. Or even deposit the money into my account. I'll even give you the routing number to my Bank of…"

"Tessa, I don't have that kind of money. I have children I live with, a mortgage, hell, a family!" His words are sharp but his voice is whiney and pathetic. "I'm still paying child support on the other two that are fourteen and sixteen. Or did you forget that I am a man with responsibilities? I don't mind helping you out with little things here and there, like the cell phone and what not, but I can't afford to be…"

I cut him off right here. "What the hell did you think this was? Love?"

He just looks at me like he doesn't speak English.

"Better yet, let me ask you another question. Have I ever asked for you to leave your home?"

"Of course not."

"For the record, I wasn't planning to. But I know you pay your wife's damn bills every month and her dry ass apparently isn't giving you shit!" I jerk my robe back up on my shoulders and tighten the belt before standing up. He stares at me and blinks a few times.

"Baby, I didn't mean to upset you. It's just that you're, um, well, surprising me with this kind of talk."

"Oh, really? Well guess what? You're actually surprising me with yours."

"Calm down. I really do like you, sugar," he says, lowering his voice. "Come sit down on my lap and let daddy whisper something nice in your ear." He tugs on the pocket of my bathrobe.

"Are you going to whisper me a few hundred dollar bills?"

"I can't do that right now."

"Like I said, we have a problem."

"Speak for yourself, Tessa. All of my bills are paid on time, I just don't have the type of discretionary cash that you're asking me for. It sounds like you're the one who may be having some problems, dear."

"I think it's time for you to go home, Mr. Turner."

His face balls up into a frown. It's an ugly one with lots of wrinkles around his eyes and mouth. "What in the world are you? A prostitute?"

"Fuck you."

"Listen, Tessa, baby. Let's not let this get ugly. But I've just never been asked to do anything like that before. First of all, you're not even my girlfriend."

I walk over to the doorway in between the kitchen and the dining room and point at the door.

"Here," he says, pulling a wad of cash out of his pocket and dropping it on the coffee table. "I have about fifty dollars on me right now. Let's not end the night like this." Then he actually pulls a small penis—maybe two or three inches long—out of his pants and shakes it at me. I am appalled.

"Get your mother fucking old ass out of my house right now!"

He's moving, but not fast enough.

I grab his blazer off my coatrack and throw it out of the door first. Then I pick up his left shoe and toss it down over the balcony.

He tucks his little penis back in and then pauses to shake his head at me before he hobbles out with only one shoe on his foot. I slam the door behind him.

I can hardly believe this shit. To have such a small dick, he has some very large balls.

I sit on my sofa and peek out of the blinds to make sure he gets in his car and leaves right away. As soon as he puts his BMW into reverse, I start rummaging through my kitchen drawers because I'm sure I left a small bag of marijuana round her somewhere in case of an emergency like this. I find it tucked away in the flour canister on the counter, but I'm disappointed to find there's only an itty bitty corner left in the small baggie. I find my cell phone and dial Steve's number. Ten minutes later, he delivers a fresh supply to my front door. He's breathing hard, I guess from running up the stairs.

"You're looking pretty, Tess. I hardly ever see you with any makeup on. I like those colors around your eyes. And it smells good in here. What you got—company coming over?"

"That's none of your business, my friend." I'm digging around in my purse to find some cash.

"You must still be dating those nerd jokers."

I pause to think about that. I look him in the eyes, which are hardly visible under his red baseball cap. "I like who likes me, Steve." I hand him fifty dollars.

"Oh yeah? Well I can't tell. I've been trying to get in your ear for a long time."

"I don't date salesmen."

"Girl, you hardly even give me any business anymore. I thought you might have found another supplier. I haven't heard from you in what? Six months?"

"I cut back."

"Got you," he says, looking at the cash. "Well, thanks for the business tonight. You can call me back later if you want to," he says, pulling my money right back out of his pocket and displaying it in his hand as if he's offering it back to me.

Am I being propositioned with sex in exchange for fifty dollars twice in one night? I find myself getting upset all over again.

"Goodnight, Steve."

"Let me know when you're ready for a real nigga."

"Like I said, goodnight."

I slam the door just to make a point and then sit down at my kitchen table to roll my joint. Not even three minutes later, the doorbell rings again. I open it to find Mrs. Brown, my seventy-year old neighbor, standing outside.

"Tessa, I was coming by to see if everything was alright with you."

"Yes ma'am, I'm doing okay. Why do you ask?"

"Because young ladies have to be careful how they conduct themselves at this day and age. There are all kinds of people out here, not to mention all kinds of diseases."

"I'm sorry. I have no idea what we're talking about."

"I just saw two men leave your door in the last hour."

"And?"

"And you should know better than to be seeing more than one man at a time. Intimacy is special, and should be reserved for people who are married."

"Since you asked, Mrs. Brown, I will tell you that I didn't have sex with either one of those men tonight."

"It doesn't matter. If you keep letting them come here then you will, eventually."

"I don't think you're in a position to tell me that."

"I've been living for a long time, and I know how this type of thing works."

"Oh, do you? Well if you know how it works so well, then maybe you should be home having sex with your own husband right now instead of policing my company through your window."

She sighs. Her chest rises and falls underneath her nightgown. She should be wearing a bra. "You need to be careful, young lady. I've been your age before."

"I know you have. Unfortunately, I'm going to have to hear about your memories some other time. I must tell you goodnight now so I can get ready for work in the morning."

"Hold on. Let me leave this with you." Before I know it, she presses a Jehovah's Witness brochure entitled "The Sanctity of Marriage" into my hand. There is a picture of a man and woman hugging very closely. There is also a lovely, light purple, watermarked cross behind them in the background.

"I do believe in marriage. Matter of fact, I believe in it so much that I feel obligated to tell you that I think you must be breaching your wifely duty to tend to your own husband. Mr. Brown seems to be working later and later these days. Sometimes he even gets in the door at the same time I do when I come home from all of my whorish dates. Does the furniture store where Mr. Brown works close at one and sometimes two o'clock in the morning?"

Her bottom lip drops down.

"Don't worry about answering that question, but tell me this instead. When did you start driving a red Jeep Cherokee? Because I've been seeing one lately that's always parked outside at about the same time that you go to Bible study on Wednesday evenings."

That same lip drops a little bit wider.

"Good night, Mrs. Brown. And thank you for the advice," I say before closing the door.

I pour myself a glass of cognac before I finish rolling my joint. Then I walk over to my sunroom to plop down on my wicker furniture and puff on it while I stare at the moon that's right outside my bay window. Halfway through smoking it I decide that I've had enough, and extinguish the remainder in my red and black ladybug ashtray. I exhale my last puff of smoke onto a purple orchid that never did bloom anymore after I brought it home from the store, and then I blow out each and every goddamn candle in my apartment before tying a scarf around my hair and getting into bed.

Karen

Christmas Lights

I HAVE BEEN GAINING, on average, five pounds a year, since my thirty-fifth birthday. I am not in denial about that. If I weren't on the border of being fat, then it might not be so much of an issue. If I didn't eat to feel better, then it could be less of a concern for my jeans. But at five feet and four inches tall, one hundred sixty pounds and on the verge of turning thirty-nine years old in January, I can't afford any more caloric intake as a result of my depression-induced binges. I won't have two or three cupcakes today, even though Lord knows I could use them, but I do think I deserve just one. I will start my diet tomorrow. In fact, I'm lucky enough to have just scored a parking space right in front of Sugarplum Bakery on this ridiculously packed and impossible to park one-way street in downtown Atlanta. That must mean it's the Lord's will for me to have this cupcake.

I can't find any change in the bottom of my purse to throw in the parking meter so I check the numbers on the screen to see if I can get by with the change that was left in there by the person parked here before me. A flashing meter screen that says "2:00 min" convinces me I have enough time to make it in and out of Sugarplum with my coveted cupcake.

As soon as my entry into the shop sets off the door chimes, I am greeted by the store owner, Tiffany. Her pink and black apron covers up her clothes. Even with the apron, her perfect silhouette is visible. The tied apron accentuates her waistline. I hate her.

But, as usual, I greet her with a friendly smile. "Hey, Tif!"

"Hey, doc! Good so see you, girl. You ain't been in here in a few days. Thought you quit me," she says with a South Georgia accent that smothers her words.

"No, honey, been trying to count Weight Watchers points. Unsuccessfully, as you can see."

"What you doing on some Weight Watchers? You don't need that mess. You look good to me. What are you having today? You still on your red velvet kick? You should try my new caramel banana pecan pie. I just started selling them this week."

I look around at every baked good on display in this shop. It's beautifully decorated in pink and black, too. I beg to differ with her about me needing to try anything new, but I don't bother to speak. She continues.

"We are in the South, honey. Don't no man want no woman without some meat on her bones. You know that. Are you still single?"

I blink hard before answering. "Yes."

"It's time for us to do something about that. I know so many single men in Atlanta who would love to have a woman like you."

I wonder exactly what she means by that, but I don't dare ask. Instead, I point to a delicious-looking red velvet swirl cake in the front of the display case. She removes it from the case and places it in a pink and black paper box.

"You single because you want to be," she continues with the unsolicited advice. "Ain't no woman like you in America got no business without a man. Probably can't nobody meet your standards."

I want to correct her English but she keeps talking before I can interrupt.

"What you like? I got a brother who's been to college. He a teacher down in Macon. Let me introduce you next time he comes to Atlanta."

"No, thank you. I hate blind dates."

"But wait, he's my brother. You didn't even let me tell you about him. He's a good, country, Southern man."

"I really appreciate the offer, but no thank you."

"Listen, girl. He can change tires, build walls out of Georgia clay, and milk cows. Probably all at the same time!" She laughs.

I smile politely and shake my head no.

"Well, maybe you'll change your mind later." Her hand moves over to another dessert tray and hovers above it. "So, do you want to try the caramel banana pecan?"

"It sounds delicious, but I'm just sticking with one today."

"It's not half as fattening as you think it is. You'll love it."

I shake my head no again.

"You're really very convincing but I must decline. Now let me ask you a question, Tiffany. How do you manage to stay so skinny when you bake desserts for a living? I mean, you are constantly surrounded by little pieces of carbohydrate heaven, but you manage to stay looking like a supermodel from Sports Illustrated. Do you eat?"

"Of course I eat, Karen," she laughs, as though I just told her a funny joke. "But I also work out like crazy. Come down to the gym with me and my husband sometime. Let us introduce you to some of those single trainers."

I smile politely because I'm tired of shaking my head and place three single dollar bills on the counter. As soon as I turn around, a woman in a blue uniform comes into my view through the shop window. I pause for a second and watch her take something out of her pocket while staring at my license plate. It takes me a second to register what I'm seeing. I leave both the money and the cupcake on the counter and run out of the shop and into the cold air.

"Excuse me!" I call out. The woman is short and round. I can't help but notice that her uniform pants are too tight. I sure hope my butt doesn't look like hers does when I wear my scrubs. She turns around and faces me, all while looking me up and down.

"No need to issue a ticket. I am right here. I just checked the meter to make sure that I had enough time in it." Shit. How long could I have been in the store? Two minutes?

"Nope, you're one minute over." Even though she looks European, she clearly has a strong Hispanic accent.

"Well, please excuse the minute, ma'am. I tried to time it exactly down to the minute but I guess one slipped by me. I'm here though. Just came to pick up something quickly, and I do not intend to stay, so please don't ticket me. I'll remove my car."

She looks down below my armpit—I'm assuming at my Michael Kors handbag—and then another look at my illegally parked Mercedes. If I didn't know any better, I would think she's deciding she doesn't like me during this very minute. Still, I'm surprised when she starts yelling. "You want to argue with me? I have a job to do just like I'm sure that you do! You can save your argument for the City of Atlanta!"

I don't know why, but I keep trying to reason with this lady. If it weren't so cold outside, this might almost be funny to me. "Ma'am, I don't want to argue with you. I just want you to hear me out…"

"I know your type," she interrupts me. "You think you're better and smarter than everybody else, huh? You bad because you drive a Mercedes? You think you're above the law just because you got some money?"

"No, I don't."

"I know you're not, that's why you're getting this ticket. You saw me out of the window. You looked at me and thought that you could beat me to your car!"

I wonder right then if this lady suffers from a serious mental illness. The professional in me wonders if she's been diagnosed or not, what kinds of medications she might be taking. I briefly give some thought to the dosage but don't have time to make estimation.

"Can you just hear me out? I really am not trying to trick you. Were you waiting on me to…" I almost finish that sentence and then realize that sharing my thoughts with her could potentially make this worse. I just close my mouth and look at her.

"You know what? I'm going to void this ticket out because I am having a good day."

I silently cheer.

She continues. "I just don't like the fact that you're lying to me. Trying to beat me to your car! Your meter is expired!"

I try not to laugh.

When she storms off, I lean against my car and try to collect my thoughts. Apparently, we have been entertaining a few of the neighboring shop owners because six or seven folks are standing outside looking. I smile at them all and run inside Sugarplum to grab my cupcake off the counter before jumping back in my car and hightailing it over to the north side of town.

One day, women are going to get over themselves and stop being mad at other women for having it going on. I didn't know I was doing anything wrong by being young, cute, professional, well dressed and classy. It's bad enough I have to hear it from family and friends, but now even the parking meter maids are tripping? Wow. See, that's why I keep my circle small. I stick to a couple of other docs I met while in medical school and a few others I work with in my church outreach committees. As a matter of fact, I probably wouldn't even exchange words with my sisters if they weren't both related to me by blood. The only reason I talk regularly with Tessa is because I know Mama would want me to check on her if she could articulate the words to ask. Tessa is the baby and still acts like it. She thinks she's so hot, but really she's not because all those fried pork chops and French fries and seafood she feels the need to drown in butter before she can eat it are making her skin break out in adult acne and what she could use is some Proactive (at least my acne was confined to my adolescence and cleared up when I turned twenty). Plus, I believe she might be a part-time whore. I don't know how many men she's slept with but I figure it's got to be a lot. She was having sex before I started which doesn't make any sense because I'm the older sister, right? I don't even want to know if she and her partners use condoms. To me, that translates into not having any scruples. And she lies. A few years ago around this time, she told me she's the one who bought herself a brand new washing machine and dryer, a brand new Honda and a diamond charm bracelet all in the same week.

"How much money does a teaching assistant make, again?" I had asked her.

"Enough to live better than your country ass," is the answer she gave.

Tessa thinks I might be jealous of her because I'm always single and she's always not. The thought of that notion is absurd, because I wouldn't touch one of her drug-dealing, thug-life, undereducated dates with a ten-foot pole. I still remember when one of her exes, Kenny I think it was, had a baby mama that threw a fire-lit wood plank through her kitchen window like the damn KKK because she heard Tessa had stolen her boyfriend. Tessa insisted the two of them had broken up before she even met Kenny, but if I had to guess which one was telling the truth, I think I'd have to believe the baby mama over baby sister.

Everybody everywhere tells Tessa how pretty she is, which makes me sick because she and I actually look a lot alike except my hair doesn't grow as long (but I am a whole lot healthier and don't smoke so my lips aren't dark from smoking which sort of evens things out). Still, I am her big sister and I make it my business to set a good example for her to follow. She just hasn't yet figured out that all she needs to do is fall in line.

Patricia, our other sister, is the oldest but she doesn't act like it. Sometimes I have a hard time believing she's really any kin to us at all.

Mama had her before she got married to Frog and you can tell she's different but we all try not to say anything. And while Tessa and I demonstrate our ambition in different ways (like her sexing somebody else's man to be able to buy some shoes versus me going to school to be a successful doctor so I can buy my own shoes, for example), Patricia doesn't seem to have any at all. She's smart, no doubt, and from what I hear does very well as an IT specialist for some big shot government contractor, but lacks drive that it would take for her to build her own business, which she very well could do with her twenty years of experience. Her husband, Gary, knows it too, but he is the one who benefits from her thinking she needs him to think for her, and heaven forbid she comes up with an idea of her own that he won't co-sign, because she'll dismiss the notion of it faster than he will. She's bossy, but only if he's not around. She's very organized and will plan anything to a T to put on a first-class event, which makes her very useful when it's time to get together for a family reunion or an occasional Sunday dinner.

I sometimes feel guilty for not visiting Patricia as often as she'd like, but I hate going to her house. She reminds me of a puppy dog that lost its master. I've tried to forget the time she disclosed to me that she has to suck Gary's dick every time they have sex, just so he can get hard.

"Every time?" I asked, just to be sure.

"Every time," she said.

I know my sister must be tired.

I've gotten pissed off during the few times I have visited Patricia's house, because her husband is clearly not handling his business as a man. For one thing, Gary is hardly ever there to cut the grass, which goes neglected, but he won't allow her to hire a lawn man. Another thing I don't understand is why something is always broken in the house because she swears he's a good provider. Last time, it was the dishwasher. The time before that it was her side of the garage door. And I swear it took him two years to get the insurance company to come out and give them clearance to get their roof shingles fixed after a tornado came blowing through North Georgia. Where does all his time and energy go? Certainly not to his wife and home. She says he's just absentminded and sometimes forgets to follow up on things. I would be concerned about that if I were her. But she doesn't seem to be, so I don't push it. And the house is so big that it feels empty. She busies herself with sorority meetings and what not, which I wouldn't have a problem with, except I know she only wants to belong to something or somebody, and it's obvious. She should have at least had some babies so I could have some well-mannered nieces and nephews to spoil, instead of Aunt Camilla's bad-ass grandkids being the only children in the family.

On the way to the nursing home to visit Mama and drop off her Sunday plate, I make a conscious effort to ignore the Christmas lights and the holiday songs on the radio. I do not want to see another Christmas movie on Lifetime nor am I interested in the newest holiday-themed family box office movie that promises to be "charming" or "warm and good spirited." I hope the hospital maternity ward staff doesn't have the collective nerve to play the Chipmunks Christmas album at the nursing station like they did last year. I am having a very difficult time believing tomorrow is the first day of December, and I actually wish I could press fast-forward and skip straight to January. In fact, right at this moment, I'm still working out my Thanksgiving macaroni-and-cheese-induced constipation and debating whether or not I want to drink another herbal tea cleanser.

I spent what feels like my entire day in church today praying for a good husband. During the Singles Ministry meeting after service, I kept looking around to see if any newbies decided to attend. As usual, no luck. Dexter, however, did invite me out for coffee this evening and, if I didn't have to be at the hospital at 6 a.m. to cover Dr. Kessinger's deliveries while she's out enjoying her honeymoon with her brand new husband, I might have been lonely enough to take him up on the offer. It's been almost a year since my own vajayjay has been dusted off. And had I known ten years ago what I know now, I would have majored in a MRS degree instead of Biology back at Florida A&M University like the rest of the girls with common sense and a mama who actually talks to them, not just barks out orders like a drill sergeant. But no, listening to my mama, who obviously values nothing except making money (and that's just because she never had any), I didn't take the time to learn the importance of or how to even begin to experience real intimacy with a man. And now, at thirty-eight, the only thing I have to console me at night is my Jack Rabbit, which is not nearly as fun as the white girl on the box makes it appear.

It's funny. In college, I remember studying the theories of child development in my psychology classes. According to somebody important, maybe Freud, you either grow up to be just like your mother or the exact opposite. I do believe there is a whole lot of truth to that. For me, my mind was made up at an early age that, although I loved her dearly, Emily Turnipseed would not serve as my role model. I hated to see her struggle with paying bills. Sometimes, although I hated to admit it, I was embarrassed to hear her cut verbs in front of my friends (in high school) and couldn't figure out for the life of me why she stayed with my daddy after I was about twelve years old. Every woman who ever knew my daddy loved him. And by loved, I mean fucked, which is how he got his nickname from what I hear. "That frog sure does hop from place to place!" the people in the street would say. And the fact that my mama stayed married to him until the day that he died has always caused me to question her IQ. Every day, I try to leave all twenty-three of my Emily-affiliated chromosomes locked up in the closet when it's time for me to go out into the world and think and make some serious decisions.

Daddy was never home. He worked, all the time, just to be able to take care of us. Mama never appreciated his efforts and probably would have been glad if he had just worked his fingers until they bled. I never saw any blood, but I do remember asking him if I could rub some Vaseline into his knuckles when they were purple and swollen. Mama never even seemed to notice, but instead, came up with a laundry list of things she needed done and an itemized ticket of the costs so he would have to go out and work even harder to make even more money for us.

"The girls all need new school shoes and sweaters," she had said to him one evening before he could even take his grease-smudged uniform off.

"Already? I thought you just bought them all brand new shoes from Buster Brown in August before the school year started."

"Their feet grow fast. And now that the spring is coming around, they need lighter weight clothes to keep them from getting chilly in class. You know they keep the air conditioner on all day long and it gets cold. If they wear those thick wool sweaters that they've been in all year then they'll sweat under their arms. Tessa's seat is under a vent and underarm sweat mixed with cold air conditioning doesn't go together. I don't even want to mention the fact that I'm tired of seeing all those lint balls stuck to them because you didn't want to give me enough money to buy the quality ones before. When you get cheap stuff the only thing you're doing is making yourself pay for something twice. Buying new sweaters is cheaper than taking them all to the doctor for the flu. And remember that Patricia has asthma."

"How much are you going to need for all of this?"

"I'll add it all up in a minute. Karen made it through the cheerleading tryouts and they're putting her on the team. Her uniform fees are coming up due, too."

"What does coming up due mean?"

"It means I need the money by next week."

"I'm sure."

"Oh yeah, I almost forgot. Tessa's class is going on a field trip and she needs the money to go plus lunch money because they eat out and a few extra dollars in case she wants to pick up something when the other girls shop."

"Since when do seven-year-olds shop?"

"Since they go on field trips to the aquarium and they want to buy toy dolphins and whales like they just saw behind the glass. That's why their parents send them with spending money. And we're going to make sure our daughter has everything all the other kids have."

"Oh, okay. So I'm borrowing money against the shop so that we can keep up with the Joneses. Anything else, Emily?"

"As a matter of fact, yes. Easter is coming early this year—it'll be here in March instead of April—and I want the girls to get their hair all pressed and curled for their programs."

"I'm surprised you haven't said anything about buying the two little ones new dresses, too!"

"I was going to get to that. But we have three daughters, not just two of them. And they have a mother who needs to look nice when she stretches her neck out from the pew in the audience to look at them. So I'll be needing some money to get my hair fixed and a new dress for me, too."

"You must think we're rich folks, Emily."

"Don't worry, you know Camilla won't rob us but we have to pay her some kind of money for doing three little nappy heads, plus mine. You know these girls get their hair texture from you, and nothing is free," she had said before winking her eye.

And after that, I doubt if Daddy stayed home long enough to take a shower, shave and change his clothes before he was back out the door.

Mama never had too many girlfriends (at first I thought it was because most ladies don't want to be around a woman who smokes and curses and that she really couldn't keep friends around long, but I found out later it was by choice that the only person she talked to regularly besides daddy was Aunt Camilla). I made sure I had plenty girlfriends to keep me company so I wouldn't look as lonely as my mama during the many days Daddy was out of town or working late. She could never understand what I got out of my Emerging Black Leaders' meetings and social club parties, and I always wondered how she managed not to rot from ignorance and lack of exposure. Right now and to this day I know she's lonely as hell in an assisted living facility when she could be right at home with me. But, of course, she's too damn stubborn to admit that and swears she prefers the comfort of Derbyshire Manor over living with her own daughter. She even had the nerve to tell me their food tastes better than mine, as best as she could get the words out of her mouth. She cares nothing about hurting my feelings.

From the parking lot, I see a Christmas tree in the front foyer of Derbyshire. The hallways are already decorated with Christmas tinsel and lights and I'm developing a headache as I get closer to Mama's room. I don't like the smell of the disinfectant they use here. I've tried talking to the Director of Nursing about switching to a hospital-grade germicide, but she swears that scented Pine Sol is just as good as the stuff that we use in my office. Of course, the Director of Nursing and I seem to have several differences of opinion. For one thing, she must have been either blind or asleep when they conducted an initial assessment on my mama and decided she was fit for residence in the West Wing, which is where folks go who need minimal care, if any. Anybody with half of a brain could look at my mama and immediately tell she needs at least Level 2 supervision, maybe even a 3. How she convinced the medical staff in that examination room she was fit for the West Wing is a mystery that goes beyond my level of comprehension. I did insist they make her start wearing the Depends adult diapers so she won't have to worry about falling while trying to hurry to the bathroom, because I doubt that she gets her Detrol on time every day. The more I think about it, the headache could be more about the fact that I just don't like coming here. I'm permanently pissed off with my mama for too many reasons to name.

I'm ashamed of feeling relieved when I enter her room and see that she's sleeping. Her reading glasses are upside down on her face. I wish she wouldn't try to pretend like she can read anymore because it just makes her look stupid. I'm sure I'll get a phone call from her telling me how I messed up again; that I brought her dinner too late. I should put the plate in the trashcan for her and save her the trouble but I just slip it into the small refrigerator in the middle of the kitchenette area, scribble a heart and my name on a sticky note and place it on the table next to her bed, then slip quickly back out of the door.

I can barely step foot out of her room before I'm touched on the elbow by a nursing assistant with some terribly outdated finger waves.

"Hey, you must be Ms. Turnipseed's daughter. You look just like her."

"Yes, I'm Karen," I say, and extend my hand to her.

"I'm Denise." When she smiles, I can see a gold tooth right in the front of her mouth. "Your mama wanted me to give you this."

"What is it?" I ask, curious about the white envelope that Denise drops into my palm.

"Her Christmas list."

I rip open the envelope and read the first three items:
#1 A power wheelchair from the Scooter Store
#2 New glasses
#3 My teeth need cleaning

I ignore the other twenty or so items and stuff the envelope in my back pocket. "Thank you," I say to Denise, and wonder who she strong-armed into writing this wish list for her. To be a disabled person, Mama writes more letters to beg for stuff she doesn't need than the law allows.

I can hear several staff members laughing and singing Christmas carols in what looks like a break room on a side hallway near the entrance of the building. In a few weeks, I'll be throwing a Christmas party for my own office staff but I'm not sure I want to go to it. I wonder if I can come up with an excuse that Pam, my office manager, will believe. She has eyes that try to look through your face and see the thoughts in your head and I will admit she's very intuitive—half the time she has me pegged down to the T but I refuse to let her know it. Ever since she married Perry four years ago she loves to tell me about the "power of love" as she likes to call it. I often wonder why it took four husbands for her to realize love's power if it's as good as she claims. Although she doesn't think I understand what she's really saying, what I get is that Pam believes my attitude sucks and I need to be sexed. She's right and I hate it. It's almost embarrassing but I keep her because she does such a wonderful job managing the entire staff and even finds time to keep my head attached to my shoulders.

Learning to date in your late thirties is not exactly my idea of fun. When it comes down to it, it's downright frightening. It seems to me (and I know I'm no relationship expert) that the black men of this millennium are the new women. Forget about opening doors and taking my coat, I want a man who can stand on his own two feet with his own career instead of salivating at the sound of me being a physician. Hell, my salary has never been all that anyway (I'm grateful for what I do have, thank you, Jesus) but by the time I take care of the overhead costs of running a business and pay the ridiculous medical malpractice insurance that is an absolute requirement these days (and I won't even think about taxes), I'm lucky if I can clear much over two hundred thousand a year, which isn't bad, but certainly isn't rich money like everybody seems to want to think these days. Still, all I hear when dating is "Oh, you're a doctor?" Like I can almost see the dollar signs in their eyeballs. But the worst ones are the docs I actually work with or have met through school or some friends. They have a case of the "I'm in the top one percentile of eligible black men in the United States so I don't have to do shit but show up because a thousand women are standing in line behind you right now waiting" syndrome and I just refuse to lower my standards for some Sugar Honey Iced Tea, as my Aunt Camilla would say.

When I enter my empty, dark house, I fight the urge to feel sorry for myself, and decide to delight in the pleasures of watching some reality TV. It is a guilty pastime. I might not indulge in loose sex, drugs and other risky behavior like some in my family, but I do delight in the pleasures of a nightly glass of wine so I grab a glass of Cabernet and start looking around for the remote control. What I'm trying to figure out is exactly how and when just looking pretty or making a sex tape or being married to a ball player constitutes talent and affords you the right to have a whole TV show and make you rich and famous. Even though I wouldn't want that kind of attention, I still just can't help but wonder. I go to the kitchen and bring the whole bottle of wine back to the living room because drinking it helps me figure out the mysteries of the world. When

I'm nice and comfy on my sofa, I scroll through the guide channel and press the blue button that says select when I see that one of my favorite music award shows is on. I am a fan of Robin Thicke and only intend to catch his performance, but then a stream of scantily-dressed women parade onto the stage, one after another, and I can't help but watch them and try not to admire their perfect bodies and beautiful faces (but fail). Despite my best efforts to stop watching, thirty or forty minutes zip by while I'm glued to the program. I only move away because I think I just heard a rapper refer to himself as Jesus Christ and I'm afraid that lightning might strike my TV set.

Some of us do possess god-like characteristics, but outright blasphemy is a sin. I prefer to think of myself as a modern-day Athena. Like the goddess herself, I was born, fully grown, out of my parents' head (I still can't decide which one, though). I learned, from one of the books I've read, that Zeus swallowed his wife while she was pregnant. A short while later, he was bothered by an enormous headache, and out came Athena, fully grown and armed. Enter me, stage left.

I can fully relate to Athena because I've had to pull myself out of ignorance and poverty row by my own bootstraps, which is why I have a difficult time feeling sorry for others who choose not to make better decisions. Take Tessa, for example. She acts as though she hates me because I'm successful and live in a nice house in Buckhead and because I have a housekeeper that comes once a week and I have real insurance benefits and a car that gets regular maintenance. But what's to stop her from accomplishing these things? And how damn long does it take to pass the damn teaching test?

After glass of wine number three, I feel like talking to Tessa and checking on her progress. At first I think she's not going to pick up the phone because I remember she was supposed to be taking online classes for whatever degree she's supposed to be getting this month (it changes about every twenty-eight days) and I think classes were supposed to start today. But then she surprises me and answers the phone and it doesn't sound like she's doing any homework.

"Hello?"

"Hey, Tess, it's me, baby sis."

"Who?"

"Karen."

"Oh." I think I woke her up.

"I'm sorry to be calling you so late, but I was just thinking about you. Haven't heard from you in a few weeks. You been doing okay?"

"Yeah, I'm alright."

"Good. You're talking sort of slow though." I pause to give her time to respond but she doesn't so I go on. "I went by to see your mama today."

"Oh yeah? I'll bet your ass got cursed out good if you didn't show up with some new sneakers. She's been expecting some new shoes. She mentioned that the last time I saw her, you know. Said her sneakers don't look white enough anymore."

"You're right about that. Except if she did any cursing, it was in her sleep. She was snoring by the time I got there, but she did write me a love letter."

She cracks up with laughter. "Our mama? Wrote one of her daughters a love letter? Yeah, right. You'd have a better chance of winning the Powerball."

"Isn't that the truth. But how about this: She had the nerve to have one of the medical assistants to write out her Christmas wish list for us."

"I thought they all quit doing favors for her because she's so rude to them."

"The girl who handed me this letter today was new. I would have remembered her finger waves if I had seen her before."

She lets out a giggle.

"Tessa? What are you over there doing?"

"Nothing."

"You're lying."

"Well, I was trying to fall asleep before you called."

"Are you high?"

"Yes."

"When are you going to grow out of that habit? It's bad for you. What if the people at your job find out?"

"The principal at my school already knows."

"And you don't see a problem with that?"

"I didn't before, but I suppose it might create an issue now that I am not giving him any. Or maybe because I cursed his ass out before I told him to get out of my house tonight."

"What did you just say to me?"

No answer.

"Tessa!"

"Did you call me to talk or to ask questions?"

"Both. Is that man actually dumb enough to try to have sex with his teachers?"

"I doubt he would try most of the teachers on staff at Cedarview, although a few of them do look like they're very hard up, but he's been pursuing me for quite some time."

"What's that supposed to mean?"

"Exactly what I said."

"What makes you so special and sets you apart from the rest of the teachers?"

"Probably the fact that I'm not a real one. Yet."

"You mean to tell me you're still not certified?'

"Yep."

"I thought you took that test last year." I'm pretending that I don't remember.

"I did."

"Oh." I'm sorry I asked her that. "But didn't you tell me that man is in his sixties or seventies or something like that?

"He is, which means that he is too damn old to be such a tight-pocket motherfucker." She slurred when she said that.

"Have you been drinking, too?" I ask.

"Is that against the law?"

"No, but I don't like to talk to you when your judgment is impaired."

"Well stop talking to me then."

"You need to get a grip on your issues."

"You read too many books."

And with that, Tessa doesn't even say bye-bye. She just hangs up the phone.

Patricia

Happy

I THINK I BOUGHT the wrong kind of buttermilk. I intended to get something low-fat, but I'm not so sure there is such a thing as low-fat buttermilk. I think the fat in the buttermilk is what makes the chicken taste good. But there is no way on earth I'm going out to Publix in this rainy weather in order to exchange my purchase, so I'll just have to experiment to find out whether or not this works out.

As I bend down in the pantry to reach for the flour, my pussy suddenly begins to feel like it has a heartbeat of its own down there. This random horniness is happening more and more since I've passed the forty year mark. I would never get this hot and bothered before and cannot understand why I'm suddenly feeling and thinking like a teenager. Sadly, I do not want to have sex with Gary. If I'm lucky, I can squeeze in a few minutes of masturbation before he comes home. I glance at the clock and realize that he's not due for about another half hour. The potatoes need at least another half hour before they're done baking. Spinach only takes a few seconds to sauté. I'm seriously considering grabbing my Silver Bullet and making a run for it up to my bedroom, but I don't want my chicken to burn.

Pop pop! The grease is hot and ready to fry. I season my flour enough to be able to see the colorful specks in the white mixture before dropping each wing into the buttermilk. It looks like the coating could be thicker but flour will stick to a wet anything so what the hell. I drop five wings into my pan at one time and stand there watching the cooking oil bubble up and through the meat. What I'm standing here thinking is that there is really no need for me to stand here and supervise this chicken because I've been frying chicken for Gary since we were married twenty years and ten months ago. I could do this with my eyes closed because I sincerely feel that frying chicken has become my full-time job. I'm even starting to think I might be better at it than I am with my real job—which is fixing on computers.

The responsible thing for me to do right now would be to sit down and plan my anniversary vacation with my husband. But instead, I'm actually looking forward to traveling to Miami in a few weeks to oversee a government agency's database migration, and find myself preparing more for that trip than my own vacation. I love that it's eighty degrees year round in Miami, and I can't help it if I'm having fun shopping for bathing suits with skirts (I need some coverage to conceal these ham hocks of thighs). I am looking forward to practicing my Spanish with the Blaxicans (that means Black and Mexican, I learned by watching reality TV). I open the kitchen drawer next to the refrigerator and pull out some packaged itineraries to Athens and compare them to some Greek island cruises that I found on the internet. Both my travel agent and one of my sorority chapter members told me the island cruise is magnificent, but I can't seem to convince Gary to give up the idea of staying in Athens for a full week. He thinks he's Greek lately because all he wants to eat is feta cheese and tomatoes and red onions soaked in olive oil. And it's not good enough to eat the Mediterranean blend by itself—oh, no—it has to go on top of everything: bread, French fries, potato chips, you name it. I laugh out loud at the thought of pouring it on top of tonight's fried chicken, but then, the more I think about it, he would probably actually like it and then demand that I cook it for him once a week.

Now, either that wind and rain are coming down mighty hard or I hear that damn garage door opening. Shit! I look at the clock again. He must have left work early. I wipe my hands on the front of my apron and walk toward the garage door to greet my husband, halfway out of routine consideration, but more so out of curiosity because I'd like to know what the hell he's doing home so early. As soon as he gets out of the car he pops the trunk and begins unloading grocery bags. I stand and watch. Then I remember to smile.

"Hey, honey, I just went to the grocery store on Tuesday. What are you doing out shopping in this weather?"

He walks over to the door and pecks me on the cheek before sliding into the house with two bags. "Can't I offer my wife of two decades and counting a few surprises every now and again?"

"What kind of surprises?" I ask while reaching for one of the Kroger bags.

"These are a few of your favorite things," he sings out in the familiar tune of that song that I can't quite think of the name of while he lifts the grocery bags over his head.

When he walks by me, I catch a whiff of seafood. The smell makes my mouth water on the spot. "What is the occasion?" I ask. Then I remember to ask about the time. "And what are you doing home so early?"

"I left the office so I could spend some quality time with my wife, of course."

I feel as though I should appreciate the effort, and I really do appreciate the steamed shrimp I'm unpacking from his Kroger bag on the counter, but I wish he had called me and told me to hold the chicken wings. I realize now that I am still going to have to cook them since I already battered them up.

"I'm going upstairs to take a shower," he says, popping open a soda can. "Then I was thinking that we could relax and watch a movie while I feed you some shrimp and fruit. Maybe order something from Direct TV Cinema. Can you check and see what's playing?"

What I know is that this really translates into is: "You owe me some pussy tonight." I know this because we are on an every-other-day sex schedule. I walk over to my wine rack and begin surveying the inventory. I have one open bottle of Patch Block Pinot Noir and one half-empty bottle of Duplin's muscadine wine in the refrigerator. I decide that neither one of these will be strong enough to put me in the mood to fuck Gary tonight, so I decide to make myself an apple martini instead.

He immediately goes into his usual routine of undressing in the living room and leaving a trail of clothes up the stairs and down the hallway. By the time he makes it to the laundry room, the only thing he has on his body to add to the basket is drawers and a t-shirt, sometimes socks. I fall right into line and begin picking up the clothes, hanging his shirt, folding his pants, and smelling them to see if they need to go to the dry cleaners right away. When he gets in the bathroom, he turns on the shower and begins talking to me through the door. "You want to put that food on some platters and set them up in the bedroom so we can eat while we relax and watch the movie?"

"Okay, I can do that. What are you in the mood to see?"

"I don't know. Maybe something with some action."

I click through the list of movies available on satellite and select a thriller that I've never heard of. Then I go back downstairs and begin placing a few wings on a platter. I find a few slices of pineapple and some grapes in the refrigerator and add it to the plate. I almost forget the steamed shrimp until I smell them on the counter on my way out of the kitchen, so I turn around and add them to the spread. Then I put some garlic salt and butter in a bowl and melt it in the microwave. When the microwave beeps, I pour the melted butter into a condiment dish and stick it on the side of my platter. When I get back upstairs I'm surprised to hear shower water still running. I put the platter down on the nightstand by the bed, take a sip of my martini and tiptoe closer to the bathroom door to peek through the crack in the door.

My husband has a bad habit of getting out of the shower and posing with a hard dick. Sometimes he even flaps it around when he thinks I'm not looking. Occasionally, just for shits and giggles, I will stand in the bedroom and peek through the crack in the bathroom door just to watch him play "Superman" by himself. I decide to peek in on the action and wait for the entertainment.

Sure enough, he's in there jerking around behind a half open shower curtain, checking himself out in the mirror. I watch him hop around like a rabbit and wonder if he thinks he's really cute. An erection slowly rises and he stands still to better check himself out. Then he begins to jerk his hand up and down, pleasuring himself. I cringe at the thought of him doing this because I know that it means that he wants to prolong our lovemaking session. I could almost find his antics funny until I hear him speak in a low, barely audible voice, "Slow down, Candy."

Who the fuck is Candy?

I open the door and stand there. His eyes are closed. Then he says it again: "Ooh, Candy, slow down."

I walk in and snatch the shower curtain all the way back. His eyes pop open and he looks surprised, but I can tell that he's still squeezing the head of his penis to get the last bit of juice out.

"Who were you talking to, Gary?"

"What?"

"Who is Candy?"

"Were you spying on my while I was taking my shower? How the hell did you see through that curtain?"

"I didn't have to try very hard. It was open. And I have the right to walk into my own bathroom. But answer my questions, will you? Doesn't your dick get tired of getting beat and pulled on? I mean, after a while, it seems like it would start to feel raw."

"Shut up, Patricia."

"I'm serious." I'm trying to stifle the smile that insists on appearing on my face.

"I don't say anything to you when you have your legs spread open underneath the bathtub faucet for ten and fifteen minutes when I know it doesn't take that long to wash your ass!"

I just turn around and walk out the bathroom door. If he didn't look so stupid thrusting his pelvis into the corner of the shower then I probably wouldn't want to laugh so hard. I make sure that I'm out of earshot before I let my giggle slip out of my mouth.

I walk around this big ass house looking for my cell phone so I can charge it up because if I don't do it now, then I'll forget and fall asleep and won't have any juice left in it tomorrow when I go to work. I'm actually breathing hard from going in and out of every room which indicates to me that I need to get back into the gym regularly. I really don't know what we need with all of this space except to show off for Gary's family whenever they come in town to visit. I tried to convince him when we moved in that we can only sleep in one room at a time and pee in one bathroom at a time, but he would not be convinced. Although I didn't get any degrees in psychology, I do believe that his need for big things comes from being raised in the projects. I once heard Oprah and TD Jakes discuss "scarcity issues" during one of their tours. They say that issue can arise from always thinking that there will never be enough of what you need to go around. Seems that a lot of us black folks try to compensate for our own damn insecurities by buying up shit, Gary and I included.

When I get back upstairs, I lie back on the bed, dip a shrimp into the butter and pop it in my mouth. After watching Gary's bathroom episode, my buzz has worn off and the tingle that had started to develop between my legs has disappeared. I am bored. I wish I had something, anything, and anybody to do other than my husband. Then I immediately feel guilty for thinking that.

One day soon, when I'm off work, I plan to cook my sisters' favorite meals and try to get them over here to spend time with me. I might even call our cousin Stacey and her bad-ass kids, Jada and Marcus, because I know they always like to order their favorite movies in the theater room Gary and I created in the basement. Karen acts like she's always too busy for me, and Tessa is only likely to come if Karen reminds her and convinces her that there will be food at my house. I think that smoking marijuana has eaten up too many of her brain cells.

One thing I do know is that Karen can be enticed with some sweets. She spends all her earned income, I'm convinced, at a local bakery that I've heard of but never stepped foot inside. There's no way in hell I would ever spend five or ten dollars on some sugar, alone, especially since baking is one of the easiest parts of cooking and I'm sure I can make anything she buys in my very own kitchen for half of the price and double the taste. Aunt Camilla loves to remind me I'm the only person in the world who's worthy of sharing her baking recipes with, but I'm sure that's just because none of her own children cook, and neither of my sisters ever cook anything worth eating.

Besides her sweet tooth, Karen loves pasta but then always has the nerve to complain about being overweight. Truth be told, I think she's kind of cute in her size twelve jeans, but apparently she's been comparing herself to too many of the white girls who are her patients, and I know for a fact she's taking her dressing cues from too many of them. But none of us have the heart to tell her that. She could be prettier than she is but she doesn't fix herself up enough, and I know delivering those babies and taking care of women who are having problems because they're getting too much sex has to be depressing for her. She talks about wanting a boyfriend in just about every conversation I have with her, but then, when I explore a little bit deeper into her psyche and hear her list the qualifications, I can quickly surmise the reason why she's alone. She wants stuff that doesn't even go together. Like, for example, men who like to cut the grass, build fences and fix toilets don't tend to be astrophysicists. Similarly, the ones who come from blue-blood money and were raised by both a mama and a daddy and got sent to etiquette school don't want to hear the rap music that she plays when she's by herself. But I don't try to tell her that, not that she would listen anyway. She will, however, listen to Tessa, the baby of the family. And why she, or anyone else for that matter, would do a dumb thing like that, the world may never know.

Tessa is a sweet person deep, deep (very deep) down inside, but you have to peel too many of her onion layers back before you can get to that soft core. For most people, including me, it's too much work. Sometimes, her common sense makes a disappearing act for days, but then she always bounces back, reeking of marijuana, and acting as if nothing has happened.

She, unlike Karen, has a new boyfriend about once a month. She has a real knack for getting them to do nice things for her, and I don't mean like changing a tire. Tessa's men buy furniture sets, put down payments on cars, and pay her school tuition whenever she claims she's going to class (which isn't often enough). Hell, I know for a fact one of my old classmates she dated left his wife in hopes Tessa would take him seriously and finally call him her man. But when he showed up at her door, she wouldn't even let him step foot into her house and told him if he was stupid enough to leave his home she didn't want him.

Pretty isn't even the word to describe her. She really is beautiful. She got Mama's big black eyes and long hair. I have no idea where that hourglass shape came from because it's not something Karen or I inherited, but she looks like a real-live movie star without even trying.

What gene pool my flat nose and long forehead came from, I will never know. And not only do I have these distinguishing features to separate me from their good looks, but I'm also a pale shade of yellow that's too stubborn to tan while the other two are gorgeous shades of brown. Either Mama really doesn't know who my father is or she has just refused to name him for forty years, but I don't even ask anymore. I got tired of her telling me that a daddy is whoever the man is that raises you, because that sounds like some ghetto shit that I've heard on one too many Maury Povich shows. I don't actually remember mama and Frog dating, but I was about six or seven years old when they got married and their wedding was the talk of the town. Frog was apparently engaged to a stringy pole-bean of a woman named Evelyn who lived across town when he met mama, whose big brown legs and thighs, tiny waist, D-cup breasts and long black eyelashes and hair caused him to fall in love at first sight. Everyone tells me they married fewer than six months after they met, and that Evelyn was found dead in her backyard about a week after the wedding. Occasionally, I'll hear a woman who's actually from this side of town mention the way that Evelyn died of a broken heart after my mama took her man. Aunt Camilla says that Evelyn died from being too damn skinny and that you can't believe half of the shit that you hear.

It didn't take anybody else to tell me that I wasn't a true Turnipseed. By the time that I was in the seventh grade and nearing puberty, I realized I was missing the Barbie-doll like characteristics that mama shared with my younger sisters. I also knew that I didn't look like the female gladiators and football players that mama always described her in-laws as being. It took me sneaking into her wine stash (and then replacing the missing fluid ounces with water) to get up the nerve to ask her about it one day when she came home from work.

"Mama," I had said after brushing the smell of alcohol out of my mouth. "Why don't I look like Karen and the baby?" Tessa was a toddler and still generally referred to as, "the baby."

"What are you doing asking me questions like this? I just got my ass in the house from work and I'm too tired to be getting quizzed by a twelve-year-old. Did you wash those dishes good? I don't smell any bleach."

"Yes, ma'am, and I used bleach."

"Good," she said, and started to kick off her shoes without making even the slightest bit of eye contact which meant she was ignoring me.

"But my nose is bigger than theirs."

"That's because you're nosy."

"My skin is lighter than y'all's, too."

"Well then take your yellow ass out in the sun and play."

My face was feeling warm and tingly, and I was getting more courage by the minute. "Mrs. Fields told our class that sometimes families have different mamas or different daddies in them, and that sometimes sisters and brothers don't look the same when that happens."

She turned all of her attention toward me and said, "Your teacher doesn't have any business trying to have those types of conversations with children. But since you want to be so nosy, then I'll tell you what you want to hear. Frog is not your real daddy, but he might as well be because he buys all of your food and clothes and pays for your cheerleading uniforms and gives you lunch money and helps me to put a roof over your head. That's all a daddy is, anyway."

"So who--"

"You'd better not ask me another damn question, especially one that I don't know the answer to. And at this point it really doesn't matter."

And that was the end of that conversation. Everybody knew that once mama had put a period at the end of a sentence, you didn't dare go behind her with a question mark.

Fewer than seven years later, I married Gary because he took care of me in a way that made him seem fatherly. I sometimes wonder if maybe I missed out on something by not having any children. I always wanted lots of them, and ended up with none. Isn't that the way things usually turn out? I've always marveled at the irony. For a long time, I thought we were just putting it off, but that it would happen eventually. When Gary got me pregnant right after we became engaged, he convinced me to have an abortion because we didn't have "the financial independence it takes to raise a child," even though all the children I know would much prefer to be raised with parents who loved them enough to offer a few hugs and words of encouragement or maybe read them a book or join them for a movie instead of just buying them stuff they don't need.

What I can say that's good about my husband is he's worked really hard to provide a comfortable life for us. And that's more than a lot of women can say these days. He has never been caught out in the streets, he comes home at night, and pays the big bills. I should be grateful, but instead, I'm bored out of my damn mind. I can't blame him if he's ten years older than I am and acts more like he's twenty years older. When I met him, I thought the age difference would benefit me by adding charm and experience. I am now woman enough to accept the fact that, what it did instead, was add cobwebs to my you-know-what.

By the time Gary makes it into the bedroom, I've finished eating half of the food on the platter. I have also reduced the slights to just a few specks in the ceiling and have a candle burning. What he does not know is that it takes all of this plus a few extra drinks to put me in the mood. Fortunately, he sincerely believes this production is for him. I am now in the bed wearing a sheer nightgown and red thong panties. Gary spares me from his sexy dance tonight, and is probably already embarrassed because I've caught him masturbating. Why get bashful now? I'm noticing that with the lights turned this low and his bald head shining, he looks sort of like Mr. Clean. I'm trying to remember what cleaning product Mr. Clean sold when Gary slides into bed. He smells like aftershave. Not the kind I bought him from the cologne counter, but something cheap from the drugstore. The smell almost makes me nauseous but I don't tell him that.

As soon as he gets into bed, I assume my usual position between his legs. I grip his soft penis and balls in one hand, just the way he likes, while using my other hand to stroke him. After two or three licks, he slowly begins to perk up. I spread my jaws as wide as I can and slowly drop my mouth and head down—all the way down—until the tip of his penis reaches the back of my throat. I bob my head up and down, creating as much suction as I can, until he grabs me by the hair and removes himself from my face before slapping me across the cheek with his dick. I am relieved the hard part is over so quickly, because I know it's all downhill from here, and slowly lie down beside him on the bed.

Gary does his usual foreplay production with a bit of kissing around my neck and shoulders, but never makes contact with my lips. Fortunately, he doesn't mind performing a bit of oral sex and I think that's what he's going to do until I feel his fingers slip into my panties to conduct the litmus test. Apparently, he must think that it's ready because I feel him slide my legs apart and enter me in what feels like one swoop motion. For the next ten or fifteen minutes, I think about the broken dishwasher and wonder if Gary remembered to call the repair man. I also think about the chicken in the kitchen and whether or not it's turning cold. I've been noticing an increase in bugs around the house lately that have skinny little bodies and about a million long legs, and I make a mental note to describe them to Google so that I can identify them and find an effective insecticide to spray. I also wonder if I should have covered the chicken with more than some paper towels, and that maybe I should have put some foil wrap on them instead, which brings my mind right back to the bugs again. I'm imagining them coming out of their cracks in the corners and sniffing their way to my chicken on the countertop. I wonder if I need to call the bug people back out to the house to administer a professional treatment again, or if I've just called too far off schedule with spraying the Ortho Max that I purchased from Lowe's. I wonder where I put the bug people's phone number—last week, I noticed that it wasn't saved in my cell phone like I thought it was. I think about the lawn man and the pest control man and try to decide which one is more attractive. I decide that the grass-cutter wins the contest and imagine him being the man underneath me. I keep my eyes shut tight for fear that Gary might seep through my eyelids and blast me back to reality while I work on climaxing.

"Did you come?" My husband surprises me by asking. His hand is rubbing back and forth across my side, traveling up and down my love handles.

"Of course I did." I roll over to face him in the bed.

"Sure? You were sort of quiet. It didn't seem like you were all the way there."

"I'm sure." I'm actually surprised at his degree of perceptiveness. "Maybe imagining Candy in the shower got you worked up for a porn scene tonight?"

Gary chuckles. "I remember when you used to put your afro wig on for me and let me call you whatever name I wanted. Candy could have very well have been you that I was imagining in the shower tonight."

"Yeah, right."

"I'm serious. And what ever happened to that wig, anyway?"

"I outgrew it."

"Buy a new one."

"So you can convince me my name is Candy?"

"No. So I can have you raise a fist in the air and yell 'black power' while you're on top of me. I think I'd like her better than Candy."

I think about his comment for a while. Just as I'm ready to tell him I've thought up my own alter-ego, one who doesn't have to wear an Afro wig or make fists, or wear blonde wigs and suck lollipops or wear plaid skirts and put her hair into two ponytails—all of which I do at my husband's request in order to turn him on—I hear him begin to snore very softly.

Later on in the night, as I'm fighting the urge to develop a hangover, I begin to wonder how many other women my age must go through such desperate measures to have sex with their husbands and I begin to feel very sad. I slip out of bed to get on my knees and pray after I'm sure that Gary is sleeping. I ask God to fix my marriage, then I change my mind and ask him to fix me, although I'm not sure what that means exactly. I start trying to find the words to describe what I want him to do, and then I feel my head begin to tip over as I realize I've actually started to doze off down here on the floor. Before I pick myself up off the carpet, I lean down further to look under the bed for my house shoes. Once they're snug on my feet, I float into the kitchen to put up that chicken that's been sitting out for the last couple hours. Unable to resist trying a juicy-looking drumstick as I tuck it in some Tupperware, I take one single big bite out of the fried chicken and wash it down with an opened Sprite that Gary left on the counter. Right before I get to the stairs on my way back up to the bedroom, I feel something crunchy under my left house shoe and jump almost a foot off the ground because I'm pretty sure that I just stepped on one of those damn bugs.

Emily

I Hate Funerals

THIS DREAM STARTS OFF just like the rest of them. In fact, I've experienced variations of it so many times that a part of me knows it's a dream as I'm dreaming it. The problem is I can't wake up until it's over. So I lie still and give in.

It only takes a moment for the pain to register.

Ouch! Camilla burns the top of my ear while curling my hair. I jerk my head to the left and pop her in her stomach with the back of my hand. "I thought you said these new kinds of flat irons don't burn your damn scalp up!"

"If your edges weren't so broken off, then I probably could grab enough hair so it wouldn't have to hurt! Sit still, Emily."

I do as I'm told—until the next time she burns me. This time, I pinch a big chunk of fat from the side of her hip. Instead of reacting, she reaches for a pack of Newports that are sticking up out of her purse and removes one, then turns on the stove burner to light it.

"Make sure you don't blow that in my direction. I'm not going around these people smelling like tar."

She rolls her eyes and hands me the comb with her unoccupied hand. "Fix your part the way you like it," she instructs, before opening a window and blowing smoke out of it.

I pick up my hand-held mirror from the kitchen table and take a look at my reflection. The curls are springy and bouncy, but my eyes catch a few strands of gray hair that must have resisted Betty's black dye. I am able to snatch two of them out before my eyes begin to water—then I stop plucking, only because I don't want to cause my eye make-up to run. I take the skinny tail of the comb and place my part in its usual spot above my left eyebrow and finger my curls into place. Then I pick up a small, black tube in the shape of a bullet from on top of the pile of makeup that is sprawled across the table and re-apply my lipstick.

"The car just pulled up outside!" Calvin's voice rings out loudly from the living room.

"Tell them we're coming," Camilla answers back.

Camilla extinguishes her cigarette and grabs the mirror and lipstick from my hand before ordering me to put my clothes on. I run through the back door of the kitchen and through the hallway to my bedroom so that Calvin won't see me in my slip and pantyhose. I make it to the back of the house right before I hear the front door slam.

"Where's Mama?" I hear Tessa asking Camilla.

"She's in her room getting ready. She'll be out in just a second."

"Why didn't she clean up the house? Doesn't she know that people will want to come here when it's all over?" That was Karen.

"We cleaned up last night. You just can't tell it now."

"Do you need me to do anything?" Patricia asks softly.

"No, baby. Just fix your slip. And put these sunglasses on until I can find you some Visine."

Honk honk!

"What time is it, Gary?"

"Ten-fifteen," I hear my son-in-law answer.

"What in the world is Mama doing back there? We need to leave here in the next couple of minutes."

"We can leave here right now," I say as I walk into the living room. I drop my shoes on to the floor and grab the edge of the sofa so that I can wiggle my feet into them.

The room is silent for a few seconds. Calvin is the last to look at me. As soon as he sees me, his eyes get as big as dinner plates.

Karen breaks the silence by saying, "Mama, you are not wearing that."

"Come on, Ma," Tessa chimes in. "You can't."

Patricia presses her lips together. Calvin looks at his shoelaces. Camilla shakes her head back and forth and begins mumbling to herself.

"Did I hear somebody say we were going to be late if we don't hurry up and get out of here?" I ask, pretending I didn't notice any of them.

Nobody answers my question.

I start pointing and talking loudly. "Patricia, turn off the kitchen lights and set the alarm. Gary, I need you and Tessa to grab those two boxes on the floor in case we run out of programs. Karen, go get in that limousine and tell the man that we are coming out right behind you."

Nobody moves except Gary. So I waltz right past all of them and go straight out the door and get into the front seat of the black car that has pulled into my driveway. I tell the driver he can close the car door and pull off if nobody else joins me in the next five minutes. But they all do. And the twenty-minute ride down Interstate 20 to the church is silent.

Exactly one hour later, I'm seated in the front-row pew of the church closest to the aisle and casket. I'm having a little talk with Jesus when a man in a black suit with all-white hair taps me on my shoulder and tells me he's ready to escort me up to view the body. When I stand up, I realize all the eyeballs in this sanctuary are on me. Some folks are whispering. Some just stare with open mouths. One or two women just fan themselves. Undoubtedly, they are all watching my every move. For this reason, I try very hard to walk in my high heels without letting anyone know just how much my feet hurt.

When the telephone in my room rings, my eyes pop open and my head begins to hurt. By the time I'm able to answer the call, they've hung up. And here I am, alone with my thoughts, without even a caller on the other end of the line to distract me from my thoughts. I prop myself up in bed to analyze my dream for the millionth time. And why? I don't know. Perhaps I'm a sadist.

* * *

Camilla wants to know what in the hell is on my mind that is so important I had to call and ask her to come by Derbyshire after work on a Tuesday.

"Don't you know Calvin and I have to meet our poker group in an hour?" she wants to know. "And that traffic coming out here is T-E-R-I-B-L-E on a week night. Makes me hot," she says while fanning herself with her hand. I don't bother to tell her she left off an R.

I turn my cheek toward her so that she can kiss it, and when she does her face feels damp. What she doesn't know is that I really wish I could avoid addressing this matter myself, but it's eating away at me. I wish there was a pill I could take to erase my fuck-ups just like there's a pill for everything else for people over sixty. I would actually swallow that one instead of hiding it under my tongue like the rest of them.

"Hurry up and push the door closed," I say, seeing Alice hunched over in her purple housecoat with an ear to her door, trying to listen in from across the hallway. I have lots to say.

When I'm finished telling Camilla my plan, she looks thoughtful. Then she opens her mouth.

"That's a stupid idea."

"What's so stupid about it?" I ask.

"I've watched enough movies to know you should never tell your grown children the secrets that you kept from them during their childhood. They'll hate you." She unbuttons the top three buttons of her blouse.

"They probably already do. I figure my stock with them can't do anything but improve at this point," I say.

"They'll hate me."

"So you can finally join my club."

"What a selfish thing to say," Camilla says. I notice a few new sweat beads forming on her forehead. "Anybody with a half of a brain would want those girls to be able to be close to their Auntie, since it's the next closest thing to a mama. And since you're so smart and you all of a sudden have all the answers on how to fix this family's dysfunctions, why do you need my help?"

"They'll take it better if you're with me. Besides, you know my words get more mumbled up when I get nervous. And don't forget I can't hold a pen anymore without dropping it. Dr. Nevarez says I may never get my fine motor skills back."

"He found what in your motor?"

"Never mind."

"Don't talk down to me, you hussy. I know more about your slick ass than you think I do. You want me to waste my good Mother's Day by playing referee between you and your kids so they don't haul off and kick your ass."

"Ma maa ma," is what comes out of my mouth, but I'm trying to tell her to shut up. This is what happens when I get upset or overly excited.

Camilla doesn't waste time taking full advantage of my disability.

"And I'll tell you another thing," she continues, while picking up a magazine from my nightstand to fan herself. "You would rather hide behind this damn wheelchair than risk rejection by those girls. You don't half way go to your therapy now, and a part of you doesn't want to get better and wants to play handicapped forever because that gives you an excuse not to have to confront the truth. You think you're fooling me but you're not. It shouldn't have taken a damn stroke for you to want to all of a sudden come clean and sit around these girls with your legs crossed singing "Kumbaya." You're only fooling yourself."

She doesn't say another word and neither do I. And as I sit here, watching her fan herself through her hot flash, I say a silent prayer that she bursts into a flame. Then I make a vow to myself that I'll make enough progress on my own through physical and speech therapy that I can write and read my own letters to my children come Mother's Day, just in case Camilla never returns from the ashes.

I-285

PATRICIA RECOGNIZED the number displayed across her caller ID, but she hesitated before picking up her cell phone. She was nervous.

"Patricia Owens," she said, after finally touching the glowing green button on the iPhone.

"Hello there, Patricia. This is Leslie Pettaway. Did I catch you at a good time?"

"Of course you did," Patricia lied, trying her best to stand still in the middle of the produce section of the grocery store. It was distracting to see so many people zooming past her, giving her what seemed to be rude looks, probably for blocking the organic vegetables. Patricia picked up a radish and fixed her eyes upon it. "It's always a pleasure hearing from you. What can I do for you, Leslie?"

"Well, I'm wondering if you'd like to purchase a ticket to our anniversary gala in March. I know the spring time seems so far away right now, but it'll be here before you know it. And seeing how you just applied for membership to our organization and all, I would think that you would want to be one of the first in line to support our fundraiser events. Am I right?"

Patricia exhaled. She had hoped Leslie was calling her to offer membership to the Golden Dove Society—the most exclusive group of women in Atlanta, and possibly the in world, as far as Patricia was concerned. Golden Doves were known to be the best dressed, most articulate, smartest, classiest and beautiful women on this side of the Mississippi River. Most of them were married to doctors, lawyers and Indian chiefs of all sorts in Atlanta, and the few who were single were known to be the most sought after women in the region.

"You are certainly right, Leslie. I wouldn't miss it."

"Very good then. And not that this should make any difference to you—we've decided not to set a price on admission this year, but to accept donations. That way, we won't limit the amount of money we can raise, because, after all, a portion of our proceeds go to charity you know. We're encouraging our patrons this year to make a five hundred dollar minimum donation per ticket. I'll reserve—what? Two tickets? Your husband will accompany you, yes?"

Patricia didn't like the way Leslie ended every assumption with a question—especially questions that she already knew the answers to—but she responded to them anyway. "Yes. Gary wouldn't have it any other way."

"How wonderful," said Leslie. "I pass your neighborhood on Wednesday evenings on my way home from Bible study. Perhaps I can drop off your tickets and pick up your donation one Wednesday in the next couple weeks. How does that sound?"

"It sounds great, Leslie. Thanks so much for thinking of me."

"You're welcome, Patricia. Anytime."

Patricia put the radish back on the shelf and picked up a cucumber. Then she picked out two tomatoes and a red onion so she could prepare Gary's Greek salad tonight with fresh vegetables. Once away from the produce section, she picked up a loaf of bread, a box of grits, and a can of Folgers coffee, which she stared at for a long time. Before Patricia could get to the dairy department to find the feta cheese, she had begun to worry. Her morning cup of coffee was beginning to stain her teeth, she had recently noticed. To Patricia, the off-white, not quite yellow clouds that were slowly beginning to appear on her front teeth looked like butter. Patricia began thinking about the Golden Doves, and how all of their teeth seemed to be pearly white. She tried hard to remember whether or not she had ever seen a Golden Dove with buttery teeth, and could think of none. Patricia picked up a tube of Crest extra whitening toothpaste before getting into the checkout line.

On her way home, Patricia passed a billboard on I-285 with an advertisement for laser liposuction. She instinctively pinched a chunk of meat on her right thigh and decided that she had had enough of thunder thighs and cellulite. There were some problems that just couldn't be solved by regular diet and exercise, and she vowed her butt and hips would be two sizes smaller by the time she and Gary went to the gala in

March. She dialed the number on the billboard into her cell phone and pressed talk. When a nurse answered, Patricia scheduled a consultation for the next day.

After making Gary a beautiful Greek salad, ironing his shirts for work, performing her wifely duties for him in bed, and waiting not long for him to fall asleep, Patricia stood in front of the bathroom mirror brushing her teeth over and over until her gums began to throb and bleed. She placed her toothbrush back in its holder and rinsed her burning mouth. Staring at her teeth in the mirror, she decided that in addition to the liposuction consultation on Tuesday, she would schedule a professional whitening treatment at her dentist's office. Then she slid into bed beside her husband, careful not to wake him.

* * *

Before it became a waxing salon, The Peach Fuzz on I-285 was a strip club called The Pink Moon. Contessa frequented them both—first as an employee of the Pink Moon, and later (after the club was closed by the government due to a rumored tax evasion) as a patron of the Peach. Her logic for going to both establishments, however, was the same. Looking good opened men's wallets.

And she had been right. After only three months of dancing, she had saved enough money to pay her rent six months in advance and to repay five thousand dollars of student loans. Now, two years later, Contessa sometimes missed the money she made from the Pink Moon, and would consider seeking similar employment elsewhere, but feels she is getting too old to be able to stay up all night and then be able to perform well on a day job the next morning. Moreover, she'd like to have a career that would put the college degree that took her so long to obtain to good use.

She didn't consider herself a loose woman: it was simply a matter of necessity.

She was reflecting upon this thought as she spread her legs apart at the Peach Fuzz, waiting for Arlita to wax her lady parts. And even though she had been through this many times before, the pain of the hair removal still took her by surprise.

Tessa returned home feeling sexy and desirable. She even pulled down her jeans a few times in front of the bathroom mirror to take a look at the smooth skin and perfectly even landing strip that Arlita had worked so hard to sculpt down there. Tessa loved the way her camel toe looked right now. She would have been willing to bet that a special man in her life would have loved the way it looked, too, but she didn't have a special man in her life to bet on.

Tessa sat down on her couch and turned on Lifetime so she could have some background noise while she studied for her teaching exam. She picked up a Kaplan test preparation book, only to close it again very quickly. Then she dialed the telephone number to the Georgia Assessments for the Certification of Educators (GACE) test administrator's office.

When a man answered the phone, Tessa asked him, "Is there a way you can bypass the class and just take the test?"

"Hold please," the man told Tessa. Tessa heard classical music begin to play on the line. She put her phone on speaker and put down the handset so she could hear the Lifetime movie, even though she had seen it before. A few minutes later, a woman picked up on the line.

"May I help you?" the woman asked.

"Yes, please. A man placed me on hold because I was calling to find out about the requirements for my teaching exam and whether or not any of them can be excused."

"Oh, yes, I think I know what you're saying. Hold on." Tessa was a little bit puzzled by her response, but she decided to turn her attention back to the Lifetime movie without worrying too much about it.

After about five minutes, Tessa forgot that she was on hold. But when the Lifetime movie went to a commercial break, Tessa remembered her phone call and feared that she had been abandoned on the line. She became upset, hung up the phone, and dialed the number back again. A woman answered. Tessa tried hard to determine whether or not she recognized the woman's voice, but by her only saying "Hello?" Tessa couldn't be sure. She wished that she had thought to ask for names. She tried to engage the woman in conversation until she could tell.

"Do you know what department handles inquiries about certification requirements?" she asked.

"That depends on what exactly it is that you want to know."

Tessa thought that this could be the woman who left her on hold, but she still wasn't sure. So she continued to talk. "I need to know what exactly I have to do to become eligible for licensure and what I can skip and if I can go ahead and take the test if I feel like I'm ready to do it."

"Okay. That's easy enough for me to answer. You need to have at least a Bachelor's Degree and complete an approved teaching preparation program in Georgia. Nothing more, nothing less."

"Well, can I bypass the preparation class?"

"No."

Tessa still wasn't totally sure she recognized her voice, but she was reasonably sure that there wouldn't have been that many female receptionists answering the telephone there—wherever the hell that was—to choose from. She decided it must have been the woman, and was upset both because the woman had been neglectful in her earlier telephone conversation and because she didn't like the answer the woman provided.

"Why in the hell didn't you tell me that the first time I asked?"

"This is the first time you asked."

"Don't play dumb with me, bitch. I asked you the same damn question before you put me on hold for an eternity."

"I'm going to have to ask you to refrain from using that type of language or I may be forced to disconnect our call."

"You're going to disconnect it any-damn-way, you lazy hag. I hate that my tax money gets wasted on you."

"Your taxes don't pay my salary, but thank you for doing me the favor of clarifying why you want to bypass the established certification process. You're probably too dumb to pass the test and too unskilled and too unqualified to teach anybody's child anyway."

And with that, the woman did the James Brown click.

The woman's words surprised Tessa and delivered an incredibly painful sting. She wondered if any of it was true. After all, she didn't have the careers and big salaries her sisters had. The only profession she ever craved was teaching math, partly because the logic and reasoning skills needed to solve Algebraic equations came easily to her, but mostly because she enjoyed the sense of accomplishment she felt when she helped young people succeed at learning. She was livid.

To calm down, Tessa smoked a joint but she was still upset. So she called Tony, a man she hadn't seen in a long time. He was a drug dealer who stayed very busy with his work. Still, Tessa invited him to come over. Tony asked Tessa to give him an hour to get there, but he sped down I-285 and arrived at Tessa's house in thirty minutes. Tessa asked him for a pair of two hundred ninety eight-dollar shoes from a Neiman Marcus catalogue and an ounce of marijuana. He handed her three hundred dollars in cash and a small bag.

Before inviting Tony to her bedroom, Tessa turned on some slow music, took off her clothes and danced for him, opening and closing her legs so he could appreciate her fresh wax job. Tony seemed genuinely pleased, and Tessa felt like something she hadn't in a while—a professional.

* * *

Karen considers herself to be a better driver than most people on the road because she is from Atlanta. This morning, as often happens, Karen is frustrated with the drivers on I-285, the interstate that makes a circle around the city. Visitors seem confused by how the signs change from "north" to "east" to "south" as they continue on the same road, so they move too slowly and without purpose. She cuts off a blue car on her right without using a turn signal because he took too long to make room for her to get over. The man in the blue car points his middle finger at Karen while honking his horn. When Karen exits, she shakes her head out of pity for the driver and wonders if he bought his driver's license from Wal-Mart. She thanks God that He made her to be so intelligent and such a good driver that she can drive for both herself and others on the road. Two seconds later, another car almost rear-ends her new Mercedes and that driver yells for her to stop slamming on her brakes so suddenly. She shakes her head and whispers a prayer for him. She feels sorry for him, too, for being both stupid and an incompetent driver.

At the Special Spot, her favorite restaurant, she orders the lox-and-bagel breakfast and asks Meechie, who during the morning shift serves as both the waiter and the cook, to put her red onions and capers on the side so she can sprinkle them sparingly across her bagel. Meechie smiles deeply at Karen because he is a breast man and Karen has big breasts. Karen looks away when he smiles because she hates to see so many shiny gold teeth at one time.

Karen

Truck Drivers

"GIVE ME FIFTY DOLLARS of Petrol on pump number seven, please."

I am pissed I forgot to grab the wallet that contains my gas card when I switched purses this morning, which means I will have to walk into the gas station in order to pay cash. The problem with this is I am spoiled and do not care to walk into the gas station where I have to wait behind dozens of lotto players who can no longer remember the numbers they dreamed they were supposed to "quick pick." To complicate matters even further, I am about six weeks past what would have been my touch-up relaxer's due date except now I'm trying to go natural but am on the verge of abandoning my efforts in this humid weather. This is the fourth day of consecutive rain this week, which, now that I think about it, is very strange weather for an Atlanta December. It reminds me of being in Tallahassee, Florida, during my undergrad studies at FAMU. As I get back in my car, I'm hopeful my hair hasn't frizzed at the top which would contrast too obviously with my silky Indian sew-in weave that's hanging down to my butt.

The supreme octane gas is chug-a-lugging into the gas tank at what seems to be the slowest possible speed and so while I wait, I begin to make a list of the groceries I intend to pick up from Kroger. I've only made it to number two—which is pita bread—when I hear a tap on the door. I jump so quickly that I hit my forehead on the window. A toasty brown man with light brown eyes and a bald head is smiling at me through the window. I do not smile back, but I do roll down my window.

"I'm sorry. I didn't mean to scare you."

I'm looking at my purse out of the corner of my eyeball, now wishing I hadn't lowered the window. If he pulls out a gun and asks for it, I'm not even going to put up a fight—I think I can just throw it at him from here.

"I saw you pumping your gas and I wanted to offer to do it for you, but I couldn't get over here in time. Let me finish this up for you, if that's okay."

I just stare at him. His lips are the darkest thing on his face. Darker than his eyes, I think. He is rough looking, but very attractive. I relax.

I leave my window down so that I can hear him talking as he holds the pipe in the gas tank. "I hope you don't mind me asking this, but are you married?"

I probably blush. I respond by shaking my head no.

"My name is Tim. You are gorgeous."

"Thank you," is all that I can think of to say.

"You mind telling me yours?" He has a gorgeous smile.

"Sorry. My name is Karen."

"Are you from around here?"

"Uh huh, I grew up not too far from here."

"No, I mean, you look kind of exotic to me. What are you mixed with?" I hate when men say that. It sounds ignorant to me. But I can't help but to like his voice. It has an unusual sound. It's deep and sort of raspy.

"My parents are black. Well, wait a minute. My mother's mother was half white, but you wouldn't know it by seeing her," I say, thinking about Emily and Big Mama. Then I wish I hadn't told him that. It's none of his business really.

"Okay, I see," he says, rubbing his hands together. "So you're just pretty. I love your skin. And those eyes are the most beautiful black I've ever seen. Please tell me you're single, even though I really can't believe it could be true."

"I am."

He rests his arm on my car door and leans in toward me in the seat. I see him take a look around the inside of the car. I'm glad I had it cleaned last week because there's usually junk everywhere.

"And you sure look sexy as hell in this Mercedes. I love to see a woman who takes care of herself. What kind of work do you do, might I ask?"

"I'm in medicine."

"Medicine? You mean like you work at a pharmacy?"

"No, not exactly that. I'm a doctor."

"Wow. So you're both beautiful and smart."

I blush again.

"Well, please let me call you later on, Dr. Karen. My homeboy over there is sort of in a hurry and I really want to talk to you but I don't want to rush this conversation."

I look over at the candy-apple red Cadillac Escalade that he had hopped out of. Sure enough, there's a joker in the front seat who's watching us like TV. I turn my attention back to Mr.—oh what was his name? Tim. The wind blows a breeze from behind him and I like the way his cologne smells. It's clean and spicy at the same time.

"What kind of work do you do?" I blurt out. It feels funny to ask because I don't want to be perceived as materialistic, but I do need to know before I give him my phone number.

"I was waiting for you to ask. I drive trucks, darling. Matter of fact, my homeboy you see over there is my business partner."

"Oh, okay."

"I'm probably not the kind of man you usually would date, huh?"

I haven't dated in so long that I don't know how to answer that. I shrug my shoulders.

"Well, you look like the type of woman who likes hospital nerds, but maybe you can learn to like somebody who's a little rough around the edges, too. Give it a try."

I smile and nod my head.

"You're so cute that I can't stop looking at you. I'm going to take you out on the road with me one day if you'll let me."

"You're asking me to ride somewhere in your truck with you?"

"Yep, that's what I'm asking."

"Is that legal?"

"I believe so. The last time I checked, you needed a license to drive, not ride." He winks.

I rattle off the phone number without thinking and figure that he won't call.

* * *

The movie *Salt* with Angelina Jolie is on television. I like this part—it's when she dyes her hair black in the hotel room and then gets ready to go out and shoot somebody with spider venom. A soon as she hits her target, I make my way into the kitchen. I'm popping some popcorn and listening out for Aunt Camilla to ring the doorbell when I hear my cell phone buzz.

"Surprised to hear from me already, huh? Well, I wanted to holler at you before you try to forget who I am. With looks like yours I think you might have a lot of men who are trying to get to know you."

"Who is this?" I pretend like I can't remember meeting him. I hope I sound believable.

"Your future husband."

"Excuse me?"

He laughs. "Lighten up. It's Tim from the BP."

"Oh, okay. Nice to hear from you," is all I can think of to say.

"So are you in for the night? Or can you come out and see me?"

I'm a little surprised by his forwardness. "It's a little early for us to do that, wouldn't you say?"

"It's not too early for me because I realize you only live once. But you can take your time. I respect that. So tell me, what is a woman like you doing in on a Friday? Oh, no. Don't tell me. You're getting ready to go out on a date right now."

I start to lie and tell him that, yes, I am, but I don't want to start off by telling untruths. "No dates planned for the evening—unless you count the one I have with two or three stacks of laundry."

"What's a woman like you doing without a husband?"

"I'm not in any hurry to get married," I go on and lie because he's forcing me to.

"Boyfriend?"

"Not exactly."

"Does that mean yes or no?"

"I guess it means no, but I do go on dates," I lie again. "Just none tonight."

"So you mean to tell me that I'm this lucky?"

"Who says you're in luck?"

"I do. I mean, I get to meet a smart, educated, beautiful woman like you while she's still single and actually get her to give me the time of day. I feel privileged."

I'm flattered. "You should."

"What do you like to do?"

"Excuse me?"

"Do you have any hobbies?"

For some reason, I'm surprised he asked such a thoughtful question. "I do. I'm on the health committee of the singles ministry in my church. I read—mostly historical fiction. And I'm also learning to play tennis."

"That's a lot. And you have time to do all this while being a doctor? I thought all doctors were too busy to have real lives."

"It does feel like that sometimes, but I've learned to find some work-life balance over the past couple years. I don't see too many obstetric patients anymore, so my hours are pretty much set, unless I'm taking call from someone else."

"I have no idea what you just said."

"Sorry. I'm a women's health doctor. I see female patients but I don't take many pregnant ones anymore."

"Got it."

"Really?"

"Yes, really. You don't have to have been to medical school to know what an OB/GYN is."

"Wow, I'm impressed."

"Why? Because you think you can't drive trucks and have a brain, too?"

"No. Because even most college-educated men don't even know what an OB/GYN is. Wait. I didn't mean to say it like that."

"That's okay, darling. I am not offended."

"I am so glad you're not. I was trying to say that most men couldn't tell you what those letters mean unless they actually—well, you know. But I wasn't trying to discredit you because you drive trucks."

"Good. Because driving trucks has earned me a pretty good living. In fact, I consider myself to be a multi-faceted business man, with being a professional driver for commercial industries just one of them."

"You're not scared to drive those big old things?"

"What's there to be afraid of, darling?"

"Carrying around all that weight and jackknifing or blowing a tire or falling asleep while on the road."

"Those are some real possibilities but I don't think about any of that very often. You'll see when I take you out on the road with me."

"And what makes you so sure I'm going to agree to that?"

"I just have a feeling you will."

"You're a very confident man, Tim. Now before you ask me anything else, tell me a little bit more about yourself."

"What do you want to know?"

"Anything. Let's see—are you from Atlanta originally?"

"I'm originally from Miami but I've been here for eight or ten years now."

"Seems everybody is a transplant these days. Did a Miami hurricane blow you up this way?"

"Huh?"

"I'm sorry," I say, realizing that he doesn't find my attempt at a joke to be funny. I'm really not sure I do, either. "What brought you to Atlanta?"

"The music industry."

I sit up in the bed. "Really?"

"Yep. Why do you keep sounding surprised? I told you I'm multi-faceted, darling."

I laugh at the way he says the word multi-faceted. I'm not sure he's using it correctly but it sounds cute.

"I've been working on an album off and on for a while now. You remember seeing my homeboy in the car with me when I met you?"

"Yes."

"He produces tracks for a lot of major artists in the area. I've sold quite a few songs, too, but I haven't been able to really break through like I wanted to until recently."

"But I thought you drove trucks."

"I do. That's my bread and butter. Really, I own three of them. I have drivers that go out for me on contract so I can free up my time and put in some work in the studio."

"How old are you?" I hear myself ask.

"Forty-two."

I am immediately impressed at his ambition to become a musician in his forties. I wish that more men were like him.

"I know you're not supposed to ask a woman her age, so let me put my question this way—would you like to volunteer to tell me how young you are?"

"Thirty-eight."

"That's about what I would have guessed."

I'm not sure how to interpret his comment.

He continues. "Do you live by yourself?"

"Yes, I do own my own home," I tell him, hoping he's equally as impressed with my ambition.

My line beeps before I get to hear his response.

"Hello?"

"Come open up the door for me. I'm outside," says Aunt Camilla.

I click back over. "Tim, I have some company. Can I call you later tonight?"

"You can do more than call me. I'd like for you to consider having dinner with me tonight."

I pretend like I didn't just hear him. I hang up and run toward the door.

Aunt Camilla has changed her hair color again. This time it's firecracker red. I also recognize the blue and white striped sweater dress that she's wearing—I let her borrow it to wear to a church event back in October. She should have returned it to me weeks ago. She looks pretty leaning up against the side of my house. As usual, she looks like she's posing for no one in particular.

"Come on in, Auntie. I like your hair."

"Thank you. I just got my lashes done, too," she says, while blinking hard. "You must not have noticed those. You know I'm trying to keep up with you young folks. I finally quit smoking, too. Those pills you gave me actually worked. You have to put in a little bit more effort to take care of yourself as you start to get older, you know."

"I know." I'm staring at her false eyelashes. I don't think it's supposed to be obvious that they're not real. They remind me of two little spiders perched neatly below her eyebrows.

"You do? Well then why don't you try coming with me to the salon sometimes? I'm ready to see you spice it up a bit. It's time for you to look your age instead of mine."

I touch my weave. "I just got this done. It cost enough money that I think I want to keep it for at least a couple months."

"A couple months? Are you crazy? You'll have a bird's nest or locks by then. Take that shit out in two or three more weeks and then get a new style. Your mama is right. You make too much money to be so damn cheap."

"Did you bring the cake with you?"

"I did. It's in the car. Did you hear what I said about your hair? It's time to cut it into a bob. Get you a style with some movement. Betty can do some pretty cuts. I watch her all the time."

I nod my head and walk outside past her to her car. I see the cake box in the back seat. I remove it from the car and take a quick peek. My mouth begins to salivate.

"Do you ever water these plants?"

I turn around to see Auntie sticking a finger deep down into the ground next to some pansies.

"Don't bother to answer that question with a lie because the dirt feels like a desert over here. Go turn on the water hose and let me see if I can bring this yard back to life."

I take the cake inside, sit it on my kitchen table, taste a little bit of icing with my finger and return back out to my front yard to do as I'm told. She's already pulled the hose out and has it raised in position over my flower bed. She waits until I cut the water on to continue talking.

"I'm giving you back your twenty dollars. You don't owe me anything for that cake," she says, while pointing the hose toward the pansies near my walkway.

"No, Auntie, I gave you that money to help out with the cost of the ingredients. I know you sell those for much more than what I gave you, so I already know you cut me a deal."

"Girl, get that money out of my pocket book," she says, pointing to the front seat of her car and almost spraying me with the water hose. "I should have made it for your birthday a few weeks ago like you asked. I've just been so busy with Stephanie and all the grandkids—carting them around to school and football and cheerleading practice and whatnot. I can't wait until she and her husband get it together so they can get the hell up out of my house."

I open her car door and retrieve the money from her bag. "Are they any closer to getting back together?"

"Don't get me to lying," she says with a shrug. "But they need to show me something soon. Calvin and I are ready to get our house back to ourselves. Start living a little. Maybe take some trips. We do still like to have sex, too, but the damn children keep cock-blocking. My period stopped a few months ago, you know."

I raise my eyebrows. "I'm surprised you've been having one for this long. I think Mama's stopped when she was close to fifty."

"I'm kind of glad mine hung on as long as it did. I'm not in a hurry to let everything dry up," she says with a smile. "And speaking of drying up, turn off that water hose and tell me what you're doing in the house all by yourself on a Friday night."

"Actually, I was just on the phone getting to know a new male friend when you arrived."

She wipes her hands dry on the sides of my dress. I think I see a smudge of mud come off but I don't say anything. She opens the front door to my house and invites herself in.

"It smells good in here. Is that a Glade plug-in? What fragrance is that? It's nice but it's too late in the year for your house to be smelling like beaches and flowers. You need something that smells like cinnamon and burning wood. Do you ever turn on your fireplace? I don't know why not. You ain't got to do nothing but flip a switch. Why are all the blinds still open? It's getting dark outside. Do you want the whole neighborhood to see what you've got up in here?"

I don't know which question to answer first. I start closing blinds in the living room.

"Tell me about this man."

"I just met him, really. He introduced himself to me at the gas station earlier today."

"Does he work?"

"Yes. He drives trucks and is working toward becoming a musician."

"Him and everybody else in Atlanta. Did he look well-groomed?"

"Very much so."

"Teeth straight and white?"

"I don't remember noticing them. I told you we just met today."

"That ought to be the first damn thing you look at. A nasty mouth means he's a nasty man."

"I'll let you know."

"Does he have any children?"

"I didn't get to that part, yet."

"Well what part have you gotten to, Karen?"

"Just work stuff, so far."

"When are the two of you going out?"

"I'm not sure. He invited me over to dinner tonight but I think it's too soon for that."

"Like hell it is. You need to get you a life. He invited you to dinner, not down the altar. You should go and see what his living arrangements are like."

"You think so, Auntie?"

"Yes, I do, unless you plan on eating that carrot cake for supper?"

She does have a point. I shake my head no.

"Go on and enjoy yourself, Karen, just be careful. You'll be an old lady before you know it. Don't waste a Friday night while you're still fine and in your thirties. You will live to regret it." She walks back over toward the door and puts her hand on the knob before turning around to look at me. "And wear something sexy, not one of those moo-moo shirts that you seem to like so much. Some jeans that fit your butt and some high heels wouldn't kill you, either."

"I would wear a certain blue and white sweater dress if my auntie didn't have it out on loan for two months."

"I thought you gave me this to keep," she says with a smile, before going out of the door.

As soon as I hear her car start up, I dial Tim's number back. When I ask him what he's doing, he tells me he's waiting for me. I write down his address. Thirty minutes later, I can hardly believe I'm leaving my house in an eggplant-purple sweater, black leggings and my highest pair of black stiletto boots. I jump in my own car and type his address in my GPS before I lose the nerve.

* * *

"Wow. Again, you look gorgeous. Please, come inside."

I hesitate for a second because I haven't been this nervous in a very long time. Out of habit, I turn around toward my car and hit the "lock" button on the remote key. When I turn back around, Tim has moved so close to me that I bump into his chest and feel his breath on my ear. I feel myself blush when our eyes meet. He definitely isn't shy. I think I smell pizza coming from inside the house. "Dinner smells good," is all I can think of to say.

"Thank you," he answers quickly. "It's from the finest chefs of Papa John's Pizzeria." He puts his arm around my waist and ushers me into his downtown condo. This place is impressive. The red and black contemporary-style furniture is a stark contrast to the classic European pieces I've collected in my home over the past six years. Actually, this already feels like a refreshing break from the monotony. I follow him through the kitchen into what looks like the living room. There is a huge flat-screen TV on the wall—I couldn't even guess what size it is—maybe a 75-inch if they make those—but the view of the city through the sliding glass door is what catches my eye. "Let me pour you a glass of wine." His voice surprises me from behind again.

"Okay. What do you have?"

"White or red?"

"White."

"Riesling."

Most Rieslings are a little too sweet for my taste. "Red," is what I say to change my answer.

"White Zinfandel?" He offers.

I wonder if he thinks that White Zinfandel is really a red wine. Apparently, he does. I dismiss my thoughts as being too petty and nitpicky. Red White Zinfandel it is. I accept the glass he pours and hands to me and take three quick sips, hoping that it helps to calm my nerves.

"I'm glad you came over here to see me. I was starting to think you were all talk."

"Here I am, in the flesh." I can't think of anything else to say.

"And beautiful flesh you are. I didn't notice you were this tall before."

"It's hard to pay attention to much detail when you've only seen a person while they're pumping gas." I'm embarrassed and feel like I shouldn't be here. I walk over to the fireplace and pretend to stare at a picture on the mantle above it. Two seconds later, I feel hands around my waist. I look down—I guess to see how clean his nails are. Immaculate. And his hands are huge. A big vein is bulging from his left wrist.

"So what do you think about my home?" Tim asks, a little too eager for a compliment. Now he gives my waist a little squeeze.

"It's gorgeous," I respond, and it really is. "Who helps you decorate? I don't know if I could do this good of a job myself."

At first he doesn't answer, only smiles a little. Ordinarily, this would have disturbed me—which is how I know the wine is beginning to take effect. "I'll take that as a compliment," Tim says, before pouring more wine in my glass. I drink half of it immediately.

Without asking for permission, I unlock the patio door and let myself outside. At night, downtown Atlanta offers a wonderful view. The junction of expressways, city buildings, lofts and restaurants lit with lights, and even small glimpses of headlights from passing cars look romantic tonight. The smell of my own perfume is intoxicating. Either the view, or this wine, or this apartment, or shoot, maybe the aroma of this pizza is making me feel extremely sexy. And right now, he is looking very Idris Elba-ish to me.

Tim-Idris grabs the pizza, two wine glasses, some plates, and joins me on the patio. A few minutes later, we're chatting and laughing like old friends. I'm proud of myself for loosening up and being pretty cool. It's just that every time he looks deep into my eyes, I think I might melt.

The next time he does it, I can't help but to blush and look away. This time I ask him, "What is it?" I don't like the way that question sounded when it came out of my mouth—it sounded much cooler in my head—so I instinctively hide my nervous smile behind my wine glass, then move the glass down an inch and take another sip.

"I'm just not used to seeing anybody this gorgeous standing so close to me is all."

"Yeah, right."

"Yeah is right."

"Why would you try to sell me on something like that? As cute as you are, I know you probably have a hundred girlfriends."

"Remember, I practically live out of a truck, darling. Most of the women I see are in gas stations or on the truck yards. And none of them look as good as you."

"What about when you're making music? I know for a fact women love that type of thing. Let me guess—they all hang out waiting to be cast in a video." I sling my hair—well, somebody's hair—over my shoulder and then immediately regret it because I bet it looked stupid. I gulp down a few more swallows of Zinfandel before sitting the glass down on the green patio table.

"Get real, Dr. Karen. Nobody has to wait for a video to be made when there's YouTube. Come on and join us in the 21st century," says Tim-Idris with a chuckle.

"So when are you going to let me hear some of your music?"

"I have a few things in production right now that should be ready for you to listen to in a week or two."

"In production? All right, okay, whatever that means. Well, you're not getting out of this one that easy. You'll just have to give me a live performance."

"Hold on. I just remembered something I do have inside you can listen to. Let me go get it."

When he walks away from me, I can see a space in between his jeans where his legs curve. I love it.

As soon as he's out of sight, I reach behind my head and make a vertical part in my head with my finger before pulling equal amounts of locks over my shoulder, and then I change my mind and flip the left side back over my shoulder. I lick my lips and almost reapply my red lipstick but I can hear Tim walking back toward the door and I don't want him to see me primping and think I'm trying too hard.

The sound of music comes floating out of the door. Since only a screen door separates us from the inside of the house where the system is playing, the sound is crisp and it doesn't take long for me to recognize the singer Miguel's voice coming through the speaker, although I don't recognize the song.

Tim-Idris picks up my wine glass and begins using it as a microphone. "Baby these fists will always protect you."

I'm feeling very warm.

"And baby this mind will never neglect you-oo."

And very tingly. He's on key and doesn't sound bad at all.

"And if they try to break us down, don't let that affect you, no girl."

I stand up so I can go to the bathroom and calm myself down. "May I have a glass of water? And where is your bathroom?"

He stands up and positions his body so close to mine that we're touching. And it feels good. So good, in fact, that I barely notice when he touches my waist and leaves his hand there. I look down at his hand, expecting him to move it away, but he doesn't. I push it away and ask him again to direct me to the bathroom. As I walk in there, I notice that my legs are a little wobbly. I decide that I've had enough to drink before washing my hands and returning to the patio. As soon as he sees me, he hands me my glass. I take one last sip before putting it back on the table.

Tim catches me by surprise by touching my chin and planting a single kiss on my lips.

"Wait a minute," I say.

Tim looks at me, slips his arms back around my waist and just holds them there. Being embraced like this feels amazing.

"This is my first time out with you. Hell, we're not even out because we're in your house. Let's just get to know each other," I force myself to say.

"Yes, let's do that," he says, while pulling me deeper into his chest and before kissing me again on my lips. For a moment, I'm mesmerized by the romanticism. Then I feel his arms begin to move south. I hate that it fees this good.

Tim-Idris's hands are sliding down into my stretch pants almost effortlessly. Before I can step back and ask him what he thinks he's doing, he finds my clitoris and begins rubbing it through my lace panties.

"We can't. I can't," I moan.

"Doesn't it feel right?"

"I'm not a whore, Tim. I don't move this fast."

"I know you're not a whore, Karen. Just relax."

I know what I should do, but I'm finding it very difficult to ask him to stop rubbing on me. It's been so long since I've been touched like this. Instinctively, I turn around and widen the space in between my legs so his hands can move more freely down there. It's got to be the wine because I'm never this weak and easy. Or horny. I feel one large finger, maybe his middle finger, head down toward my vagina and encircle the opening before finding its way back up to my other parts. I actually begin to tug at my own panties and pants to pull them down. He makes brief eye contact with me before grabbing my waist and kneeling down on the ground. Right here, on this patio, outside for the neighbors and whoever else to see, he begins to lick on me. I unbutton my own shirt. He yanks off his own pants.

His dick is big and black and thick and long. Before I can think about what's happening, he pulls me down on top of him, right into his lap. I ease down slowly. It's been such a long time and my body is responding favorably by giving me just enough juice to glide up and down and around all on top of him.

As soon as I think that I am starting to find my rhythm, he stops me.

"I want you to lay back."

"Huh?"

"I said that you need to lay back, beautiful. You're in control all day every day. I want you to surrender to me right now."

"Okay."

He places his hands around my waist and lifts me up carefully, very gently. He inspects my entire naked body. I feel a little self-conscious and try to suck in my stomach. He stands up from his seat and touches my face with two hands before looking me in the eye. "Karen, you are the most beautiful woman I've ever met."

"What?"

"Everything about you turns me on," he whispers, while laying me on my back. He places what feels like twenty kisses on my collarbone before meeting me in the eye again. He is still for a moment and touches my bottom lip with his index finger. Finally, he speaks again.

"You're sexy because of your brain," he says, and kisses my forehead. "I love how smart you are. And you should see these big brown eyes the way I can," he says, before kissing my eyelid. "Your breasts are perfect, like two volcanoes full of hot lava." One warm kiss follows another, then another. I plan to say, 'Come on. Yeah, right,' but then when he starts to kiss on my stomach, I forget to talk.

Between my legs, his mouth feels like a warm massage. He's still talking, but I have no idea what he's saying. He sucks and licks and rubs and touches on me for several minutes and with a pressure so steady that I come quietly and quickly, without warning. When I put my hand over my mouth to stifle my whimpers, he tugs it away and laces my fingers through his.

As soon as my leg stops shaking, he parts my thighs again. This time, he enters me more forcefully and quickly. Once he's all the way in, his strokes become long, deep, slow and tender. With each thrust, he aims himself toward my bottom and massages everything on the way up before landing on what I think might be the top edge of my cervix. I can't remember the last time I was with a man whose penis could reach all the way back there! Without even trying, I begin to rotate my hips toward him to catch every bit. He pushes and I pull with every muscle that I can find down there. I had no idea I could ever feel this good.

And then Tim suddenly stops moving.

I grab his wrist and pull it, anxious for him to continue pushing himself inside of me. But instead of pushing deeper inside, he withdraws.

"The condom broke," he announces solemnly. As if to prove it, he holds a piece of what looks like cling wrap up for me to see, then removes the now-detached plastic ring from the base of his penis and tosses it over the balcony. "That was it," he says. "That was my last condom."

Tim starts to stand up, but my body is having none of it. My legs are beginning to shake and the pit of my stomach feels like it might explode if he doesn't quickly lie back down on top of me. I know I should know better than to say what next comes out of my mouth, but I can't help it. I've been dickmatized. "Come back inside. You can pull out when it's time."

Tim doesn't ask me if I'm sure. He doesn't even pretend to be hesitant or thoughtful. He just pushes my thighs apart. And dammit, I let them fly right open. He eases back inside with such grace that it's almost poetic.

His chest, against mine, feels protective. His hands have joined with mine, over my head. My legs open wider and wider with each of his thrusts, because I want to feel all of him. I'm squeezing and rotating and shivering and pulling him deeper into me, all at the same damn time. After a few more strokes, I'm ready to come again but this orgasm is much stronger than the first. I bite my tongue in order to keep my mouth closed and from making eye contact, because I don't think it's supposed to be this good, this can't be right, he must have put something in my drink. This man—this bald-head, muscular work of art—is hitting the right spot every time he enters me. He doesn't miss—not even once. For a minute, I'm tempted to say I love you.

"Do you like it, darling?" he wants to know.

"Yes, I do," is what I attempt to say.

"Are you sure?"

"Oh, baby, I'm sure."

"I want you to be mine."

"You can have me. You can have all of me."

Tim licks my left nipple, and then my right. He goes back to the one on the left and stays there, gently sucking, until my hips stop pulsing up and down against him. And I could swear to God, that at this very minute, right now, the earth stands still.

Patricia

Old Receipts

THE LAST TIME I kept my workout clothes on this long after my spinning class, I ended up with a yeast infection that resembled a diaper rash. I should have changed my panties, at least, a long time ago but I was too busy listening to Carolyn, my yoga teacher, gossip about her twenty-something-year-old boyfriend. Todd, I think she said his name was, apparently has a very strong back and even stronger third leg. I tried not to become jealous as she boasted on how long he could love—and by love, I mean make love. I've been imagining myself in a steamy shower scene like the one she described during my whole fifteen minute drive home. And come to think of it, I've probably aroused myself into getting even more extra moisture in my panties. I unbuckle my seatbelt before I get in the driveway good and prepare to make a bolt out of the car even though I'm tempted to stay in and listen to my favorite song by Sade that just came on the radio.

I'm straining my voice by trying to sing low and raspy even though I'm now out of the car and don't have Sade's voice to lead me back to the right tune. I have absolutely no talent for singing, but it makes my soul feel good. I believe it is true that we, like God, are composed of three parts: mind, body and spirit. I've been making more of a conscious effort to nurture all three parts ever since I turned forty and started subscribing to the Oprah e-newsletter.

For example, working out with the girls at the gym always works to heal both my body and my heart. As much as I never feel like getting started, I'm always so grateful I did by the time I finish. Not to mention the fact that I owe my whole social life to these ladies. I never was too good at making and keeping friends, but for the past five or six years they have accepted and loved me for who I am.

I'm so anxious to get in the house that at first I'm not sure if I applied enough pressure to the garage door button when I pressed it. With the second push, I'm sure there was no mistake. At first I think the battery in the remote opener must be dead, but then I remember I had it replaced at the car dealership fewer than six weeks ago. It takes three or four minutes for the truth to register with me: that Gary, the Negro that I live with, my husband and supposedly my provider, let the damn electricity get cut off in my house. Again. He can be so forgetful. I wish he'd let me take over the bills.

I'm reminding myself of Mama with all the curse words that I've thought up by the time I make it in the house. I check the kitchen drawer, the bathtub soap basket and the kerosene oil lamp drawer hidden in the shelf in front of the tackle box before I finally circle back out to the garage to find some candles. I hear a box of something that sounds like tools topple over and land on the floor where I normally park my car. Reaching for the box's splattered contents, I stump my baby toe on a box that I couldn't see in the dark and holler "shit!" as loud as I can in hopes that screaming will relieve some of the pressure from the collision. Now hopping on one foot, I manage to light enough candles around this garage to be able to see what I'm doing. While bumping around in a drawer next to the tool shed in the garage, I notice a piece of paper lodged firmly in between an empty plant pot and the storage ladder. One day I'm going to get rid of all the meaningless paper that haunts my purse, garage and trunk, but, hey, Rome wasn't built in a day. I yank it out of place will full intentions of running it through the shredder when I notice it's a receipt dated 2009 for Babies"R"Us.

What in the world?

The text is hard to make out because the ink has faded. But if I didn't know any better, I would believe I saw Huggies diapers and Dr. Brown bottles itemized on the white piece of paper I'm holding with Gary's name and last four digits of his credit card printed across the top. I almost convince myself I'm overreacting to this bullshit until I notice two more receipts folded neatly behind it, one a baby jumper and another for—my eyes must be tricking me so I squint, as if doing so will rearrange the letters that I'm seeing into a different word—a baby crib.

Just as I'm trying to replace the receipts to the exact same spot where I think they may have fallen out of the toolbox, my eye catches a faded, yellow envelope below some rusty nails and tools I cannot identify. I scratch my middle finger while trying to dig beneath all of this metal in order to get my hands around it. The paper nearly tears in two as I fish it out of the box.

The envelope is halfway open and appears to be old because there is absolutely no adhesive left on it. I start to feel a little bit guilty for snooping in Gary's personal items but I quickly talk myself out of it and point my little flashlight at the stack of twenty or thirty personal check and store receipts that I retrieved from inside the envelope. My heart starts to beat quickly, so I put the envelope down on the top of the tool box, look around in the garage until I find a stool, open it up and take a seat on the top step. I take a deep breath and begin to shuffle through the papers.

The one on top is a carbon copy from Gary's Bank of America checkbook in the amount of $150. It's dated this past July 1. He's signed it, but there doesn't appear to be anyone's name on the recipient line. The memo line says "childcare" in his cursive handwriting. The next paper is a receipt from Toys"R"Us dated last November. The third and fourth are illegible—the ink has rubbed off.

The next words I see written across a different piece of paper make my heart bleed, and I have to re-read it twice to make sure I didn't make it up. It is another carbon copy from his checkbook. The recipient line is blank just like the other and the dollar amount on the check dated February 1 is four-hundred dollars, but the memo line clearly reads: Child support payment. I swallow hard and then almost choke on my saliva.

I stand up and then sit back down. I stand right back up again and then tuck the receipts into my pocket and walk back into the house. Then I decide to place them back in the garage and have almost returned them in the exact spot I found them in his tool box before I change my mind a second time.

This time, when I re-enter my home through the garage door, I feel the immediate urge to shit. I sit down on the toilet and try to calm my nerves and collect my thoughts. By the time I'm finished and have washed and dried my hands, I have decided there must be a logical explanation for these receipts and replace my evidence back outside where I found it and wait until something else warrants the need for me to bring this shit up to Gary. I stand in front of my bathroom mirror and wonder, out loud, what friend or family member he's helping out and why he chose not to discuss it with me because I know there's no way my husband could have had a real-live affair, much less fathered a real-live baby, without me having a clue. Gary loves me. He goes out of his way to make that clear to me on a daily basis. Right?

I pour a little bit of Gary's Remy Martin over some crushed ice in my wine glass and drink it straight while I talk to the automated phone system for Georgia Power. The two-hundred-nine dollars and forty-eight cents that were overdue are now posted to my American Express card, and I don't even bother to write down the confirmation number. I hang up on the computer lady right after she tells me my electricity will be restored within twenty-four hours, and fall out on the chaise in my bedroom. I thank God the temperature is in the sixties today, and that I have a gas fireplace in my bedroom I can always turn on if I get cold tonight. When my vagina begins to itch, I remember to take off my exercise clothes. I jump up and peel them off. I pile them up into a little hill at the foot of the bed, lie down and stick my foot on top of the pile to examine my now purple toe.

In fact, I'm still lying on this bed butt naked when I hear Gary's truck pull up in the driveway. The front door slams when he walks in. I can hear his clothes hit the steps as he simultaneously climbs them and disrobes in his evening ritual.

"What happened to the garage door?"

"It works on electricity."

"What in the hell does that have to do with anything?"

"Apparently, a lot. Ours was cut off today."

He grimaces and drops his head. "I'm sorry, Pat. I knew I was forgetting something. Where is the cordless phone? I promise to have it back on by tomorrow."

"I already called Georgia Power and made the payment."

"How much was it? I'll put the money in your account tomorrow."

"Two hundred."

"Well, let me have one of your deposit slips out of your checkbook before I forget." He bends down and kisses me on the cheek.

"I'm not worried about the money. But tell me this. What's on your mind so much lately that you would forget to pay something as important as the electricity? The last time you did this, you had been fired from your job and had been trying to hide it for almost six weeks. Should I ask you if you went to work today?"

He doesn't answer me, but instead goes back downstairs and pours himself a glass of what smells like cognac with eggnog—the festive kind that they only sell in December—and lays down behind me on the bed. I wish he would get up and take a shower. It doesn't matter that I'm not clean. I try real hard to remember if we had sex yesterday but I can't. If we did, then I'm off the hook for tonight.

"What happened to your foot?" he asks, apparently noticing my purple toe for the first time.

"I bumped it in the dark."

"Do I smell liquor on your breath?"

"Do I smell it on yours?" I'm not trying to be cross, I just can't help it.

"Okay. I deserve that. I know I'm supposed to take better care of my wife than this," he says, while rubbing a hand over my cheek and neck. "But was your day okay, I mean, besides your forgetful and getting-old husband forgetting to pay the bills on time and allowing the electricity to be cut off in your house?"

"It was," I say, in my best attempt to soften up.

"Clark finally accepted my client's offer for the system they wanted me to build."

"Is that right?"

"Yes, indeed. So you know that my bonus commission check is going to be right on time for Christmas, right? You still haven't told me what you want."

"Lights and heat."

He shakes his head and gets up and goes into the bathroom. I feel incredibly relieved.

As soon as I hear the glass shower door go BAM, I immediately begin looking for his iPhone. It takes me two or three tries to find it because I have to look in different pockets of his pants, which, of course, are strewn across the steps. What immediately pisses me off is that it has a code on it. I don't have a code on my damn phone and smell more trouble. Anger turns to relief when I guess the code—his mama's birthday—on the first try. What I'm looking for exactly, I don't know. Anything. I'm down to the Z's in his contact list and haven't seen any names that look even remotely suspicious.

I'm getting ready to put the phone down when I see an envelope pop up on the screen. I sit down on the bed and touch it. The text message envelope opens up. I sit still for a minute because I didn't know Gary even enabled his text features. What I see next makes my heart skip a beat:

Vanette: You left something here I think you'll soon miss.

Without any context I have no idea what this means, so I scroll up to read more of the conversation. My eyes land on his writing, which displays in the color blue.

Gary: Send me a picture.
Vanette: Okay, I'm driving. Wait until I get home.
Gary: Don't forget.
Vanette: Hope you're sitting down.
Vanette: This picture file is too large to download. Compressing...
Gary: I didn't get it. The file is too big.
Vanette: For real? It says it went through. Let me resend it.
Gary: Still nothing. That ass is too fat to send through a phone. LOL.
Vanette: You'll just have to come and see this for yourself then.
Gary: Leaving work in 10 minutes. Call you when I'm outside.
Gary (again): Wowsers!
Vanette: You left something here that I think you'll miss.

I back out of this message and see about ten other conversations floating around in his phone. This motherfucker is the king of texts. And is obviously too stupid to delete them. No, wait a minute. I must be the stupid motherfucker in the room. And to punish myself even further, I continue to read them. While reading, I feel as though I've been personally introduced to Sandra, Jada, Shoniqua, Deloris and somebody programmed under the name "Banana Split."

Gary steps out of the shower and puts on his robe and slippers. He comes into the bedroom where he must have forgotten about the electricity problem because he immediately picks up the remote control. Without thinking, I jump up, snatch it out of his hand and start hitting his stupid ass over the forehead with it. Out of what I think looks like a reflex, he raises his hand back like he wants to hit me. He pauses for a second before grabbing me forcefully and restraining my arm, but not before I kick him in the shin.

"What the fuck is wrong with you!?" he screams.

My lips want to form some words, but nothing is coming out. For a minute, I wonder if I'm having a stroke. I am breathing hard and on my back with my hands pinned down. Finally, I am able to push out, "Get off of me."

We stare at each other for a few long seconds.

"Who are all these women in your cell phone?"

He looks down at the cell phone that fell on the floor as if he's just seeing it for the first time. "You've been going through my phone?"

"Yes. Who are they?"

"I don't even know what you're talking about. Who is who?"

"All these women who you've apparently been texting while I was stupid enough to think you were at work until 7:00 every night."

"What are you saying, Pat? You don't think I've been working because I've sent a few texts?"

"I said who the fuck are they?"

"Just friends."

"I sure as hell don't text my friends at 8:00 every morning. And I certainly don't ask them for pictures or tell them that I'm on my way to their houses at 5:00 in the damn evening."

"Pat, what point are you making? And why are you even in my damn phone? And how did you get in here? You've been hacking my privacy?"

"Hacking your privacy doesn't even make sense, you stupid motherfucker. You need to rethink that phrase while you're rethinking the lie that you're trying to sell me. How many women are you talking to like this? No, scratch that. I have a better question for you: Are you seeing a woman with a damn baby?"

Gary turns around and walks back toward the bathroom in which he just took a shower. He doesn't even answer me—just walks real slowly into the bathroom and pauses in front of the mirror. He looks like he's about to choke. For a real minute, I believe he might not be breathing. Serve his black ass right. I just sit there and wait with my back propped up against a pillow.

I run out of the bedroom and start jumping down the stairs two at a time. When I get to the bottom, I slip and almost fall on the hardwood floor because I'm wearing socks. In less than three seconds, I'm in the kitchen, feeling around under the dark kitchen sink.

My fingers identify the object I'm reaching around for before my eyes have a chance to confirm it. In fact, I don't even look down at all. I just shake the jug around to make sure it's not too close to being empty before I dash back upstairs and to my bedroom.

I hit the switch in the closet to turn on the lights, then I remember that the electricity is cut off. I walk out and grab the flashlight from the bedroom before re-entering the bathroom to access our closet. Gary's clothes are on the left side. Mine are on the right. I can feel his eyeballs behind me, staring, wondering what I'm about to do next. But for some reason, instead of slowing me down, the thought of him anticipating my every move just fuels my rage. At first, I begin by taking shirts and pants off of the hangers. After one of the hangers catches my robe and doesn't easily give, I get aggravated and I grab a big armful of clothes off the rack. It's not until I release the clothes into a pile in my bathtub that Gary is able to see the blue and white Clorox bottle in my hand. He lunges toward me, but the top is already off and I forcefully sling the contents of the jug onto the pile of clothes and stand back and wait for a reaction as if it were a baking soda volcano and I just added the vinegar. Then he tackles me like I'm a football player. All of my muscles tighten up in anticipation of him hitting me, but he doesn't. Instead, he screws the top back on the bleach, then looks me square in the eye and just says, "Patricia, calm down."

I jump up. "Calm down?" Then I remember the scissors in the drawer behind me. I almost break the knob while slinging the drawer open to grab them, and briefly wave them in the air at Gary. "I'm going to calm down right now. Matter fact, I'm already calm. I'm so cool, motherfucker, that you don't even understand it." And then I walk into our closet and begin to slash the arms and collars and buttons on every goddamn suit, shirt, pair of pants, and blazer I can get my hands on.

"Maybe I should leave."

I turn around. "What?"

"I said it's probably best that I leave. I can understand you being upset, but there's no need for you to get ridiculous." He's not looking at me. He's looking at the scraps of clothes on the floor.

"Oh no you won't be leaving me, nigga. You're not leaving me because I'm leaving your ass first! But answer me this, before I go. How many children do you have floating around out here?"

"I don't even know if this baby is mine. She tried to trick me into being with her and has been upset with me ever since she realized I wasn't leaving you."

"That's not what I asked."

"How many? Children, you mean?"

I take the top off of the bleach again.

"One."

"So you're out here populating the world and don't even have the decency to inform your wife, the one you won't even allow to have any of your babies. I see. This all makes sense to me now."

"It's nothing like that, Patricia."

"It's everything like that, Gary. Why didn't you take her ass to the clinic like you took me?"

"I didn't even know she was having the damn baby until he was born."

"Having the damn baby," I repeat. "You are a sorry excuse for a man, and a much worse excuse of a father, you know that?"

He directs his gaze to the empty closet behind me.

"I wouldn't wish you on anybody's baby. I mean, it's one thing to be a whore, but it's another to halfway acknowledge your own child. I never knew that you were such a coward."

Gary turns around a leaves the room. I have no idea where he goes, but I'm glad he's out of my sight.

A few seconds pass before I notice his phone is still resting at the foot of the bed, and has the nerve to be lit up at the moment. A silent call must be coming through. I pick it up and answer it. Gary either doesn't hear me or doesn't give a shit. The caller on the other end hangs up. Finally, I do too. Then I decide to drop his phone in my purse, pull on my slippers, grab my car keys and walk out of the house. I don't even know where I plan to go when I hear myself start the car's engine. But before I back out of the driveway, I put the car in park, throw on the emergency brake and hightail it back into the house. The knife I have in mind is glistening, smiling at me from on top of the knife rack. I quickly snatch it out of its place and for some stupid reason grin just to see if I can catch the reflection of my teeth to see if they look like they belong to me because they suddenly feel bigger—too big for my mouth—before heading back out of the door. I stab the tires on Gary's Range Rover one at a time, twice in the last one, before taking a deep breath and jumping back in the Camry. Tears spill over the side of my eyeballs before I can catch them and I call myself dumb out loud for staying married to a motherfucker with the nerve to go out and get a baby on me and for being too damn stupid to notice until today.

Emily

Go Fish

CAMILLA AND I are lying across my bed playing Concentration with Go Fish cards. We spread all the cards out, face down, then turn them over one at a time, hoping to get a match. The cards belong to her granddaughter, but we find playing with them to be more fun and mentally stimulating than five-year-old Jada does.

I turn over a card that has a purple fish wearing a pink wig and red glasses. Do I really even need to go through with this whole production? It certainly sounded more useful in my head before I actually started putting the plan into play than it does now. Physical therapy hurts like hell. Kicking those little blocks and boards around in that whirlpool is not nearly as fun as it looks. And squeezing that tennis ball fifty eleven times a day is making my whole left side hurt. Plus, I can think of a few good reasons why I should quit going to physical therapy and speech therapy all together. The next card I turn over is a blue dolphin wearing a neck tie. I flip both of them back over, face down.

Reason number one to bail out: The girls already think half of me is crazy and the other half handicapped. To let them tell it, I only had a few working marbles prior to my stroke. I'm off my rocker, at least in their eyes. And it's almost easier to keep things that way, because people tend to be nicer to you when they believe you to be slow. God looks out for babies and fools, is how the saying goes. I'd rather be the baby, but I can't help that I keep having birthdays.

Reason number two: What if they don't like me? What if, after peeling away my defenses and lowering my guard, they believe me to just be weak and pathetic? Isn't that worse than being mean? It might be, for me at least. Then I'll get absolutely no leniency at all, if on top of not liking me, they find out I can take care of myself. Shit. I might need to rethink this whole strategy. Camilla might be right about something for the first time in her life.

I'd better not let her hear me think that just in case she's half as psychic as she thinks she is. I scoot away from her on the bed so she doesn't pick up anything from me through osmosis.

She doesn't seem to notice the space I've put between us. She's too busy cheering because she just won the game.

Karen

Labor and Delivery

THIS MORNING, I'm flying like a bat out of hell because I am late for work. I hate being late for work. I hate being late anywhere.

What annoys me more is the fact that Dr. Mignon didn't bother to give me a status report on her patients before she left town this morning for her island destination shotgun wedding. She knows better than to turn her patients over to me without a courtesy phone call. And for some reason today, I'm not in the mood for surprises. It could have something to do with the sleep deprivation that I've noticed accompanies my dreams lately, most of which involve lions and tigers and snakes and bears. And, oh yes, fish.

Last night, for example, I had the most difficult time falling asleep. When I finally did, I had a dream I was a mermaid swimming alongside hundreds and hundreds of fish. There were big fish, small fish, and everything in between. I counted them all and named their colors, just like a Dr. Seuss book. I met a seahorse who could juggle seashells and a jellyfish that could squirt red velvet cupcakes out of his butt. A lovely dolphin named Otis allowed me to ride on his back as he took me on a tour of the entire ocean. It was an amazing and wonderful adventure until Otis suddenly turned into a huge shark and tried to eat me. I swam away so fast that I woke myself up and had to catch my breath, feeling even more tired than I was when I went to sleep. I am sure this is a sign of either anxiety or depression, perhaps even both.

I swipe my badge through the digital sensor as soon as I arrive on the fourth floor of the hospital and race back out to the parking lot to move my car to any space that doesn't say handicapped on it before I get towed. By the time I get back upstairs, change into my scrubs in the locker room, and head back to the physician's lounge to get morning report it's already 6:00 a.m. As soon as I hit the unit, my pager goes off and I immediately recognize the number to the emergency room. I turn right back around smack dab in the middle of the hallway without even looking for Dr. Mignon's patient charts. This time, I take the stairs down instead of using the elevator, hopeful that increasing my heart rate and circulating my blood a little more quickly will help me shake off my case of the sleepies. When I enter the suite from which I've been summoned, I see, in a bed, a young woman who's tossing, turning, moaning and groaning while holding her right side.

"I've given her morphine twice already," says her nurse to me without ever making eye contact.

"How many weeks pregnant is she?" I ask.

"We don't know. She doesn't remember her last menstrual period. The ultrasound transporter hasn't come yet to pick her up. We wanted you to take a look before we turned her over to them."

"I'm writing an order for Fentanyl."

"Fentanyl? Don't you think that's a bit much for a miscarriage?"

"Perhaps, but not for an ectopic pregnancy."

"How do you know that without seeing her ultrasound?"

I pull the young woman's bed sheet away from her bottom, revealing the pool of dark purple spotting that has collected beneath her for both of us to see. She should have recognized the classic symptoms of an ectopic pregnancy before she even paged me. I start to answer her question, but then I decide not to waste my time. I can't make up for what she didn't learn in school. Not today.

Without even reviewing her chart, I begin to stroke the young woman on her forehead and tell her that she'll be feeling much better soon. "As soon as you get this new medicine, you'll begin to relax. I know that you're hurting, and this is the closest thing I can give you to cocaine, legally. I believe I know what's happening with you, sweetheart. Depending on what comes back on your ultrasound, we may have to go to do some surgery today. But try not to worry. You're going to be fine."

She looks up at me through bloodshot eyes. "Did I do something wrong to make this happen?"

"Nothing. Absolutely nothing at all."

"But I tried so hard to get this baby."

"I understand."

"My husband went home to bring me a change of clothes. Can you wait for him to come back before you do anything to me?"

"I believe we can. Call him and tell him to grab a few things for himself, too, just in case you have to stay here another day or two." I start to talk to her about what she can expect during the ultrasound, but her eyes begin to close as the last of the drug is pushed through her IV.

Claudia Houston is her name, I soon discover. I learn in the operating room, as I'd already suspected after reviewing her ultrasound results, that her ectopic pregnancy has ruptured her right fallopian tube, but I hadn't expected quite so much blood to have collected in the cul-de-sac. I didn't have much tissue to disconnect and remove—it was one of the worst cases I've seen in a long time. I take a quick peek over at her left tube before closing her up. I'm relieved to be able to tell her it looks normal, and she can likely still have a baby when she's ready to try again.

Once I'm back up on Labor and Delivery, my eyes go from my watch to the assignment board that has already been written on. I say a quick prayer in my head to ask for something reasonable today, maybe a scheduled C-section or a vaginal delivery by a twenty-something-year-old mom without complications, because I haven't been feeling quite right for the past few days and, after my marathon swim meet last night, I am absolutely exhausted and don't think I can handle anything too challenging. When I finally spot my patients' names and conditions on the board, I realize I will be having no such luck today.

Room 819's nurse, Sylvia, comes out and stands in the hall right in front of me. She's an extraordinary nurse and seems very experienced. Still, I believe she looks much older than she really is. She might have had a hard life before she came over here from Mexico. I have to make myself stop tracing her frown lines around her face in order to pay attention to what she's telling me.

"I don't understand this," she says. "The girl is eighteen years old and acts like she's completely oblivious to the situation—like she doesn't even realize she's having a baby. I asked the mother about her daughter's acceptance of this pregnancy and she just shook her head 'no' but still hasn't explained what that means. Her sister is there with her, thank God. You'll get more conversation out of her than you will Ms. Gonzalez. And she doesn't speak any English so you'll probably want to page Sabrina to help you through. And, oh yeah. I almost forgot. Do you have any gum that you can chew while in you're in the room?"

When she asks me this I realize that I must have missed something important in the conversation. I guess I started tuning her out without realizing it. "Gum?"

"Yeah, to help you with the smell."

Shit. I hadn't had a chance to go through her chart yet but there was about a 90% chance that an IUFD with a bad smell meant that there was some type of infection. "Yes, I think I have something in my bag. Thanks for the warning."

"You're welcome, *chica*. *Adios*, and have a good day." With that, Sylvia grabs her book bag, hits the handicapped automatic door opener sign, and leaves the maternity ward. At this exact moment, I decide I'm quitting teaching hospitals and going private. Somewhere where I can bill insurance companies instead of waiting for the county or Medicaid (if we're lucky) to pay the bill. And, oh yeah, somewhere I don't have to learn to speak Spanish.

I walk into 819 to introduce myself but no sooner do I cross the threshold do I walk right back out the damn door to fill my lungs with fresh air. The smell is rancid, something worse than hot shit. I haven't even seen the patient.

"Hello?" A girl's voice calls from the room. She must have already seen me.

"I'm sorry, I forgot something very important," I call back through the door. I jog back down the hallway and into the locker room to look for some gum. After four years of medical, another four years of residency and five years of looking up inside my patients' booties all day long one would think I'd have become immune to most smells, but I see that I'm really going to need some help with this one. I rummage through my "Smart is the New Sexy" bag that I always bring with me. No gum there, but I do find three broken pieces of peppermint at the bottom. I quickly stuff one of them in my mouth and find solace in the eucalyptus mint flavor.

The second time I enter her room I see that the patient, Ms. Gonzalez, has turned toward the door in her seat. She is a petite Hispanic woman with bleached-blonde hair and doesn't look a day older than fifteen. The girl who is perched on the window with her legs crossed is probably the older sister. Neither one of them says anything but they both have an urgent look in their eyes that suggest they are waiting to see who will start talking first.

Ms. Gonzalez doesn't say anything, but her sister speaks up as I'm writing my name on the dry-erase board on her wall. "I'm her sister. She doesn't speak much English but I can help her. She needs something for pain." I'm glad that she reminded me to check the front desk to see if Sabrina has returned my page at the nurse's station.

I look back at the patient lying in the bed and ask, "*Tiene dolor?*" She still doesn't speak but nods her head. I walk to the head of the bed and hold out both hands, wiggling my fingers, to let her know I am preparing to touch her. After conducting a brief physical assessment, I point to the pain scale on the wall. "*Que numero es dolor?*" I ask. Where is the interpreter when you need one? Ms. Gonzalez doesn't say anything but she looks at her sister and they conduct a brief conversation, speaking Spanish so quickly that I don't catch anything. Her sister turns to me and says, "Ten." This is a little unlikely considering most of our tens are in the middle of pushing a head out of their vaginas. Ms. Gonzalez is not crying, frowning or even rubbing her belly in that protective reflexive gesture that is most commonly reflective of pain. I wonder if they understood my question.

"*Diez?*" Someone repeats from behind me. I turn around to see Sabrina, the Spanish interpreter, standing behind me. Praise the Lord that she finally felt like showing up.

"*Si.*"

I open her chart to the physician's orders tab to see what Dr. Mignon has ordered for her. Nubain for pain and Phenergan for nausea. I decide to push the narcotic through her IV and give it a few minutes to circulate through her bloodstream before doing her vaginal exam. I pull the drugs out of the PIXIE system, pop the vial on the Nubain and draw it up through a syringe. After disconnecting the needle, I twist it onto the port on Ms. Gonzalez's IV, using my left hand to steady her wrist. Her hand is as cold as ice. "*Frio?*" I ask? No answer. Her eyes close as I push the last of the drug into her veins. If she was cold before, this will warm her right on up. I look over at Sylvia who is busy writing in the chart for me, and ask her to let Ms. Gonzalez know that I will be right back.

Feeling lightheaded from taking tiny sips of air while in Ms. Gonzalez's room, I sit down to review Ms. Gonzalez's chart. I am saddened to see that the psychiatric tablet is the thickest one of them all. Inside, I learn that Maria Gonzalez has been pregnant by her stepfather four times, beginning when she was eleven years old. Her mother, who refused to believe he was molesting her, put the teenager out of her house once she learned of this pregnancy. I flip to the history tab and find out she also has been diagnosed with chlamydia four times, corresponding with each of the pregnancies. The anger I felt toward her apathy is immediately replaced with sympathy. This child has been through more in her eighteen years than what is reasonable for eighteen people to experience in eighteen lifetimes.

My reading is interrupted by the moaning coming across from 819, which is room 820.

I am immediately surprised when I walk in the room because, by the last name, I expected to see another Hispanic patient in the bed. Instead, I'm looking in the face of a woman who is as black as I am. She is by herself, clenching the bedrails, and moving her legs up and down under the sheet. I lift the sheets back and see the bloody mucus and bubbles oozing between her legs. She's ready and I haven't even set up for the delivery. "Hello, Ms. Vasquez, my name is Karen. Do you mind if I give you a quick exam to see how far along your cervix has opened?"

"Aye yaye," Ms. Vasquez says.

After removing a sterile glove from the drawer next to her bed, I slide it on with one hand and apply the sterile lubricant with the other. Carefully inserting two fingers inside of her, I feel nothing but the anterior lip of her cervix. Just as I suspected.

"Ms. Vasquez, your baby is almost ready to come out. I want you to take some deep breaths and try not to push while I call your doctor and set up what we'll need to deliver the baby. Will you be okay if I leave the room for a few minutes?"

"*Tengo mucho dolor,*" she tells me. Shit. She can't speak English. I run out of the room yelling for Sylvia, the interpreter, while dialing Dr. Morgan's pager number. A resident I've never seen before gets up from her chair in front of a fetal monitor and follows me back to the room. "I'm Dr. Daley and I'd like to assist with the delivery" she says.

"Where is your attending physician?"

"Doing a delivery at Teglar Regional."

"Shit. Okay. If you want to go on in, you can. I'm going to grab a delivery package from the stock room."

Dr. Daley stands in the middle of the hallway like she's lost. "Room 820," I say. She turns and goes toward Ms. Vasquez's room.

I run back to the stock room and almost right into my friend and favorite nursing assistant, Corrine. I grab her and the delivery pack before running back into the room. Thank you, Jesus, for small miracles.

Corrine doesn't ask any questions, just immediately starts unwrapping the packing and arranging the tools on the silver examination tray. Dr. Daley stands in the middle of the floor, but just close enough to the patient to still be in our way. I start preparing the baby's setup by turning on the heat lamp and connecting the suctions for the baby's lungs. While doing this, it occurs to me I don't even know the sex of the child. I walk out to the medication cart and grab some erythromycin and Hepatitis B vaccine and when I get back in the room I ask, "Ms. Vasquez, have you signed your consent form for the baby to receive his or her medications at birth?"

She offers me nothing except a blank stare.

I forgot that damn quick that she don't speaka no English. Where in the world is that damn interpreter? Before I can look for her, Ms. Vasquez starts pushing. The resident doesn't seem to notice, as she's distracted watching the contractions rise and fall alongside the heart rate on the electronic fetal monitor screen. Done with preparing a sterile field for delivery, Corrine passes the sponge and betadine over me for my preparation of the mother. She's the best, and I am so glad she's working my shift today. I am so not feeling my job. I think I should have gone to school for social work.

Less than two minutes later, Ms. Vasquez's baby is crowning. Aside from rhythmic moaning and some soft crying, Ms. Vasquez is impressively calm and quiet. I say a silent prayer, thanking God that one of my two assignments is going to deliver a baby with few complications. I moved out of the resident's way to let him do the rest of the catching, satisfied that her bottom was still intact.

Ms. Vasquez's baby girl was already out and on my table getting her measurements when Sabrina finally decided to show up after her hour-long vacation. With no apology or explanation for her recent AWOL status, she immediately went to the mother's bedside and began speaking instructions to her in Spanish. I am thankful I can finally catch a break and do some charting, but then I remember my patient in 819. There is no rest for the weary.

So I'm walking out of the room, confident the resident can handle a placenta delivery on his own and resolving to report his attending physician to the hospital administrator when Corrine says, "Dr. Karen, I think we have more than afterbirth left in there."

"What do you mean?"

"She looks like she still hurting to me and I see bubbles, as you would say, coming out."

I turn back into the room and do not believe my fucking eyes. Ms. Vasquez is crowning again. Another baby really is in there.

"Who in the hell did her ultrasound?" I yell out to nobody in particular. Then I remember that I haven't even had time to read her chart. For all I know, it could have been spelled out on the front page.

"You'll need to give gentle massage to help that placenta separate and come out," says Dr. Morgan, who just magically shows up in the room and is obviously unaware of the crisis.

"And you need another gown on to catch this second baby," I scream back at him before walking out of the room to check on my second patient.

Forgetting about the stench, I walk in the door and immediately dry heave. I am embarrassed that she sees me, because I didn't mean to hurt her feelings. I turn and face her sister who has now moved from the window to a chair in the corner. She is eating a burrito from Taco Bell that she probably got from the food court downstairs. The thought of eating a taco right now from anywhere makes my stomach turn over. "Please let her know I'm getting ready to check her to see how far along she has dilated."

Fortunately, her cervix is only 4-5 centimeters dilated, but as I look down to remove my hand I notice she has green fluid leaking from her bottom. This time the heaves in my own stomach are stronger than they were the last time, and I can't help it—I throw up on the bed. I am so embarrassed that I snatch the sheets off the bed before I can think good and expose her whole bottom half naked. I apologize, although I doubt she can understand me and, since Sabrina has already left my patient's room next door, I don't even bother to call her back because I know she has probably already gone back into the black hole where everybody seems to be disappearing today. I walk over to the nurse's station and almost yank the door off the blanket warmer to open the door and remove two warm sheets and blankets. Embarrassed, I walk back into room 819 and carefully cover the patient back up. In fact, I proceed to set up the delivery tray, cover it back up so that it can be ready for its next user, Dr. Peters, who's covering the evening shift, and get ready to take my black ass home.

I peek in on Claudia before I leave the hospital for the day. She's still a bit hung over from her anesthesia, but perks up when she sees me standing over her bed. A man—I'm assuming her husband—is lightly snoring on the sofa next to her bed.

"How are you feeling?" I ask the pretty girl.

"Weak."

"I can imagine you do feel that way. You had a lot of internal bleeding. You were very lucky to have recognized something was wrong and make it to the hospital."

"You mean I could have died like my baby?" she asks, with big, inquisitive eyes.

"Although I hate to say this, yes, you could have. What you experienced isn't quite the same as a miscarriage. Your baby didn't travel to your uterus before it began to grow, but instead, it stayed in your fallopian tube." I point to a diagram on the counter to help illustrate my point as I'm talking to Claudia.

"Will I be able to have another one?"

"I believe so, but it's impossible for anyone to be one hundred percent sure about anything like this. What's important right now is that you go home and allow yourself to heal. Let that man over there give you all the TLC you can stand. When it's time for you to try again, you'll know."

Claudia's eyes well up with tears. "I wanted my baby more than anything."

"We both did, Claudia, but I don't know what I would have done if something happened to you," her husband surprises me and says while walking toward her bed. He kisses her on her nose before turning to me. "Thank you, doc. For saving *my* baby." He kisses her again, this time on the forehead.

My own eyes begin to sting with tears but I'm not sure if it's due to my joy or sadness, and I make sure I leave the room before either of them notice. I am so thankful to be reminded that black love is still alive and well. Still, I am sorry for their loss, and whisper a little prayer that their next baby gets to see the light of day.

As I'm exiting the Labor and Delivery suite, I notice the executive conference room doors are open and soft Christmas music and loud voices fill the air. I poke my head in the door just to be nosy and see Sylvia, Sabrina, Dr. Daley, Dr. Peters and a few other attending physicians, all partying their asses off underneath a large banner that says "Tis The Season!" I don't know if I'm pissed because I just vomited on a pregnant patient, because I couldn't find the real doctors until now, or because I didn't get invited to the damn party.

* * *

It's been several days since I delivered the IUFD or performed surgery on a ruptured fallopian tube. In fact, I haven't even been on call at the hospital all week, and, therefore, cannot blame this morning's vomiting episode on the smell of my patients' infected bodily fluids. I stop by the CVS to purchase a pregnancy test for myself. It's more to clear my mind than for any other reason because I know for certain I'm not pregnant. But if I didn't know any better I would think that something was wrong with me because I can't remember the last time I felt this tired or this sick.

When I sit down on my toilet to pee on the little stick I almost make a mistake and shit too because I see two lines forming instead of one. I instinctively stick my finger up in my own vagina and suddenly feel light-headed enough to fall into the water when I realize my NuvaRing isn't in there.

"How late is your period?"

"Late enough," I tell Tim, whom I now consider my boyfriend.

"You might just be counting your days wrong. You think that's possible?"

"Nope," I say, while staring at the curly black hairs on his chest.

"Cool," he says, before putting his arms around me.

I pause for a minute and wonder if I heard him right. Just to be sure, I ask, "How do you feel about that?"

"I think that's great news. I'm ready for a baby."

"You are?" I look up and into his eyes to see if he's telling the truth.

"Yes, I am. And I can't think of a woman that I'd be happier to have one with."

"Really?"

"Really." Tim kisses me on the lips.

"But we haven't been dating for very long. I've been worried that maybe we're moving too fast."

"Karen, the last few weeks have been some of the best I've experienced in a long time. I am a grown man. It doesn't take me years of dating you to figure out how I feel about you."

I am so relieved I could cry. I put my arms around his bald head, so that we're embracing each other in my bed. "Thank you," I whisper to both Tim and to God, happy that my prayers have finally been answered.

"Think you might be ready to get married, soon?" Tim asks.

"I do."

"Good."

"Wait. How soon?"

"I'll let you make that call. If you feel like doing it before the baby, then we can. If you want to wait until after my son gets here, then we can."

"How are you so sure it's a boy?"

"Because you ride me all the time."

"So?"

"So it takes more than pails and snails and puppy dog tails to make boys. It also takes an ambitious, independent woman to be the mother."

"And what in the world does that have to do with bedroom positions?"

"Everything. Those women happen to love being on top. And I doubt we were in the bedroom when we made this baby." He smiles and touches my stomach.

"Thank you for educating me."

"Anytime. I'm surprised you didn't know this already. Didn't they teach you anything in medical school?"

"Only the not-so-important stuff."

"Obviously," he says with an irresistible smile. "So tell me. How am I going to take care of my future wife and son if you're living way over here across town?"

"I hadn't thought that far ahead yet."

"It's time to." And with that, he pulls me on top of him. Again.

Emily

G.

"**DEAR GIRLS.**" I say out loud, hoping to convince my fingers to cooperate. I stare at the piece of white, lineless paper in front of me for a couple seconds before positioning my right hand at the top of the paper. With my left, I slide a blue ink pen in between my right thumb and index finger. Then I fold my index finger over on top of the ink pen and push it. Hard.

I make it to the capital letter G before my hand contracts into a ball with a hole in the center, much like a doughnut. The pen falls straight through the passageway in the middle of my fist and drops down to the floor.

Denise, who has been standing behind me while scratching my dandruff and greasing my scalp, bends over, retrieves the ink pen, and places it back on the table in front of me without offering a word.

Tessa

Change of Status

THE PINK PIECE of paper in front of me says "CHANGE of EMPLOYMENT STATUS" across the top.

I blink once, twice, then a third time to see if I can make the pink paper disappear. The neatly typed memo reads something about being required to take an administrative leave per some earlier conversation that I did not fucking have about my not being licensed to teach. I wish I had left the damn envelope in my mailbox in the administrative office instead of bringing it back here to read. Kids are already starting to file in and take their seats. I look at the clock over the whiteboard. It's 8:29.

I push straight past Mrs. Baker and out of the damn classroom before she can notice my cheeks are wet. As luck would have it for me, the bell is ringing, signaling to these pubescent wackos that it's time to get to class and causing them to shuffle through the hallway like roadrunners on a cartoon just as I make my way to Mr. Turner's office. I do not even turn around to see who poked me in the butt as I'm nearing the administrative suite in the high school.

I arrive in front of Mr. Turner's door just in time to see him stand up to close it. I am sure, nope, make that positive, he saw me before he slammed it shut. WHAM! I am surprised at how much noise the wooden door makes when I throw my first shoe into it. Klunka klunk is the sound of the second shoe. The cheap ass heel pops off and I find myself staring at both pieces of my shoe on the linoleum floor, concentrating on not crying when I hear Glenova, the school secretary, ease the phone off of the cradle so she can call security. I lift up my skirt and turn around to show her my ass.

My nose hairs itch and I sneeze, then curse out loud at the office staff because they stood there and witnessed it and didn't even have the decency to say bless you. I hear Mr. Turner say something that sounds like "call security" through his door. Ms. Wood, an assistant principal, comes out of her office and reaches for my hand. I don't know her very well, but she offers me a warm smile and a motherly expression. "Tessa," she whispers. "I don't know what got into him this morning. The board had an emergency meeting with him on Friday to discuss personnel issues and budgets but I had no idea this was coming. Calm down, and I'll work with you a little bit later to help you figure something out."

I look up at her salt-and-pepper-colored hair and talk to her bangs because it is very difficult for me to take eye contact with anyone right now. I don't even yell. I just ask her calmly, "Figure something out like what? Who else got a note like this? Did he put you up to this shit?"

"Of course not. And I'm going to try and help you get your job back, but I need for you to calm your temper a bit until I can decide what's best to do next."

"What kinds of decisions are you weighing out, Ms. Wood? Whether or not you're going to pass out a collection plate around here to help me pay my bills? It's Christmas! Do you know how much my gas and electric bills are? And I'm in school! I don't have anybody to help me!" I wish I wasn't crying.

"My daughter works in the unemployment office downtown. I'm going to have her call you."

"I don't want any damn welfare checks. I want my job." I wipe my face with the back of my hand.

"And you will have it again in due time, but you have to cool it! You are a brilliant young woman with a bright future ahead of you, but you can't allow your mouth and attitude to get you in trouble."

She must think she's talking to one of the students. I put my hand up and wave at her as if to say, "shut up." All of a sudden my pantyhose itch, so I pull them down and off of my bare feet right there and leave them on the floor.

"Tell Mr. Turner there's no need to call security on me because I can walk myself out the door," I tell the crowd that has gathered around me in the office. I march straight toward the door without looking at any of their faces. Before I leave I holler "little dick!" through the door and pray Mr. Turner heard me.

I have to sit in my Honda for two or three minutes just so I can stop shaking and try to gain my composure. I'm on my way out of the parking lot when I pass a police car with the blue lights on as he's turning into the school. I drive past him slowly and cautiously and am relieved when I make it out of the gate at the end of the school campus. I just know these motherfuckers did not call the law on me. I'm going to sue all of their sorry asses before they even know what hits them. Mr. Turner's black ass will be the first to pay for my harassment charges, and it will cost him much more than those fifty damn dollars he tried to give me.

I stop by the Citgo gas station and run in to buy a Black and Mild cigar, hoping that the nicotine will help calm my nerves. It's not until I've smoked the whole thing that I remember that I haven't had any breakfast.

After I arrive at the restaurant I find that I can hardly eat a bite because I'm too busy thinking up a way to contact Mr. Turner's wife at home. This is the only thing that makes me feel better—imagining Mr. Turner explaining to her what a cunt-sucking bastard he is—when I notice Brown Eyes looking at me across the bar in Applebee's. Hell, Mrs. Turner probably already knows. But just in case she doesn't, I'm going to make good and sure. Brown Eyes looks like money. I'll bet Brown Eyes knows what to do to keep a woman. And to think that I've been wasting my time on brown-nosing-cocksuckers with gray hairs in their dick bushes makes my stomach hurt.

Brown eyes makes eye contact with me, then throws both hands up in the air like he's asking a question. "Can I come over?" he appears to be saying. Depends on what you mean by that. I nod my head up and down and motion the bartender to bring my third French Connection.

Brown Eyes is wearing a black cotton jogging suit and some black and white tennis shoes but I don't recognize the name brand. The closer he gets, the better I can see his beady little brown eyes. The parts of them that should be white are red. He sits down in the vacant seat next to me and immediately starts asking me questions.

"You drink like a man all the time and this early in the day?" His voice sounds much higher than I expected.

"Just on Mondays and when shit happens," is my reply.

"You're pretty. You should smile more. In fact, you look upset. Are you angry?" He's obviously not from Atlanta. He sounds a little California-ish to me. He pronounces all of the "r" sounds at the ends of his words.

"You could say that."

"You need somebody to drive you home?"

I just look at him. I would give this some serious thought, but I can't. First of all, he's too forward. Second, he looks weird up close. I've got to pee. Having an orgasm always improves my mood, but damn, he looks like a horrible lay. I get up without answering him. When I pass by a window on my way to the bathroom, I notice a police car in the parking lot.

I come out of the bathroom to see Mr. Officer sitting at the bar. He waves for me to stop as I'm getting ready to pass him.

"Didn't think I would catch up with you, huh?"

"What the world are you talking about, officer? I don't know you."

He shakes his head as though he's disappointed. "I noticed you flying out of the high school down the road like a bat out of hell and turned around and put my lights on you and followed you here."

I hadn't noticed I was being followed—much less by an officer of the law with blue lights and a siren on top of his car. What took him so long to come in here? I immediately feel myself begin to sober up. "Listen, I'm so sorry. I didn't see you, I swear. I had a terrible day. I can't go to jail, officer."

"What is your name?"

"Tessa. Contessa. Turnipseed."

"Do you know what day of the week it is?"

"Today is Monday, December 17th, sir."

"Sir? Now I didn't ask for all that. I don't look that old, I hope." He certainly is from the south. He takes a long time to say his vowel sounds, a lot like I do.

I look down at the floor and start tracing the circles in the carpet with the big toe on my right foot, relieved he's being so friendly.

"Did they call you to come get me?" is all I can think to ask.

"Who is they, Contessa?"

I look up but keep my mouth closed.

"What were you doing at Cedarview? You look like you're too young to have children there."

"I work there. Or, I used to work there until today."

"I see," he says, connecting the dots. "We have resource officers that patrol the campus and the parking lot. You're very lucky none of them noticed the little stunt show you put on with your car."

"What stunt?"

"You sped out of the parking lot like the gangbusters."

"I thought I was driving the speed limit."

"Maybe that is the speed limit on the Daytona 500 racetrack. Consider yourself very lucky today."

"So you didn't come here to arrest me?"

"I came here to be sure that you weren't having a real emergency—"

"My job is a real emergency."

"You cut me off. I wanted to make sure you weren't having a real emergency and to make certain you weren't getting ready to harm anyone. Now what I absolutely should do is arrest you. But I'm feeling very generous today and also maybe a little bit sympathetic."

I pause so he can continue to explain. While I wait, I direct my gaze in the direction of Brown Eyes. He's staring at me. Now down at a credit card slip. He signs it. Points to his watch like he's letting me know that I'm taking too long.

"I'll wait here with you until your ride arrives."

"I didn't call anybody yet."

"You will."

"My date is over there waiting for me."

"If I didn't know any better, I would think you don't even know him, ma'am."

His southern accent is turning me on. I forgot how much that I've missed hearing southern accents, seeing that nobody in Atlanta is from Atlanta anymore.

"And how is it that you know that, officer?" I ask, trying to flirt a little.

"My job is to make accurate observations about folks, ma'am." Nope, didn't bite.

"Okay, well let me step outside and call one of my sisters to come and pick me up."

He shakes his head. "I'm not letting you go outside for you to run to your car and jet out of here. I've already spent enough taxpayer money on burning gasoline while following you today. You can sit here or in the back seat of my car and place your call, ma'am."

It's not until I'm bending over to get into the police car that I notice the way he's looking at my behind. Every few blocks I see him looking at me in the rear view mirror and, if I'm not mistaken, even smiling every now and then. I tell him to slow down and then stop when we near my apartment building. He sort of shifts in his seat and then looks at me like he's waiting to be invited up and into my home. I grab my things and ask to be let out of the backseat. Without speaking, he follows me upstairs.

When I reach the door, I thank him for the ride.

"You're welcome. I was feeling very generous today, Miss ... um, Tessa."

"Turnipseed," I offer.

"Anybody else would have and should have arrested you, Ms. Turnipseed."

"I know."

"Do everybody a favor and promise yourself you'll let go of whatever it is that's bothering you, and start over, sober, tomorrow."

"I will."

"I've already let Freddy at the bar know your car will be parked in his lot for at least the next few hours. I'm patrolling the area today so I'll keep an eye on it, too. The deal is off after 7:00 this evening, though. So make your arrangements before then, young lady."

"Okay."

He stands by the door and smiles at me like Mr. Ed, the talking horse, for a full second. It is obvious to me that he wants to show me all of his teeth. I'm sure I could count thirty-two if I had the time.

I almost don't, but then decide to follow my carnal instinct. "Would you like to come inside?"

"I guess there's no harm in scoping out the place to make sure you're safe," he says with a smile.

As soon as I let him in and before I can hang my purse up in my closet, he's reaching for my blouse's buttons. Unbuttoning them. With a look of fire and urgency in his eyes, he rips the last two on my shirt. I look at him. He won't look back. He's too busy diving toward my breasts. He scoops the left one out of my bra with his mouth, and begins to suck on my nipple very quickly. He cups it with his hand and wiggles the bra down with the other. I inch over toward my bed so that I can support myself.

The police officer whose name I've forgotten at the moment unsnaps the bra and turns his attention toward the other breast. He sucks aggressively, almost too hard. I tell him to slow down. He just grunts.

After a few minutes of his horrible mouth play and with nipples that are on the verge of being raw, I place his hands on my waist and guide him to ease down my panties. As soon as I remove my hand, he snatches them off. I'm not sure whether I should be turned on or afraid. I look down at him for a clue but he won't let me get any eye contact. After feeling me stiffen, he asks if I'm okay.

"Slow down," I tell him. He does, but only a little.

Fortunately for both of us, he positions himself down in between my knees and spreads my legs apart with both of his elbows. I begin to throb down there with excitement but am quickly disappointed by the sloppy, light strokes of his tongue that start and end nowhere in particular. It makes me wonder if this is his first time eating pussy.

This foreplay sucks, but I'm still excited enough to want to have sex and even more eager to orgasm, so I direct him back up and place my right hand on his dick. It is definitely hard but not quite the sizeable tool I was hoping for. I am also sobering up very quickly. I lean down to his ear and whisper, "put it in baby."

He does. And at first I think that this shit is a joke. He slips it in very slowly, and then pulls it right back out, almost mechanically. In again, then right back out. On the third time that he goes in, I sort of grab his butt and push him inside of me deeper, hoping to coax him to stay there. He does and sighs loudly. I look up at him hoping that he didn't just come. His eyes are closed. Then, sure enough, he pulls it right back out.

I'm getting pissed off.

"Let me get on top," I say, as calmly as I possibly can. He looks at me, realizing this is not a suggestion, but instead, a directive. His expression is a cross between reluctance and defeat. I could really call this whole thing off, just off of the principle of him being such a disappointment. But my determination to get something out of this whole episode is what persuades me to climb on top of him and ease back down. It takes a second before I get him in the exact spot that I want, and then I proceed to try and gain a rhythm to ride him. At first, he fucks that up too by moving his own pelvis too much.

"Be still!" I say, and then almost laugh at myself for yelling at a police officer. Then I catch a glimpse of myself in the mirror and don't find anything funny anymore.

I'm on top of him with my back to his face and I can see myself going up and down in the mirror that's attached to my dresser. I am quite sure that if I were sober I'd be halfway embarrassed by the dark circles under my eyes and my hair sticking up like it wasn't combed this morning, and I could get depressed with my decisions because fucking (or refusing to, now that I really think about it) is very likely what got me in this predicament. I believe I want to cry but I feel myself starting to come and so, fuck it, I close my eyes and feel everything tighten and even hear him moaning in response to the seven or eight seconds of my orgasm. He is right behind me. If I didn't know any better, I would think I feel semen in me. I jump up. I rub my eyes and look down. I do not believe I actually fucked this stranger without the notion of a condom running through my mind until now.

"What's wrong with you, baby? Aren't all you girls on the pill now?"

Of course I am but I won't tell him that. "Absolutely fucking not you nasty ass short dick ass little boy ass man! Get out of my house!" He looks at me as though I am crazy. When I look down at my naked ass and back up and at the man who I just let put his thing in me, I wonder, for a split second, if I might be, too.

"You heard what I said."

He gathers his shit and hurries up. I don't even peek out of the blinds to make sure he gets in there. I just roll over to the side of my bed and grab the trash can to spit in it. I can't remember if he kissed me or not but I don't want to take any chances of swallowing any of his spit.

On Tuesday, he calls me at seven in the morning. At first I have no idea how he got my telephone number, and then I remember he is the damn police. "Good morning," he says. I hang the phone up immediately. Even though we just had sex yesterday, I go to the drug store and buy a First Response. I feel better to see that my pregnancy test is negative, even though the box says that you can't detect a real baby until your period is due.

On Wednesday, I'm taking my first shower in forty-eight hours, hoping some of my depression will wash off my body and down the drain. I also have intentions of going down to the county unemployment office to apply for some benefits before meeting Karen for lunch. No matter how bad I seem to be feeling about myself, hearing her sob stories about her own stupid ass lonely life have a way of reminding me how lucky I am to have some common sense. Even if she does make more money than I do.

Just as I'm finishing my business and washing between my legs, I notice a tender, itchy spot. Make that three, four, maybe five if I count that sore area close to my ass (which happens occasionally when I have anal sex but I'm sure I would recall fucking in the ass even if I cannot remember his name). I turn the water off and towel dry, anxious to get a mirror and see what's between my legs. I haven't recently noticed any hair bumps, but at least a few become ingrown each time I get a wax. I stare at the image produced on the mirror for ten minutes I'm sure. My brain can't hardly process the tiny red sores that have erupted overnight and now cover my thighs, vagina and both ass cheeks.

I pretend that I didn't just see those bumps as I throw on some panties, jeans and a blouse and hop in the car. I drive straight over to the unemployment office and the first person I catch sight of is a social worker named Kathleen who I actually recognize from high school. I am delighted to see that age and time have not been very kind to her because she was as pretty as a mermaid back then but now she looks more like a beached whale. I immediately feel guilty for wishing harm on her but sometimes it just feels like some girls have all the damn luck and I do believe that in getting so much they must have taken a little bit of my share, like maybe they stole it when God was handing out scoops of it and he wasn't looking and I was too busy forming in my mama's womb to notice or be able to cry about it. As if it's not bad enough that I'm comparing her high school yearbook picture that is etched in my mind to the chubby girl with dry, cracked lips who is standing in front of me, I can't hear a word she's saying because instead of asking her if I brought the right documents or when the checks will start coming or if I can sue anybody, I start imagining her becoming one of those red dots down on my booty and I want to ask her what the fuck it is. Kathleen tells me I won't become eligible for unemployment assistance for another two weeks and then, out of nowhere, the answer to the butt bump riddle comes to me. I forgot that I recently tried a laundry detergent sample that I got in a gift pack out of the mail. Yes, that's it! I know I'm not supposed to use anything except one scoop of Tide or Gain like Mama taught me, but I hadn't had a chance to make it to Walmart and the value pack of samples and coupons made it to my mailbox right on time. I'll flush it out with some Benadryl.

By the time I meet Karen at the Special Spot she has already been seated and is sipping on a soda. I assume she's ordered her food because she hates waiting on people. She's so impatient. As always, she looks like her jeans and T-shirt came from the clearance isle in K-Mart. She didn't even bother to iron the wrinkles out of them, but she does have an expensive bag tucked under her arms. When she asks me what's going on, I don't bother to answer. I have no intentions of telling her about being fired from my job, the occurrences of this shitty ass week, or even my allergic reaction to the cheap laundry detergent sample that came in the mail.

Meechie smiles at me from behind the counter. I love to see his gold teeth sparkle. For a short moment, it brightens my day.

Karen gulps down the remainder of her drink and tells me what I think sounds sort of like, "I'm pregnant."

The only response I can give her at the moment comes out as, "I have some bumps on my pussy that itch. Can you give me anything stronger than Benadryl?"

Emily

Keeping Secrets

CAMILLA PUSHES my wheelchair into a very comfortable blanket of shade, just underneath the big oak tree in her back yard. She almost forgets to put the break on the wheel until I start sliding forward.

"Girl, don't you go sliding down that hill. I can't fish you out of that ditch today. You know I've already had two or three beers," she says and laughs while pushing the lever forward. I don't find her comment particularly funny.

She unfolds a green and white lawn chair and knocks off the spider webs with a dish towel before plopping down in the seat next to me with a red, white and blue can in her hand. "Now, Emily, are you sure this is the right time to tell these girls the truth? I mean, they seem to have an awful lot going on in their own lives right now. And to be quite honest with you, I still think it's sometimes best to leave well-enough alone," she says, followed by a sip of the Budweiser.

"Don't tell me what's going on in their lives, sister. I raised every last one of them nearly by myself—certainly without much help from you or anybody else. They're making messes out of their lives right now and I'm starting to think that not telling them the damn truth about this family has done more harm than—

I am immediately interrupted by Jada, Camilla's granddaughter, who is five going on twenty. Her mama, Stacey, ought to be out of the house any minute to catch a ride to the grocery store with Tessa and Karen. Pat should be pulling up to Camilla's house any minute—that is, if she decides to show up today.

"Auntie Emily! Hey! Are you here to eat some crabs?"

"Hey, baby. Yes, I am. You're growing up big!"

"Mimi." She turns to Camilla. "I can't understand what she said."

"She said you've gotten bigger since she last saw you and that you're very pretty."

"Thank you," she says, and smiles at me. "Do you want to see what I can do?" Before I can answer, she jumps up and then down on the ground and into a split. My bottom hurts just by watching her.

I nod and clap in approval.

"Jada, go in the house and tell Paw-Paw I said to give you ten bucks so you can ride with your mama and your cousins to the store and buy that glow-in-the-dark butterfly nightlight you asked me about."

"But why can't she talk good again?"

"Because Auntie Emily had a stroke."

"What does that mean?"

"It means that she got real sick and some blood bust in her brain and her mouth can't keep up with her head that good."

"Do I have blood in my brain?"

"Yes, you do, but that's not what I meant to say. I should have said that she had a blood tube in her brain that broke. But don't worry about that right now. Go get the money from Paw-Paw so you can catch them before they go to the store."

"Okay," she says, but she doesn't move her feet. She looks at me, then back at Camilla. "Mimi, how do you understand what she's saying?"

"Because she's my big sister and I've been talking to her for so long that I can understand most of what she's trying to say, and I can almost read her thoughts straight out of her head. Now go."

"Can you read my thoughts, too?" she asks. Her eyes have gotten big.

"Yes, and I can also see into the future. And right now I see a behind whipping coming up if you don't hurry up and do what I told you to."

Instead of walking, Jada turns cartwheels all the way to the front door in search of her granddaddy, and almost kicks her mama in the face because she didn't see her coming out of the house. Stacey dodges her daughter's foot and walks right over.

"Hey, Aunt Em," Stacey sings. She kisses me on the forehead. "I didn't know you were here. Don't you want to come in the house instead of sitting out here fanning these awful bugs with Mama?"

"It is a hot ass December, ain't it?" says Camilla. "I can't remember the last time I had to fan flies and mosquitoes in the winter time, even if we do live in the South."

"It's technically not winter yet," Stacey says, correcting her mother. "December just got here. We have until the twenty-first before we can call it that."

"You like sounding smart and talking over me, don't you? Since you know so much, how about figuring out how and when you and your children can move up out of my house?"

"I like it," comes out much more clearly than I expect it.

Stacey ignores both me and her mother and walks over to the pot of steaming water that's resting on a gas cooker a few feet away from us. "I know my auntie better than that. You're out here supervising the crabs, huh? I don't blame you. Nobody here can cook them as good as you could," she says loudly for my benefit. That is a true statement, but it's also true this blue sky doesn't have a single cloud in it and I'm enjoying the outdoors today. But what's more important and requires the privacy we're seeking is the serious business my sister and I need to discuss. I wish we could get a minute alone.

"Excuse me?" Camilla pretends to be offended at her daughter's comment.

"Yeah, Mama. You heard me. And if Daddy didn't make you come out here to do your drinking then you'd probably be in the house, too, yelling cooking instructions for me from out of a window," she giggles and hands Camilla some spices. "Can you get the water seasoned up for me while I start moving the crabs?"

"Yes, I will do that, but first let me go on record of saying that your daddy doesn't make me do a damn thing. I go outside to relax because I need my peace of mind and a break from you and your bad-ass chillun."

"Understood," replies Stacey as she goes back toward the house.

"Shit," says Camilla.

"What?" I ask, but before she can respond, I look around and see the answer myself. What looks like a busload of family, mostly children, come whirling past and in between my sister and me. They are chewing gum, twirling braids, throwing balls and water balloons, and some complaining about how hungry they are and asking how long it's going to take before the fish is done frying and the crabs are done boiling. Best of all, I am greeted by the hugs and kisses of many—especially those who don't take the time to visit me in Derbyshire.

"Why didn't you tell me all these folks were coming?" I ask, halfway annoyed.

"I'm not the one who put the announcement in the newspaper. You can thank Stacey for that one. She's been talking for some time about wanting to get the family together more often. What makes it so bad is that she isn't the one who's feeding them—I am!"

I laugh because I understand what she means. Tessa liked to invite what seemed like everybody in her high school class over to our house on the weekends. I felt sorry for her because her older sisters had already moved out and she always seemed lonely, so I allowed it.

"Hey, Mama. Hey, Auntie Camilla," says Karen, seemingly out of nowhere. I take a good look at her in some blue-jean shorts that I know I've seen before. She has gained weight. And her titties look bigger.

"Hey, baby! I'm glad you stopped delivering those babies long enough to come out and spend some time with your family! I miss seeing you. You're still tiptoeing around like a cat, I see." Karen winks at her and plops down in the first vacant lawn chair she can find, pretending to be interested in the blue crabs that are crawling around in a wooden crate near the pot.

Calvin, Camilla's husband, has the nerve to be seen out here—I don't care if we are family—in a muscle shirt and some rather short, cotton shorts. I am staring at his ittie bittie chicken legs so hard that I almost don't hear him when he speaks to me. He is throwing too much salt on the fish while he's waiting for the grease to get hot in the cooker. I look over at Camilla and notice she has hidden her beer between her ankles, tucked away under her long skirt.

"Patricia! You came!" Camilla stands up to extend her arms out to my daughter. I squeeze her hand and stick my face out for her to kiss my cheek. I look behind her for her husband but don't see any sign of him. She bends down to hug me, and squeezes me on the shoulder.

Immediately after that, she assumes her role as the bossy cook of the family and starts giving orders: "Tessa, start slicing these onions. You can put that cutting board in your lap right there in that chair. Man-man, bring her a wet wash cloth for her fingers. These bugs are too damn bad out here today. Uncle Calvin! Where do you keep the Citronella candles?

And what happened to the tiki sticks I brought over here last time? What? You burned up all the oil in them already? Well, just bring me whatever you have. Anything will help at this point. Jada, you and your brother grab those red peppers I left in the kitchen sink!"

"Oh, Auntie, do I have to go with him? He still has cooties from having the chicken pops."

"Your brother got over the chicken pox a year ago, Jada," answers Pat. She places her hands on her hips and sighs. "Go get the peppers without him but you're going to have to make two trips because you won't be able to carry them all in two hands."

"You didn't buy any peppers, did you? You must not have seen my garden around there on the corner of the house," Camilla says.

Everybody seems to be talking at one time.

"I grow my own, Auntie," replies Patricia.

That girl has my mannerisms. And in a few short minutes, the seafood pot has reached a rolling boil and smells of salty water, Old Bay, lemon wedges, onion and an assortment of peppers and spices. My mouth begins to water when Calvin walks over to the pot and dumps in two or three pounds of shrimp and some cut up sausages.

Camilla sneaks another beer out of the cooler, but this time, pours the straw-colored foamy liquid into a Styrofoam cup. She leans in to me and continues where she left off. "I'll do what you want me to, but I want to go on the record of saying it's unnecessary. Too much water under the bridge now."

I struggle so hard to form the words that I want to say that I give up. I make a fist with my good hand and bang it on the side of my chair.

After taking several more gulps, she goes on, this time more loudly. "And tell me this: Who even cares at this point? A mama is the woman who raises you, not just the person who births you. The one who stays up with you all night, feeds you, gives up her life so you can have one. Teaches you about periods. And boys. And how to cook and grease your scalp and roll up your hair. You did that, Emily. As far as I'm concerned, you are her mother. I never had any business asking you to give her back. She had really become yours by then. I'm old now, Emily. I know that."

Calvin walks over to us with a finger over his mouth. "Camilla, are you out here drinking? You're talking mighty loud."

Camilla shows her husband her empty Styrofoam cup. Calvin rolls his eyes and rejoins the gas fryer.

"I was sixteen years old. What in the hell was I going to do with a baby? I'll answer that for you. Absolutely nothing. Don't you remember that I threw myself down the bleachers at school and took four or five dry mustard baths behind trying to get my period to come back on? Well I did. So there you have it. I was too young and stupid to even get rid of her right. You did us all a favor by taking her in."

"Shut up, hear?" I think she got that.

"You stop telling me to be quiet. Your ass is too bossy. You want me to help you plan to fuck up my good Mother's Day with some bullshit. This is just as much my business and decision as it is yours."

The shriek of a child pierces the air. "Mimi, call 911! A crab done got ahold of Jada!"

Of course, all forty or fifty of us who are outside in the yard look over there. And, sure enough, Jada is waving her tiny hand around in the air and jumping up and down while a crab hangs onto her index finger with his pincers for dear life. I don't know which one to feel more sorry for. Calvin tries to rid his hands of the fish he's carrying by quickly dropping three or four pieces into the grease at one time, and then he curses when the hot grease splashes up and pops him in the hand. Stacey, who I thought had finally gone to the store, comes charging out of Camilla's house as if she'd been watching everything through the window. She opens her hand enough to reveal an ice pick just before punching the crab through its back. The crab drops down into the grass, but the pincers remain wrapped around Jada's finger. Stacey carefully opens up the crab's claw, tosses it in the nearby pot of water, then examines her daughter's finger to determine the extent of the damage. All this happened without the child even crying one tear.

Camilla yells, but doesn't get up out of her seat, "Baby, are you okay?"

Her mother answers for her. "I see one little drop of blood on the tip. She'll live."

"That hurt, Mimi! I'm going to eat that crab!"

"Only if I don't eat him first, baby."

Camilla turns back around and looks at me like she wants to go back to pleading her case, but now there are too many people standing within listening distance of us. If Camilla says another word, then I'm going to try to kill her.

"I'm through talking," she says, reading the expression on my face and rolling her eyes at me.

"Who wants some hot fish?" asks Calvin. I want to motion for him to bring me a plate of something without bones in it, but I forget what I was getting ready to say each time I look at him. His legs are a distraction.

"Not me, Uncle Calvin. I'm waiting for those crabs to go in," says Stacey. "But put that piece that's in your hand on this plate for the kids. Jada and Man-Man, did you wash your hands? I already know that you didn't. Get two pieces of bread from out of the bag on that table. Don't touch anything else."

The kids run over to the table to get plates and bread, eagerly awaiting their fish. In fact, most of the adults are hot on their heels and ready to feed their own bellies. Patricia and Tessa are at the back of the food line. Karen is in the front. And now that I can see her good from the side, it's easy to tell that she's gaining weight. If I thought she had sex on a regular basis then I would swear she was pregnant. Good thing I know better.

As if she's reading my mind again, Camilla asks, "Has Karen been missing periods?"

"How the hell should I know?" I whisper. I'm hoping she'll take my hint and lower her own voice.

"You are her damn mama the last time I checked. Or do you have some secret that you want to reveal about that, too?"

I ignore my sister and take the plate of fried catfish Stacey brings me.

"This is the warmest December I've ever seen. Weather like this is scary. Makes me feel like something's getting ready to happen," Camilla says in between sips of beer number three. I don't acknowledge her comment. I just motion for her to pass me the mustard and hot sauce.

"Turn that up! That's my song!" somebody yells.

"Marcus, go find my playing cards. They're in the house somewhere. Look in all the kitchen drawers until you find them," says Stacey.

"What happened to all the damn beer?" somebody wants to know.

"That music is too damn loud. This is not the nightclub," yells another adult.

"What happened to all the damn fish?" I believe that was Tessa.

"Are those crabs ready yet?" asks a voice I can't identify at all.

"I hope you dropped some eggs in there, too, Pat. I don't see anything but corn and potatoes floating around at the top of this water," says Calvin.

"Karen, you look like you're gaining weight in your breasts. Are you pregnant?" yells Camilla, as a joke.

"Yes."

We all turn and look at Karen to see if that was a serious answer she just gave. It was. Somebody stops the music. I wonder if this is another damn dream.

"Well, congratulations, honey! When were you going to say something? How far along are you?" That sounded like Stacey's voice.

"Not far," says Karen, glancing in my direction to see if I heard her. I look down at my fish sandwich and pretend I didn't.

"You see what I'm saying? Karen must have finally gotten herself a life and now here you come wanting to disrupt shit. You waited too long to try to get holy. Folks always want to do this when their asses get old and they start getting scared that they're going to die soon. Have you been taking your diabetes medication? Probably not because you're too hard-headed and I've also noticed you're sitting there drinking that grape soda and I know that ain't no doctor in his right mind give you permission to do that. But tell me again, why is it so important to you all of a sudden to even make this kind of announcement to Pat?"

I wish I had the strength or the energy to communicate that I can't stand to watch our daughter drown. More than that, I wish I had the clarity of thought to know exactly why I think she needs to know about this. I wish there was an easy way to tell a person that parents are not superheroes, even though their children expect them to be, but she was still loved in the best way we knew to give it to her. I wish I could tell her how much I loved her when I first laid eyes on her, even though she hadn't emerged from my own belly. I wish there was an easy way to tell her that by trying so hard to not be like me, she became more like me. In fact, all of them did. But most importantly, I wish I knew for certain that sharing this information will do more good than harm for Pat, Karen and Tessa. But I don't—I'm taking this chance based completely on gut and instinct. I just pray that Camilla cooperates, and that they will hear me out.

Calvin announces that the crabs are done cooking, and family, even the children, start spreading out at the picnic tables lined with newspaper.

I also wish I could crack a crab with my back molars like I used to. But instead of attempting to verbalize any of this, I just say, "She doesn't know how much her mama loves her. None of them do."

Camilla looks down at the ground and makes a swirl in the dirt with the toe of her shoe. She wants to ask me which mama I'm talking about—me or her—but she doesn't. Instead, she looks me square in the eye and says, "You've been watching too much television in that damn old folks home. You make me sick. I'm going to do this your way but I don't want to. Now you're going to have Patricia being mad as hell with me for giving her to you in the first place." When she shakes her head at me, the curls in her head tumble back and forth and the meat on her arm jiggles. Her hip bumps into my wheelchair when she gets up to put more food on our plates and she knocks me backwards, but she either doesn't care or doesn't notice. I begin rolling slowly, but not too fast to miss what happens next.

Camilla barely makes it two feet away from me before Patricia stops her dead in her tracks. She speaks loudly enough that I can hear her. "Aunt Camilla, what did I hear you just say to my mama?"

At first Camilla is speechless. Then her bottom lip drops open and she lets out a little hiccup. She looks over toward me, and then her face displays an expression that looks like a cross between panic and surprise.

I am unable to hear her reply to Patricia's question because I am rolling, then accelerating, then flying down a hill at the edge of Camilla's yard at break-neck speed on what feels like one tire of my wheelchair before being catapulted into some thorny bushes. And then, all of a sudden, everything goes dark.

* * *

"What in the hell do you mean by that?" asks Tessa.

"Excuse her language, doctor."

"What I'm saying is that your mother was not seriously injured by her fall. She read every word that's printed on my name tag and badge to me this morning just to prove it. She can continue to do all of the things she enjoys, but perhaps a bit more carefully. That ankle might be swollen and a bit bruised for a while, but she's very lucky to have only sustained a soft tissue injury."

"Get out of here," says Tessa.

"I thought this would be good news for you," says Dr. Nevarez.

"Did I just hear you say she could read?" asks Patricia.

"She memorized whatever he thinks she read. Mama is slick, you know," says Karen.

"Yes, I did just say that she can read. Her cognitive abilities are probably still comparable to all of yours. I think she prides herself on being a spry sixty-year-old, even after her brain attack occurred."

"Come again? That's not right," says Patricia.

"Could you rephrase your question? I'm sorry, I don't know what you're asking," Dr. Nevarez says.

"My sister didn't ask anything. What she's trying to tell you is that our mother hasn't been able to read, write, speak or think or move well since she had her stroke last year, and that your assessment must be off," offers Karen.

"I'm sorry to have to disagree so much with you. Your mother's stroke did leave her with a mild degree of dysphasia, but I'm starting to think those effects might only be transient. Even still, it hasn't affected her ability to do much besides speak clearly. The right-sided muscle weakness that she initially experienced has improved significantly, which is why I've expanded her activity privileges here in the West Wing. I can understand her becoming fatigued with all of the excitement when she's at home with you ladies and wanting to retreat to the comfort of a wheelchair from time to time, but I really think she might be best served now by ambulating on her own just having a walker or cane nearby."

I close my eyes and pretend to still be asleep because I can hear their voices nearing the door to my room.

"What is dysphasia?" asks Patricia.

"Google it," says Tessa, before the doctor can answer the question. "The man already told you the important part which is that Mama was not as slow since her stroke as we've been thinking."

"I don't mind answering any of your questions, ladies," Dr. Nevarez says. "In your mother's case, it means she can understand and process language very clearly, but she has a difficult time articulating her thoughts."

"And if I'm not mistaken, you also said she can walk," says Karen.

"Yes, she can. While her stroke certainly left her with some right-sided muscle weakness, her condition has improved tremendously over the last several months. She's been working very hard with her speech therapists and physical therapists. Together, they've made some beautiful progress."

"Which means what, exactly?" Patricia asks.

"Which means that, if she continues progressing through the regular use of physical therapy, she should soon be able to walk for longer periods of time independently."

I wish I could open my eyes and see everybody's posture and facial expressions when the room goes silent. Then I hear Dr. Nevarez excuse himself to check on another patient.

"Why in the hell would she pretend to be so bed-ridden and confused all the time, I wonder," mumbles Tessa.

"The same reason why she would wear a red dress to my poor daddy's funeral," says Karen.

"We come from a family full of lying, sneaking sons-of-bitches and I hope I don't take a damn trait after any of them," says Patricia.

Then I hear several feet stomping followed by the slam of my room door. And as much as I wish I didn't care, I am heartbroken. Now, in addition to being mean, disconnected and crazy, my children believe me to be a phony. There's no way in hell they would believe that my plans were to surprise them even if I tried to explain.

I open my eyes, hoping to find that at least one of my children decided to stay here with me. And even though my eyeballs are now stretched wide apart, I still can't see anything in the room because too much water is coming out of them.

Patricia

Leftover Ass

MY PLANE RIDE to our Miami field office was smooth, especially after two glasses of Riesling. While I was in the air, I leaned my head against my window seat and made up stories about everybody who was sitting near me. I took guesses about the kind of work they did, relationships they were involved in, the money they make, the houses they live in, the sort of sex they have, their relationships with their siblings. I even wondered which one of their parents they might have favored more than the other. One thing they all had in common, in my made-up biographical sketches, was they had real parents and a real family.

Then I found myself getting angry.

How is the decision made, while we're still being stitched together in our mother's womb, who gets selected to go to what families? How are some of us less worthy of having parents who love us and are happy to conceive us than others? What could the unworthy of us have done differently while waiting in heaven to get blasted down to earth that was so deserving of such familial dysfunction?

When my eyes fall on a twenty-something black Barbie Doll lookalike with a silver locket around her neck inscribed with the word "Daddy" sitting in the row across from me, I want to throw my paper cup at her. I'm willing to bet money that having a father in my life would have helped me land a much better gig in the dating world. I feel foolish to have looked for love in Gary now that I know what it is that I was doing. I am almost embarrassed for the younger me who married him and wish there was some way I could replace his memory of her for the new and improved me who doesn't give a damn what he thinks—at least not as much.

I am not as much upset as I am afraid. I'm afraid of not being able to find another man to love me. Plain Jane, thick-hipped, boring old me.

It was Gary who took care of me when I caught pneumonia and ended up in the hospital. He picked up my antibiotics and made sure I took them on time and called my job for me and doctored up my Campbell's soup. He's cleaned up my vomit and unstopped the toilet when I had diarrhea and used too much toilet paper. He's blow-dried my hair when I was too tired after I shampooed it. He put the down payment on this house and has paid the mortgage and all of the utility bills (even though he sometimes forgets to mail the checks on time) for the last ten years. That's got to be some kind of love.

Gary is a member of Omega Psi Phi fraternity, and has been popular in the community since we were in college. Being his lady has always made me feel worthy and accepted. He played football in school and was chased down by many a cheerleader and popular girls. The more I think about it, he is the one thing is this world that has made me feel as though I accomplished something—that I've finally come in first place. And look at what has happened.

I could resent his ass if I wanted to. I always took the vacations Gary wanted us to take because he said they were cultural and insightful, not meaningless and frivolous, like the Caribbean all-inclusive resorts I always wanted to try. I read the books about slavery, politics, travel and arts he thought were befitting of upper-middle class black folks, instead of the black literature I always thought was a more interesting and entertaining way to spend my free time. I stopped relaxing my hair because Gary watched a television special on the effects of sodium and calcium hydroxide on the scalp and decided that in order to put that cream on my head, I must actually hate my blackness, when in fact, I just don't have soft wavy hair that can easily be pulled back and I actually want to just wear ponytails. I watch the science channel on TV about astronomy and comets and black holes so I can sound intelligent when his geek-squad friends come over to dinner. I wish I wasn't tired of wearing this Halloween costume, but I am.

My hotel is on North Beach.

Before I can even empty my bladder for the first time since arriving, my cell phone rings.

"I thought you were going to call me when you got there," says Tessa.

"I would have, but you beat me to the punch."
"How was your flight?"
"Uneventful."
"Where are you staying?"
"The Trump Hotel on North Beach."
"Why in the hell would you want to do that? Do you know that he asked President Obama to produce his birth certificate to prove his citizenship?"

I have to think about that for a second. "I forgot about that. But that wouldn't have influenced my decision to stay here one way or the other. It's a nice hotel."

"Well your nice-hotel money is probably financing the tea party movement that's in the middle of shutting down the government as we speak."

"I thought that the budget was functioning with a continuing resolution."

"Which expired last night. Don't you watch the news?"
"Not lately because it depresses me."
"Everything depresses you, Patricia."

I just take a deep breath and exhale loud enough to let her know she's getting on my nerves.

"Well, I wanted to make sure you still had a job to do down there, with nobody going to work and what not. Otherwise, you need to bring your black ass home and sit down and talk to Auntie Camilla. She's driving everybody crazy because you won't answer her phone calls, you know."

"I don't feel like we have much to talk about."

"You sound like a crazy person. You just found out our auntie is really your mama and nothing is up for discussion?"

"I don't know what's left to say when you're forty-two years old and find out your mama gave you away."

"You heard her say she was young and stupid and scared. I don't see what the big damn deal is. She could have done something else with you like left your ass in a trashcan. You must not watch Lifetime, either."

I imagine that. "Maybe she should have."

"You either need to get you a prescription for some Zoloft or Paxil like all the high school kids take now or smoke one of my joints when you get back. I can see the cloud over your head all the way from Atlanta. I recommend the weed because it settles your nerves a whole lot faster."

"I've actually been thinking about scheduling some counseling. It wouldn't hurt me to talk to somebody about my divorce."

"Girl, I wish I had your problems. We should trade one day."

"Bye, Tessa. I've got to go to the bathroom."

"You need to watch the news," she says, before hanging up.

And when I do, I'm disgusted to learn government operations are in fact shutting down and there's a high likelihood my clients won't be getting paid for working tomorrow, and neither will I.

I march downstairs with my bag and promptly check out of the Trump and into the Marriott, just in case Tessa knew what she was talking about.

* * *

When I return to Atlanta, my friend and co-worker Nadia, who is an informatics specialist for another contract and who also has the body of a dancer, tells me a friend of a friend of hers would recommend Dr. Jamison to me if I was seriously thinking about getting the liposuction I had mentioned. It was important for me to understand she had never had any cosmetic surgery performed, Nadia had told me, but she had heard Dr. Jamison was really, really good. I thanked her for the reference and told her not to worry, because I had no intentions of exposing her friends nor her friends' friends, and that their secrets, even though they didn't have any, would be safe with me.

I'd already decided I didn't want to have my procedure performed by the first doctor with whom I'd consulted after I visited her office and saw the operating room was in the same building as a massage parlor and a gym. To me, it didn't matter what they called it or how they described it—I just didn't want to be on an operating room table in one room while somebody would be sweating on a treadmill in the next.

Dr. Jamison's office was pristine, though. And his staff all looked like brick houses. For this reason, I felt very comfortable, excited even, as I waited for him to enter my room and begin our consultation.

"So you only want me to remove some fat?" he asks, with emphasis on the word remove.

"Yes."

"From your hips? Right here?" His hands are gripping the meat on my upper things.

"Exactly. I want you to cut the tips off," I say while pointing to the outermost edges of my hips.

Dr. Jamison smiles.

"What's funny?" I ask.

"Nothing, really. By the way, I like that description—tips. It's just that most of my patients come to me because they want me to put some tips on their natural hips and buttocks."

"Who would want to do a thing like that?"

"You'd be surprised."

"Where do you get a tip from? I mean, the meat—where does it come from?"

"I can usually graft fat tissue from most anywhere on the body where it exists in excess."

"Like hips?" I ask.

"Like hips. Although, like I said, most women want me to transfer the fat to those parts of the body that round them out, giving them a more curvy appearance—not take it away."

"You mean to tell me you're how every woman in Atlanta is getting these perfect breasts and butts?"

"Women come in many different and beautiful sizes and shapes naturally. The only thing I do is work to enhance a woman's perception of herself, simply by borrowing from something she has a lot of and putting it in a place where she feels she is lacking. A lot of them find that idea to be liberating. I like to think of it as a Robin Hood approach to beauty. So no, I can't take responsibility for all the voluptuous women you see here, and many of them born that way, although I have been complimented on my work by many."

I think about all of that for a second. "I don't want any fat added anywhere."

"Then I wouldn't suggest that we transfer any."

"So how do you remove it? Is it like trimming chicken fat?"

Dr. Jamison chuckles before sitting down on a stool. "I suppose you could say it is. But I will be very careful in how I remove your tissue. And before we trim anything, I'd like to make sure you're really comfortable with having this procedure done and all your questions have been answered. We can spend the next few minutes discussing everything you need to know in as much detail as you'd like. And if you think of any more questions after you get home, either I or my nurse will be happy to answer them by email or telephone."

I like Dr. Jamison much better than the lady with the operating room inside the gym. Or was it the other way around? And, at any rate, I feel comfortable scheduling my procedure with him. I sort of like the idea of taking my fat from one place and sticking it in another, but truthfully, I don't know where I would put it. I would donate my own fat to help spread someone else's ass if I could, but I'm sure most women would find it unappealing to become so intimately acquainted with another woman's leftover piece of ass.

I take that thought right back as soon as I remember all the women whose names appeared in my husband's cell phone.

Karen

What Happened to Your Townhouse?

"WHAT HAPPENED to your townhouse?" I ask Tim through my cell phone. I have just arrived at the address that he told me to come to.

"Oh, I let somebody rent it out from me for a little while, darling. I'm just staying here temporarily until I close on my new house. It's real big and nice—out there in Niskey Lake off Cascade."

I shut my cell phone to disconnect the call, and see Tim walking outside the front door. He is wearing a wife beater, baggy jeans and no shoes or belt. He smiles when he sees me but I cannot smile back. This is not a townhouse, penthouse, apartment-house, or even an outhouse. This is the fucking projects.

"Come on in here, baby. Those all the bags you got?" He's just looking at the duffel bag on my shoulder. I shake my head no.

I pop open my trunk and motion toward the two suitcases. Tim comes over to me, grabs one bag, and hollers back toward the house, "Black! Get yo ass out here and help me, nigga!" Black must not have heard everything Tim said because I see him open up a window and stick his head out. "Oh, she moving in?" I hear him ask when he sees me standing outside my car with the trunk open and a bag on my shoulder. My car. Dammit. Where do I park my car? His head goes back inside, and the window shuts. I guess he's on his way outside to help.

"Tim, baby, who was that?"

"Black."

"I understand that much. Does he live here?"

"Yeah, that's temporary, too. He's my sister's boyfriend and he just got out of jail. He's trying to get back on his feet."

"I didn't know you had a sister. Does she live here?"

"Yeah, Quita. She's in the house. I got three sisters."

I have to stop myself from correcting his English—I've never heard him talk like this before. But instead of doing that, I just silently pray that the two other sisters don't live in this tiny apartment, too. "Where do they live?"

"They stay together. They down in Albany in school. But you asking a lot of questions today. How's my baby doing?"

I rub my stomach. "We're fine." Now Black comes out of the house with what looks and smells like a ham sandwich hanging out of his mouth. He walks over to where Tim and I are standing and looks me up and down before grabbing the other suitcase. I look at Tim. He didn't seem to notice.

I follow the two men in the house and, to my surprise, immediately almost trip over a baby in the floor. I want to know who she belongs to, but I'm almost afraid to ask. Before I am able to think up a tactful way to phrase the question, Tim yells into the back of the apartment, "Talitha, come get this little girl! She bout to get stepped on!"

Talitha appears from out of a dark hallway. It is a wonder that she could fit through it because she looks to be the size of a small door frame. She smiles politely at me, picks up the baby, grabs a bottle of what I guess is milk from out of her back pocket, and disappears back down the hallway.

"Come on, baby. Let me show you to your room." Tim flashes his million dollar grin my way and grabs my hand. One of my bags falls over onto a cloth sofa that looks like it's one hundred years old. I say a silent prayer that bed bugs aren't waiting to jump from it and into my luggage. He leads me through the kitchen, which smells like burnt cheese, and takes me to a room that lies just behind the refrigerator. I couldn't even tell that it was back here. The room is small, but is neat and clean. A queen size bed and two dressers fill the entire space. There is a tiny bathroom to my left, and a television on a small table just in front of me. As soon as I unzip my bag and prepare to get settled into my new room, I hear a crash that sounds like it's coming from above me. I jump and I imagine that the baby does, too.

"What's that?" I ask while rubbing my belly with my right hand.

"Damn, probably just some children playing upstairs. When did your ass get so scary?"

I don't say anything and just start unpacking clothes.

"Black, you got my money for the Pampers? Reesey just shitted on his last one." I hear the voice coming from down the hallway. It must be Talitha.

"I'm about to make a quick run, T, but I'll be right back with it." His voice comes from the other direction in the hallway.

"I guess I can tape one of my maxi pads to him. That ought to hold him for a little while."

"See, I knew you were smart, girl. That's why I got with you. I'll be right back." He isn't yelling anymore. In fact, I think he's standing right outside of my room.

"Okay, and bring me something, too." I hear them kissing. Tim shuts the door and helps me unpack my clothes.

My mind is racing a million miles per minute as the two of us bump around this room. For one, I'm hoping that Quita and Talitha are the same person. I don't think anybody else can fit into this house. Something else I'd like to know is how Tim manages to speak correct English while everyone else's verbiage is so poor. And I just have to know why in the hell he would offer to rent out the beautiful, contemporary dream house where I fucked him and managed to get pregnant right after he offered to let me move in. I hope he closes on the new one soon. Then, all of a sudden, another thought occurs to me. "Tim, it doesn't look like you live in here at all. Where are all of your things?"

"I've been in and out for a couple weeks while I'm working on the new house. You're going to love it."

Three hours later, we're finishing our fish filet sandwiches that I drove out and picked up from McDonalds. It's 7 p.m., and I'd like to stay up to watch the comedy show that is playing on TV in the living room, but I just can't. Everybody is in there laughing, including the baby. I still haven't seen Quita. Note to self: Find out if she and Talitha are the same person as soon as I wake up from this nap.

* * *

My nap turns into an overnight slumber. When I get up, I quickly discover that Quita and Talitha are in fact, two different people. Turns out that they are both the mothers of Black's children (I still don't know if that's his real name, but I certainly hope not), but Quita is Tim's sister. Apparently Quita doesn't live here but visits frequently because she and Black are still dating one another. Talitha gives me the rundown on all of this as she helps me unpack my clothes. She also explains that she's living here temporarily until she can get on her feet, but she didn't explain what all that entailed. I didn't ask.

Talitha is a very soft spoken woman, and comes across as being very nice and extremely helpful. She scrambled me some eggs and fried a few slices of bacon before making herself a grilled cheese sandwich. When I asked her if she had to work, she shook her head back and forth and said, "I do hair."

I'm a little bit surprised to hear this because I'm sure that blonde thing on her head is a wig she's wearing and most of the hairstylists in Atlanta I've ever known keep their hair done. "Where is your salon?" I ask, peeking through the blinds and noticing there are no cars parked outside.

"I do it here in the kitchen. See?" And with that, she opens a cabinet under the sink and proudly shows me her collection of shampoo, conditioner, color, and other hair products that I don't recognize.

Because we are the only people in the house I suggest we go to Lenox Mall to get some fresh air. She squeezes into a pair of jeans and a cotton shirt that's about two sizes too small. I want to suggest she lose some weight, but it's really not any of my business.

We pull up to the mall and I park my car in the garage outside of Bloomingdales. When we get inside, I immediately see the Maui Jim sunglasses that I've been searching for and purchase them. As soon as the saleswoman gives me my receipt, Talitha asks me right away, "Are you really rich?"

"Not even close. And where on earth would you get an idea like that?"

"Black told me you were but I didn't believe him because you don't dress like any rich lady I've ever seen. But, hell, now I have to really wonder because I don't know anybody who buys three hundred dollar sunglasses like that."

"I don't think anything is wrong with spending money on the things you like if you work hard to earn your money."

"Yeah, you're rich."

"No, I'm not."

"Come on. Let's go into one of those name-brand stores I hear about on the radio so you can buy something out of there. I want to know what they look like on the inside."

"I don't buy my clothes in those stores." As soon as I say that, I spot a big red leather pocketbook through the window in Macy's. I hold up a finger to tell Talitha to hold on while I run inside and feel it. It's beautiful, but I refuse to buy it in that color. I'm back outside the store in thirty seconds.

"Okay. You say that but I see that you like high-priced purses and sunglasses, so what kinds of stores do you like to buy your clothes from?"

"TJ Maxx and Stein Mart."

"I lell, you ain't no better than me. I used to shop out of there too before the last baby put all this weight on me. I wasn't this fat before, you know."

"I believe you." I'm not sure if that came out right. "How many children do you have?"

"Three."

"Wait a minute. I only saw one baby in the house."

"Yeah, that's Little Black. We call him LB. He goes to Head Start during the week."

"Well, what about the other two?"

"Black told me a long time ago that he didn't want to be raising anybody else's children so I sent them back to their daddies."

If I could fight, I would punch Talitha in the nose right out here in this mall.

"I know what you must be thinking," she continues. "I really am not a bad mama but they were better off with their daddies at that time, anyway."

"Why? Were you on drugs or something like that?" I notice a woman covering her child's ears as she passes by us. I make a mental note to lower my voice.

"Hell, no. I ain't never been on no drugs. But at that time, I was participating in the type of behavior my children didn't need to be around."

"What kind of behavior was this, if you don't mind me asking?"

"I was gay for a little while."

"Oh." I am immediately uncomfortable and wish I hadn't let her cook for me this morning.

"But I stopped when I got saved."

"I understand that," I say, but I really don't mean it. "But how was it that you were dating Black and, um, being with women at the same time?"

"That wasn't a problem for him. He helped me find them."

Hearing this makes my stomach hurt. "Do you want to get something to eat?"

"We just ate breakfast."

"I know, but I'm getting hungry again."

"Sure, if you're paying. I don't have much money because business has been slow lately. Folks don't get their hair done much around Christmas and the holidays. But I thought I was the fat girl between to two of us. Where are we going?"

"There's a Chick-Fil-A in the food court. Let's walk down there."

And we do.

"Talitha, you mind if I ask you another question?"

"Sure."

"What's Black's real name?"

"Black is his real last name."

"Well what's his first name?"

"Eldorado."

For a tiny second I feel stupid. I wonder what I'm doing out here with these people and why I'm actually trying to reason with this woman who lives in a house with her baby daddy's other baby mama, and who's boyfriend actually shares the same name as a Cadillac. Then I shake my head back and forth to dismiss the hormone-induced negativism that has been creeping into my thoughts left and right since I moved in with my fiancé, and sit down in a chair in front of Chick-Fil-A while Talitha stands in line for both of us.

* * *

Pregnancy has made sex feel even more incredible. I didn't realize that was possible until this morning when I woke up extremely horny and was able to achieve an orgasm in less than five minutes. I don't recall

Tim getting in bed with me last night, but I sure was glad to be able to wake up and roll over on top of him. It feels like my sensory receptors have been fine tuned to detect and respond to even the slightest amount of stimulation—I'm sure that I can attribute this to the increased pelvic vascularization that is characteristic to gravid women at around eight or nine weeks gestation—and I was feeling so good that I was starting to feel bad over our excessive amount of fornication, which is how I ended up approaching the subject of weddings.

"You know what we're doing is wrong."

"Nothing about this feels wrong to me, darling," Tim had said while rubbing my thighs.

"But it is. We shouldn't be playing house. It's time for us to move forward with planning this wedding, wouldn't you say?"

"I would, except that weddings cost a lot of money and we both know that we have some competing priorities."

"So how long?"

"Not long."

"I know, you've told me that. But how temporary is this supposed to be? I don't like living with other people. I feel like I have to bite my tongue when we make love so I don't wake up the children in the room next to me."

"You can yell as loud as you want to, baby. These walls ain't that thin."

"Yes they are, but that's beside the point, Tim. We need our own space. I still think we would have been better off had you moved in with me."

"Hell no we wouldn't have. I'm a man." His hand stops rubbing me. "You act like you're bad enough as it is because you've been to school for a few years and make a decent paycheck. I can't move into my girl's house."

"But you can move me into your boy's house?"

"See, there you go with that shit. You always find a way to put a nigga down."

I immediately feel bad. "No, baby, I didn't mean it like that. I know that you're doing the best you can. I didn't like my house all that much anyway. It barely had a back yard and I was starting to notice problems with the plumbing."

He puts his arms around my waist and gives me his sexy smolder. "Nothing would please me more than to put my wife in the brand new house of her dreams."

I love it when he calls me his wife. I just like the way the word sounds when it comes off of his tongue.

"And that's exactly what I'm planning to do," he continues. "There are just a few more pieces of business that have to come together first."

"Okay, like what? Tell me what I can do to help."

"Nothing, Karen. I don't want you to worry your pretty little head. Let your man take care of this."

"But I don't mind, really, baby. I'm your partner, remember? We're a family," I say, thinking about my little zygote and getting lost in Tim's beautiful eyes.

"I guess you could, um, front me a few dollars to help out with the construction of the house."

"I thought you said the house was already up."

"It is, but they're still doing some upgrades, you know?"

"Sure, I understand. How much is a few dollars?"

"Maybe ten or fifteen thousand. You said you have a savings account at the hospital credit union, didn't you?"

"I did."

"Okay, well break it out of there for me, darling, and I'll replace it before you even notice it's missing."

I kiss him on the lips. "That's no problem."

* * *

I think I must be dreaming when I wake up at two in the morning and hear muffled voices coming from the front of the apartment. After lying in bed for a few minutes, I realize I recognize at least one voice—Tim. Although it's hard to make out exactly what anyone is saying, Tim's voice is much lower than the other, which makes me want to know what he could be talking about at this hour.

This mattress on this bed creaks every time I turn, so I put some real effort into easing up just in case anybody can hear me through these paper-thin walls. As soon as I stand up, I remember the floorboards creak, too, so this adds another two minutes to my commute toward the door.

Fortunately, the hallway is carpeted. The moonlight peeking through the windows in the house illuminates my path so I don't need any light, and also allows me to see the front door is open. Just as I suspected, Tim, Black and the baby are all outside on the stairs and stoop of the apartment. I don't know why, but my heart begins to beat faster. I stand at the end of the hallway, toward the left side where some shadow remains, and pray nobody hears me breathing. I hate to eavesdrop, but I wonder what kind of family meeting they could possibly be having at this time of night.

"You sure this shit is going to work? I mean, she don't look that dumb to me," Black says as he bounces the little girl in his lap.

"I'm sure. I can handle everything on my end. You just make sure you come through with your end of the deal."

"I already have. I done talked to the white folk over there at the lot three times now. Billy said the truck is yours as soon as you make good on the money you owe him. We're going to be back in business in no time. I can feel my palms itching now, if you really want to know the truth. Oh, and Monkey 'nem sent me some fire ass beats yesterday. Pull up your iPad so you can listen."

"This ain't the time for that, man. Right now I'm trying to make moves and get me a truck back out there so I can secure me some contracts."

"I feel you on that, partner. I'm going to be needing a few extra dollars myself soon."

Tim looks at Black as if to say, what's up?

"Quita says you have another niece or nephew on the way."

"What? You lying. I thought you said you were done."

"Hell, I thought she said she was done."

"Does Talitha know about this?"

"Not yet."

"She still looking for her own place?"

"Yeah, she says she is. But I think she knows she's got it made over here. She don't have to work. She can eat her food and drink her liquor and Quita will babysit Trinity anytime she wants."

Tim shakes his head. "You oughtta be glad you have some cool-ass baby mamas. I know plenty of niggas getting drug through the damn mud about child support and catching hell about the new girlfriend."

"T is pretty cool. Everybody knows that. She might be a lazy motherfucker, but I ain't never say she wasn't cool. It wouldn't hurt her fat ass to get up and find a job, though."

"You sure you ain't still dipping and dabbing in that?"

"Naw, man, that's done. You acting like you don't live here half the time and see it for yourself. We just have a cool-ass living arrangement."

"I know that's all it better be. Let me find out that you break my little sister's heart then I'm have to shoot your ass in the nuts."

"Man, stop talking crazy. I'm in love with your sister. I'ma marry her pretty ass after I get this record deal."

"Cool."

"I'm changing the subject," Black says, then takes a sip of his beer. "This is what I want to know: What kind of shit are you doing to that girl to make her come over here and pay the note on this house while you're making all these investments? You've got to be doing more than calling her stupid ass darling all the time."

"Lower your voice, nigga."

"Okay," Black whispers. "Now tell me."

"What you mean?"

"People think the shit they see with me and my girlfriend and baby's mama all living in the same house is weird, but you're setting a new record right now. That lady has been spending cash on you for the last two weeks like it ain't no tomorrow. She even bought Talitha a new crib for the baby and Quita says she gave her some money to buy a new wig."

Tim laughs. "Only thing that I can tell you is that I put that old-school dig in her ass the way my daddy taught me. I be stroking."

"I be stroking too, but damn, I ain't never had no college-educated bitch to do no dumb shit like what you done talked her ass into doing."

"I told you to keep your damn voice down, nigga."

"Alright, but for the record, I know you've got to be licking more than her titties. Stick out your tongue, boy. I know it must be long."

Tim tries to stifle his laughter. "It ain't as long as my dick."

"You and every other motherfucker in the world."

"Except the difference with me is that I'm telling the truth. Ask your mama."

"Don't start that shit unless you want me to tell you how deep your sister is."

"Don't bring that shit up no more unless you want your nuts in your mouth. If you weren't my homeboy then I'd dump your damn body back there in them woods and fertilize the trees with your ass."

"You started that shit talking about my mama. She been dead for ten years. That shit wasn't even funny."

"Alright, partner, we gone be cool. But that was real talk about my dick. You know my daddy is from the islands."

Both men chuckle.

I quietly tiptoe back down the hallway to my room, pick up a trashcan, and throw up in it.

Patricia

Recovery

NOBODY TOLD ME having some fat chopped off was going to make me feel like I have been hit by a bus.

I am in a dark room with a blood pressure cuff attached to my arm and my bottom half is stuffed into what feels like a strait jacket. To top off the pain, I am suddenly hit with a wave of nausea that is enough to wake me right up from the anesthesia-induced doze I've been drifting in and out of for the past few minutes. Then I catch a glance of the clock on the wall in here and I believe that it says 5 o'damn clock, meaning I've been in surgery for the past three hours. There is a nurse in the corner. I ask her if I can go home yet. She tells me to close my eyes and take another short nap. I take a series of them for another two weeks.

On the Monday morning I am supposed to return to work, I call my job and ask Nadia to tell Wendy, my contract manager, that I still have the flu. I hang up the phone, take another Vicodin, and cover up my head with a pillow and go back to sleep.

After another three lonely days go by, I get up with plenty of energy and decide to host a dinner at my house to try bonding with my sisters. Cooking has always made me feel good about myself—probably because it is one of the few things I ever felt I was really good at doing.

But maybe inviting Tessa and Karen over right now may not have been a good idea, I begin to think as I inch through the grocery store shopping for all of the specialty items my recipe requires. I'm sure Karen is busy with her new fiancé and the pregnancy, and Tessa is busy with whatever Tessa stays busy doing. I want to be close to them—they're such admirable women. Karen is brilliant and young with a life pregnant with promise. And Tessa has always been a happy, loveable free spirit. I can remember hearing her name being associated with trendy and popular people all throughout the neighborhood. All my life I've wanted to fit in with that crowd.

I'm embarrassed to be thinking this thought, but pleasing Gary became the point of my existence. I know women who won't boil water, but I had to be the best at frying chicken on this side of the Mississippi River. Nearly a virgin when we got together, I started watching porn movies when he wasn't at home so I could feel as though I was competently screwing my husband while emulating the jerks and rolls that some adult star on a movie called *Soft Chicks and Hard Dicks* was demonstrating for the camera.

But I'm determined to change that, starting today.

Now that my scallops are done broiling, I cover them with foil to keep the juice from drying up while I finish sautéing the asparagus. Nothing is worse than feeding people some crunchy vegetables unless you plan to serve them with ranch dressing. On my way to the bathroom in the hallway, I stop and peek out of the blinds over the sofa in the living room just to look out at the neighborhood. I glace up the street and wonder if my sisters will arrive on time. I can just make out the right tip of the gate and hope that they'll remember my instructions for entering. I think about calling Karen to make sure her GPS is able to pull up my neighborhood, but I stop myself for fear of feeling too anxious for company. She assured me they would be here between 6:30 and 7:00 p.m.

After scrubbing the scent of garlic off my hands with vanilla-scented hand soap, I stir a little bit of milk into the mashed potatoes to keep them from getting stiff. I glance at the clock: 6:45. I hit a button on my cell phone to make it light up so I can see if I've missed any calls. None. Just for the hell of it, I touch the email button to see if any new emails have come through. Nothing but sale offers from Bed Bath & Beyond and New York & Company. Another one pops up right in front of my eyes from a sorority sister on the local listserv wanting to know if anybody has successfully removed red wine from carpet with baking soda; she's been trying for an hour and thinks she's missing an ingredient. She wants to know if perhaps it's vinegar but maybe she's thinking about one of her children's science projects instead of carpet removal techniques. Another two pop up by the time I finish reading the first one. Looks like answers to the baking soda question.

By 7:00, I tune in to Lifetime and watch a movie I've seen before so I don't mind catching it exactly halfway through the story. Although I remember it's an entertaining picture, I can't recall what happens when the baby goes back to her real mother in the end. It makes me begin to wonder why I could never get back to my real mother in the end, and if I would ever have really wanted to. As far as I'm concerned, neither mother (biological nor adopted) really cared enough about me to see to it that I was properly cared for, so I'm not sure if it even matters. What I do know, as much as I hate to admit it, is that not having a real mother has affected my ability to process normal things that normal adults with mothers do not have trouble processing. How do I know? Because I don't see other women my age struggle with the same types of questions I do. They are able to pick out clothes confidently in the department stores because their mothers have taught them a little bit about style or flair or how to match them up and even coordinate jewelry and tell the difference between what is tasteful versus what is not. I watch them when I'm in the checkout line and then silently debate if my items, selected fresh from the clearance rack, could ever compare to the ones thrown over their arms. I wonder, when I run into them at the movie theater, restaurant, or even in the produce aisle at the grocery store, if my clothes will still look "mammy made" just like they did when I was tortured in high school for wearing clothes I had worked hard to sew the weekend before.

I get up again to check the clock—it's now 7:45—and pour a glass of wine from the bar next to the refrigerator and fix a small plate of scallops and vegetables. I sure hate to be rude and begin eating dinner before the guests arrive, so I play with the arrangement that just came out of the broiler and reposition the remaining sea scallops to make it look like I haven't been picking through them. I'm hungry. I bring my cell phone with me back over to the sofa and stare at it for a full thirty seconds as though I can will it to ring. At 8:01, I decide I've been selfish and feel immature for thinking that calling will make me look anxious when really I should be checking on their well-being. Karen answers the phone on the second ring. She sounds surprised to be hearing from me when she answers.

"Hi, there."

Silence.

"Karen, are you there?"

Nothing.

"Just checking on you. Actually, I'm wondering if you're able to find the subdivision okay, a lot of systems don't pick up an accurate system and I know I'm kind of far out of the city."

"Oh, Pat, I'm so sorry. I got tied up with some Christmas shopping this morning after coming off of a twenty-four hour shift and came home and passed out without setting an alarm to wake me up."

"You mean I just woke you up?"

"No, not really. I've been up for a few minutes but I completely forgot about the dinner."

"What about Tessa? Is she with you?"

"No, Tessa should be at home. Did you try calling her?"

"I thought you were bringing her out here. Is she going to come by herself?"

"Shit. I forgot that, too. I was supposed to drive us both out to see you, wasn't I? Girl, it must be this pregnancy brain. I wonder why she didn't call me and remind me."

"Okay," is all I can think to say.

"Listen, I am so sorry. How about a rain check? What are your plans for next weekend?"

I feel myself beginning to get choked up. I want to hurry and hang up the phone.

"Next weekend will work even better, Karen. You go on and get yourself some rest."

I return the cordless phone to its base.

Why should I be surprised Karen and Tessa have forgotten about my invitation for dinner? I bought the groceries and cooked the food, but asking them to simply show up was still too much of a strain for them, wasn't it? They're probably thinking, as usual, sweet Patricia will understand. The sign on my forehead that reads "Use me and abuse me because I'm not special" apparently is still visible.

I would love to know what the secrets are of the women who get ahead. My mother never gave me the mystical and classified instruction reserved for beauty queens, for popular girls, for the sexy and flirty women who can steal your husband away from you right in front of your eyes. I wish to God I knew what it is they have that I don't.

I pour a glass of muscadine wine, take a few sips, and decide that today, I will go find out.

I blink past the tears that are stinging my eyes as I pack up every last piece of food into my brand new red and clear storage containers and throw them into the recyclable grocery bag that I keep in the trunk of my car. Before I stop to really think, I type the address of Gary's baby mama into my car's GPS system and back out of the driveway so quickly that my tries squeal. Ten minutes later, I'm sitting outside of a raggedy apartment building that says 1105-1149 on the brown pillar. I'm nervous but not quite scared and can't quite figure out what I'm doing or where the courage is coming from, but I knock on the door. I hear footsteps running around inside the house and so I pause for a second before knocking again. A woman who looks about thirty years old and tired as hell with a scarf tied around her head wearing sweatpants opens the door. For a few seconds, I cannot speak. I just stare at her. She is the first to talk.

"I thought you were Keisha coming back with the Pampers. I ain't trying to buy nothing."

I straighten up my back before responding. "My name is Patricia. I'm Gary's wife."

She looks surprised at first and then mad. "Don't be coming around my house starting no damn shit lady. I ain't even seen Gary's trifling pussy-eating ass in two weeks, and when I do see him, I don't won't nothing but the damn money he owes me. You can trust and believe that. You can keep your husband."

"I really don't know why I came," I start. And then I realize I don't know her name. "May I ask for your name?"

She looks me up and down while she contemplates answering my question. And why should she? "Sharon," she surprises me by answering.

"Sharon," I repeat. Sharon. I wouldn't have thought of that. In my mind I had imagined a Tina or Candy. Something that sounds more like a stripper. Sharon. Sharon is my husband's child's mother. Sharon. I don't even remember seeing her name in the cell phone.

Sharon looks at me like I'm crazy. As if on cue, she asks, "What exactly may I help you with, Patricia?"

I can tell she's trying to speak properly, probably because she notices I'm speaking proper English.

I look behind her without trying to and see a cross-eyed baby with thick glasses crawling on the floor toward Sharon's right leg. I can't tell whether the baby is a boy or a girl, but as soon as he or she touches Sharon, she shakes her leg to free herself of the baby's grasp. In the background, I hear even more children. I ask for permission to come into her house.

I step inside the house and realize I'm in the family room. None of the furniture matches so I pick the chair with the orange and white flowers to sit in. I hear a clink-clink noise and turn my attention to a boy seated in the kitchen next to the family room. He is sitting at the table eating a bowl of crunchy squares I assume to be cereal, except I don't see any milk. The shape of his face and slant of his eyes tells me he might have Down syndrome. I look back at her to try and guess her age because I think that she is too young of a mother to have a child as old as he is (maybe thirteen?) and with a chromosomal abnormality.

Low and behold—a baby who's not even old enough to crawl yet awakens from a nap in a swing by the window and begins to cry. The smell that follows tells me exactly what he needs. I peek into the green and yellow swing to see if I can spot any of Gary's features but I can't. Maybe he or she is too young to tell. I am disgusted by the brown smear I see on the side of the baby's diaper.

It suddenly dawns on me that I am feeling a rather odd emotion. It's something similar to sympathy, but just without so much of the feel sorry part. I dig down through the bag and produce the dinner I just cleared off of my own kitchen counters. I can still feel the warmth through the plastic. I try to hand it to her but she looks at me through big, black, cautious eyes and asks if I'm trying to poison her. I tell her I'm not and just ask if she likes scallops and asparagus.

"I like anything that comes out of the ocean but I don't know about asparagus. Aren't they the little cabbages?"

I explain that she's thinking about Brussels sprouts. "I've never tried that before."

The toddler on the floor holds his hand out to ask for some. She hands him one. I keep waiting for him to spit it out, then choke on the large piece of meat, but he doesn't. It appears to have gone done in one single gulp.

I decide to go straight for it: "Which one of these children did you get by my husband?"

She swallows a scallop whole after putting it in her mouth with two fingers. "He sleep. Got a cold and just had his medicine." She points to the back of the house.

I'm almost afraid to ask my next question but I have to. "May I see him?"

She hesitates, not as though she doesn't want me to see the baby, but because she doesn't want to put down the plate she's eating from. After another swallow, she gets up from the sofa and disappears down a short hallway. She comes right back with a toddler over her shoulder. I stand up to see his face. Immediately, after recognizing a widow's peak and Gary's chocolate brown skin tone, I become teary eyed. The girl eyeballs me suspiciously and returns her baby to his room just as quickly as they came out. She plops back down on the sofa and surprises me with her next comment: "I didn't know he was married at the time we started, um..."

"Fucking," I surprise myself and say.

"Well, yeah."

I can't come up with anything more intelligent to ask except, "How much child support does Gary give you?"

She rolls her eyes. "How much as in how often or how much as in how much money?"

"Both."

"A few dollars every now and then when he feel like it. Don't worry, we ain't taking no food off your table." She stops chewing her food and places her hands on her hips. I look closely at her face and suddenly recognize the expression: shame.

I survey her tiny apartment. My eyes hurt each time I see that sofa. Another look at the shitty diapered child on the floor and at the one who is currently searching for more cereal in an empty bowl. My eyes go from the stain on the carpet in front of me to a matching stain on the sofa. I wonder why my husband fucked a woman in such desperate condition and hid the baby and denied his child a decent chance at a more privileged life. I refuse to ask any more questions and instead, tell Sharon I'm going up the street to Walmart to pick up diapers for the baby.

When I stand up to leave the apartment, the cross-eyed baby grabs around my ankle and holds on for dear life. I bend down to pick him or her up, which is painful because my thighs are still sore. Now that I'm up close, I'm pretty sure this one is a girl. She has beautiful big black eyes which she obviously did not get from her mother. Just to be sure, I check this baby's face to examine it for any possible resemblance to Gary. I don't see any.

"Take her with you," Sharon says with a half of a smile. I don't smile back because I don't know if she's serious or if she's joking. I place the baby in her mother's arms very gently and she begins to cry, softly at first, then louder. I grab my purse and exit the apartment anyway.

I am full of so many emotions that I cannot remember which side of the store carries the non-perishable items I came in here to get, even though I shop here at least once every other week for my own household supplies. It takes me four trips around the store to figure out what I think I came here to buy. After an hour and a half of shopping and idle walking, I finally purchase diapers in three different sizes, two extra-large containers of Enfamil, one gallon of whole milk, a super-sized box of Cheerios, a jug of apple juice, eight or nine cans of soup, a box of Saltine crackers, a variety pack of potato chips, some pasta noodles, a pack of cheddar cheese, two dozen eggs, and a bag of oranges. It's not until I reach the checkout line that it occurs to me that I should have written down a grocery list. I put the food into the trunk of my car, then decide to go back in the store to the clothing section to pick out some children's outfits in various sizes.

I manage to get lost on my way back to Sharon's, but I refuse to turn on my GPS. When I finally make my way there, I've already made up my mind that I'm not going back inside. It takes me three trips back and forth to the car to carry everything out of the trunk and leave it on her front door step. I push the doorbell button and pause for a moment to make sure somebody heard the bell go ding-dong before turning around to head back to the Camry.

As I step back into my car, I take one last look toward the door. I could be mistaken, but think I see a crooked eyeball peeking at me through the front blinds. I do know for a fact, however, that I'm not just hearing things when I roll my window down and hear her older children scream that Santa Claus must have come to their house early.

Karen

Didn't I Tell You?

"**DIDN'T I TELL YOU** that nigga was full of shit?" asks Tessa.

"Shut up and pick her clothes up before these people get back," snaps Patricia.

"She's right," I say. "You told me. I didn't listen."

"Wait a minute. Where is your furniture?" Tessa wants to know.

"I left some of it in my house for the renters. The rest is in storage."

"So where are we taking you now, exactly?" asks Patricia.

"Back to my house."

"What are you going to do with the new tenants? Just put the people out?" asks Tessa.

"Not exactly. They hadn't moved in there yet. It cost me some money but I was able to void out the contract."

"You're too damn old to be falling in love with penises," Tessa continues. "Where did you get your doctor degree so I can go get me one?"

"You're being ugly," says Patricia.

"No I'm not. It's about time somebody listens to me instead of thinking I'm the dummy of the family. I might not have as many degrees as you two but I ain't never let a man make no fool out of me. And why the hell does it smell like burnt cheese up in here?"

"Grab that suitcase over there," I say.

"If Mama could talk then she would curse your ass out good," Tessa says.

"Mama wouldn't have room to talk with as many women that used to call our house looking for daddy in the middle of the night. You two were too young to remember," says Patricia.

"Well that is a good thing so none of her stupid could rub off on me." That was Tessa.

"Oh, you're stupid, alright, but in a different kind of way," says Patricia.

Tessa points her middle finger at Patricia.

"You better pray to God that the little girl in your stomach is listening to everything going on in here so she can break the cycle. Either that, or let her spend a whole lot of time with me."

"I'll bet it is a pretty little girl," says Patricia. "And her Auntie Tessa needs to only get to make supervised visits," she giggles.

"There won't be any babies coming out of this stomach anytime soon." Tessa and Patricia both drop their bags and look at me.

"What have you done?" asks Tessa.

"Nothing, yet. But I'm making an appointment for one day this week."

"You'd better not be planning anything except a baby shower, Karen," Patricia says.

I look at the ground. "I've decided it's probably best for me to have an abortion."

"Like hell you will," says Patricia before throwing a suitcase on the bed. "I'm seeing to it that this baby gets born if it's the last thing I do."

Therapy

"I STILL DON'T KNOW why we're here," says Tessa, just before placing her hand on the doorknob of the therapist's office. She turns to Patricia before asking, "And where did you find this man? I'll bet he's white."

"I work with his wife and, yes, he is white, not that it makes any difference," answers Patricia. "She suggested we try some family counseling and promised he would offer us a discount."

"That's because you tell your co-workers all of your damn business. Speak for yourself next time you want some sympathy. I don't need any counseling."

"Welcome!" says Eugene Brown as he yanks the door open. He looks Tessa in the eye and gives her a warm smile as if he heard her comments through the door. "I was just looking over the registration paperwork you provided to me online. Please have a seat."

Karen and Patricia sit on a small sofa. Tessa sits in the chair. Eugene snuggles in behind his desk and begins writing even though nobody has given him any information to document.

"Tell me what it is I can do for you ladies," he finally says while looking over the top of his glasses.

"We want to find a way to get closer and understand each other as sisters," says Karen. "None of us want to be anything like our mother—we all have that in common—but we could use some help in learning how to be better support systems for each other."

"I want to know why I never felt like I was a part of this family," says Patricia.

"I just think both my sisters are spoiled bitches who are looking for sympathy," is the only truthful thing Tessa can think to say.

"Okay, that's fair. Well let's start by talking about where the three of you ladies come from. Tell me about your childhood, and your experiences while growing up together."

"You want to hear the truth or some bullshit?" asks Tessa.

"I'd prefer to hear the truth."

Karen adds, "Patricia feels sorry for herself because she doesn't have the same biological mother and father as we do. As far as I'm concerned, she got the good end of the deal. Tessa is a whore but I don't know why. Our daddy was in our lives."

"Excuse me, bitch? A whore? Well what does that make you? Certainly not a cast member on Married to Medicine. Let the good doctor tell you about her drug-dealing boyfriend who got her pregnant at a BP station." That was Tessa.

"I hear that you've fucked in a few public places, yourself, but you probably stay too high to remember," shouts Karen.

"Take some of that K-Y Jelly out of your office, lube up your fingers, and see if you can remove that stick out of your ass," replies Tessa.

"Excuse me. I want you ladies to feel comfortable expressing yourselves, but there's no need to be vulgar and disrespectful in this office."

"I'm sorry, Mr. Brown. Initially, I thought it might be a good idea for us to come here and talk out some of our issues, but apparently we're not ready. Forgive us for wasting your time," says Patricia.

"Is your insurance paying for this?" Tessa asks Patricia.

"No."

"Well, you sit your black ass down and tell this man why you're depressed all the time. Getting your ass and titties done and shit. You're already going to get a bill from this quack, so you might as well make him listen to the Turnipseed family violin's sad ass song."

"You've recently had some surgery, Patricia?" asks Mr. Brown, clearly ignoring Tessa's putdown.

"I have. But not my breasts."

"But it is some shit you don't need, am I right?" asks Tessa, of course.

"I had my thighs liposuctioned."

"Do you feel better about yourself after having done this? Maybe more confident?" asks Mr. Brown.

"As a matter of fact, I do. I like the fact that I no longer look like a pear in my jeans."

"Karen looks like a damn potato turned sideways in hers, but that didn't stop her from getting a man. You just don't like yourself. Tell the man the truth," Tessa demands.

"I do like myself. But the fact of the matter is I am different from the two of you."

"Different how?" asks Mr. Brown.

"Different that we don't have the same exact lineage. I don't come from Emily and Frog," Patricia says.

"Frog?" Mr. Brown raises his right eyebrow.

"That's what everybody calls daddy. I mean their daddy," offers Patricia.

"Why do they call him a frog?"

"Because he looked like one," Patricia answers.

"Because he was whorish and hopped from woman to woman," says Tessa.

"Don't listen to them. He was nicknamed Frog a long time ago because his real name is Kermit," says Karen.

Mr. Brown looks quizzical.

"You know, like the one on *Sesame Street*?" asks Karen.

"Oh."

Patricia clears her throat before saying, "I didn't find out who my biological mother was until very recently. I have no idea who my father is and, unfortunately, my real mother can't tell me because she doesn't know either."

"What she doesn't know is that she's really the lucky one out of the bunch not to have our parents' DNA," says Tessa.

"Really, she does. Aunt Camilla and Mama have a lot of similarities. It's not like Patricia came from a stork or got dropped off on Mama's doorstep from an anonymous sender. She's our damn auntie. And she's always been in our lives—sometimes more like a mama than Emily. I can think of worse things to have a pity party over. And if you want to know the truth, Patricia had her issues before all of this even came out."

"Thank you for making that point, Karen. It's important to acknowledge that we all have issues. I happen to think that Patricia is quite normal. And that having a nip here and tuck there doesn't translate into self-loathing behavior. I'll even share with you ladies that my wife had her breasts lifted when she turned fifty. And I paid for it as her gift."

"How much did it cost? Maybe I wouldn't mind building me some titties," says Tessa.

"See? As hard as you are on your sister here, you may be the one with the insecurities. Could it be that you envy her for having the guts and the money to improve her perception of her physical self?" asks Mr. Brown.

"Hell no, because I saw her ass limping around the house when it was over," says Tessa.

Mr. Brown seems unfazed by any of this and turns his attention to Karen. "On your questionnaire, you indicated your sister was going through some traumatic changes in her marriage."

"I did."

"Would you mind elaborating on that?"

"He has been hiding a baby from her for the past few years. A toddler, I think. And it's a boy," says Karen.

"Wow, I imagine that must have been very difficult for you," Mr. Brown says to Patricia.

"Not really."

"Oh, yeah?" asks Mr. Brown.

"Yeah. I was excited to hear about the new addition to our family. I always wanted an outside baby of my own to brag about."

Mr. Brown makes a face.

"Let me put the question this way: How did receiving the news make you feel?" he asks.

"Angry," says Patricia.

"Hell, yeah, I would have been mad as a motherfucker," says Tessa.

"Tessa, please," says Karen.

"Sorry."

"And then relieved," says Patricia.

"Relieved?" ask Mr. Brown, Karen and Tessa at the same time.

Patricia is surprised by her answer, too, so she thinks about it again before answering the question for a second time. "Yep, I think so."

Mr. Brown nods.

"I haven't wanted to be intimate with Gary in years. I do it because I'm his wife and I know I'm supposed to. And to be honest, I've been thinking that something has been wrong with me. Maybe it's my hormones."

"That's a real possibility. How old are you?" asks Mr. Brown.

"Forty-four."

"Many women your age begin to complain about peri-menopausal symptoms, which sometimes can include a lack of libido."

"But I want to have sex when he's not around."

Mr. Brown smiles knowingly. "I see," he says.

"Let's get Patricia out of the hot seat," says Tessa. "Karen here, who's supposedly the brains of this family, went and got knocked up by a street hustler. She's lucky getting her pregnant was all he did."

"The thing I most want for Patricia and Tessa to understand is that I am human. I do not even attempt to be perfect, so they should cut me some serious slack about the situation I'm in," says Karen.

"What is that situation exactly?" asks Mr. Brown.

"I fell in love with someone only to find out he's not exactly who he says he is."

"That must have been heart breaking," says Mr. Brown.

"It was. And it still is."

"Don't forget to talk about the fact that you're pregnant," says Tessa.

"Wow. Pregnancy is definitely a major life change," says Mr. Brown.

"So I've noticed," says Karen.

"How do you feel about your pregnancy with this baby?" Mr. Brown asks.

"I'd prefer not to talk about it right now."

"Okay. I can accept that. But I would like to offer to you that many of us suffer heart breaking losses over the course of our human experiences. I would even imagine your sisters have experienced similar feelings of loss, only through different situations and a different pair of eyes. If the three of you can learn to listen to each other, then you may realize that you have more in common than you realize."

"I think that could be true for Patricia, maybe, but I don't know about Tessa," Karen says. "I sometimes wonder if she has a real heart in her chest."

"Of course I do. What kind of silly question is that to ask this man?" asks Tessa.

"I wasn't asking him. I was just sharing a thought."

Mr. Brown turns toward Tessa and says, "What I think I'm hearing your sister say is she feels you are somewhat insensitive toward others."

"That couldn't be farther from the truth. You're talking as if you don't know me at all."

"I know enough. Like how you're not just cold to me, but to anybody who really tries to get close to you," says Karen.

"Like who?"

"Girlfriends. Which is probably the reason why you don't have any."

"Women don't do anything for you but try to get in your damn business. I must be like my mama. She never had any either, and didn't seem to miss them," says Tessa.

"Well what about men? Are they not worthy of your companionship without having to buy it?" asks Mr. Brown.

"Absolutely not."

Mr. Brown raises an eyebrow. "Is that right, Tessa?"

"Hell yeah, that's right. I don't need a man to come flopping his ass on my furniture and breathing up my air and eating up my food and putting his thing in me if he can't contribute to my financial well-being. Paying bills is mandatory."

Nobody says anything.

"If I could have a different man for each bill in my house I would," Tessa continues.

"That's the reason why she's by herself," says Patricia.

"And she has herpes," adds Karen.

"I knew I should have asked a real doctor instead of coming to you about my damn problems because you were just going to put my business out in the street and you probably don't even have the diagnosis right. I still think it's a rash from my laundry detergent and maybe a few hair bumps. But do this: Tell me how many women you know who haven't slept with a damn man and ended up taking something permanent from what was supposed to be a temporary-ass relationship. And neither one of y'all in this room better not raise your hand to say you know any."

"That's true, but I just treated you for Trichomoniasis last year," says Karen.

"I caught that from a toilet seat. And what is your point, bitch?" asks Tessa.

"That you keep bumping your head on the same tree branch."

"And she supposedly went to somebody's real school to be able to make these kinds of assessments?" asks Tessa before frowning. Nobody answers that question.

"See? That's what I'm talking about. It's always cold in there," says Karen.

"Tessa, do you like Karen?" asks Mr. Brown.

"Sometimes."

"That was a serious question," he says.

"And you got a serious answer. Sometimes. Today? Not exactly."

"Well, tell your big sister however it is that you do feel about her."

Tessa faces Karen before saying, "I love you, but I'm tired of you acting like such a goodie-goodie. So what if you finished college in four years? And if you went to medical school on a full scholarship? So what if you don't drink or smoke weed or party or never get in trouble? You still put on your pants one leg at a time just like the rest of us."

"Is that all?" asks Mr. Brown.

"You are not any better than I am," continues Tessa.

"Anything else?" asks Mr. Brown.

"Stop trying to be everybody's favorite everything."

"Keep going."

"I'm finished," says Tessa.

"Tessa, I hadn't planned on interjecting my comments until the very end of this session, but I cannot sit by and miss this teaching opportunity."

All stares.

Mr. Brown goes on. "Your perception of your sister is clearly distorted by your own insecurities."

"What?"

"I mean that if you really liked yourself more, then you would be less concerned about what Karen thinks of herself. Or of what anyone thinks of her, for that matter."

"You clearly have me confused with Patricia."

"No, I don't. One of the things I like about Patricia is she has lots of emotional intelligence. She's very perceptive."

"If that's true, then how did she manage to miss the birth of her husband's outside baby?"

"Actually, I doubt she missed it. I think that she just chose not to look at it."

"Are you serious or was that a joke?"

"I'm very serious. But what I'm more interested in exploring is why you feel the need to point out the shortcomings of others." He flips through his chart. "It says here you're the baby of this family. Sometimes, the youngest child feels her or she has to fight in order to be noticed. Would you say this is true?"

"With all due respect, I don't think you have any idea what you're talking about," says Tessa. Her eyes look a bit teary to her sisters.

"I'm not surprised you feel that way."

"Good. So you won't be surprised when you see I don't come back."

"I won't now that you've told me, but I hope you consider changing your mind. Sometimes therapy feels uncomfortable for a while before it begins to feel helpful."

"That might be true but I still know bullshit when I see it. Karen, this gentleman owes you a refund."

"Do you mind going back to the part about how I was supposed to have known my husband was cheating on me?" asks Patricia.

"I didn't say that exactly." He rolls his pencil around in his palms and looks up at the lights in the ceiling. "But it does sound as though you no longer thought he was deserving of your love. And I have to wonder if that's because you knew deep down he wasn't right for you in some very important way."

The women can hear a door out in the hallway open and close, which means that another patient has just arrived for a session with Mr. Brown.

"You look very thoughtful, Patricia. Before you leave and lose your train of thought, tell me what it is that's on your mind so we can continue with it during our next session."

"I can't tell you what she's thinking but I sure do want to tell you what's on my mind," Tessa blurts out. "We have spent all of thirty minutes in this office for you to rattle off some stupid-ass theories you read out of a book that's probably old as hell and smells like mothballs. If you're getting ready to collect any amount of money over twenty bucks, then I know for sure that all this time I've been trying to enter into the wrong profession."

Tessa

Better Late Than Never

EVEN THOUGH I HAVE a pounding headache from sleep deprivation after staying up tossing and turning until almost 4:00 a.m., I do not hit the snooze button on my alarm clock when it rings at 7:00. I am taking my ass to somebody's church if it's the last thing I do.

I take a pill for my outbreak before I even brush my teeth and pause to look at myself in the mirror. My mind goes back to the embarrassment I'd felt when filling the prescription at the pharmacy when I recognized the pharmacy tech who rang me up and I prayed he didn't remember me from Karen's office party last year. I chase the Valtrex down with some water and follow it up with a St. John's wart pill. My women's daily multivitamin rolls forward in the drawer as if begging for me to swallow one of those, too. The lady on the front of the bottle is smiling at me. I politely smile back.

I put on a black dress today because I'm feeling very dark, and, in fact, I have been since I participated in that stupid-ass therapy session with Karen and Patricia. Even though none of what that little man said was true, it hurt my feelings to know I could be perceived the way he described me. I change panties three times to make sure a line won't show across my butt. It takes me another fifteen minutes to get the right amount of makeup on to cover the dark circles around my eyes from having cried all night.

Finally satisfied with my dress, makeup and hair, I head off for church. I'm early, so I park right in the front. On the way in the door, I run right into Stephanie Morman, a classmate from high school. I don't feel like being phony, so I try to pretend like I don't see her.

"Tessa, is that you? I don't believe it! Come here, girl, and give me a hug!"

"Hey, Stephanie." I try my best to sound both happy and surprised to see her. She's put on weight since I last saw her. "How are you doing? You look great. I love the red dress." I lied. Mama would say she looks like a prostitute (even if it is the holiday season).

"Thank you, honey. I've been trying to lose some baby weight. Three babies in five years will really do it to you. But you're still pretty as ever!" I see her look down at my left hand before she asks, "You're still not married?"

I ignore her question. "So how long have you been attending church here?"

"Oh, two or three years. We fell in love with Pastor Simmons a while back when we saw him on the news helping to rebuild homes after the river flooded. What about you?"

"I'm just visiting. My sister is a member here."

"Who is your sister?"

"I don't think you know her. She graduated a while ahead of us."

"Oh. Well you'll love it. And at least three or four of our classmates are members too, so I'll tell them to look out for you. Maybe you can join the singles ministry. Do you remember Tera Fields?"

"No."

"You don't? She was captain of the drill team."

I shake my head no, to say that I still don't remember her.

"Well, girl, I'm going to have to re-introduce you. She is the chair of the singles. Right now she's planning a retreat to Callaway Gardens you should definitely participate in."

"That sounds great," I say, trying my best to sound sincere.

"You know what? My husband is in the annex with the boys getting folks registered for the holiday donation drive. He'd love to meet you! Are you going to be standing right here for a minute?"

I look around at the Christmas tree that I'm standing next to in the back of the sanctuary and wonder if that was a serious question. "I was going to try to take my seat soon, but I'm sure I can catch up with you guys after the service."

"Wait, hold right here for just a sec. Let me grab them—it won't take but a minute. Charles Junior—we call him CJ—just lost his two front teeth at the same time. It's the cutest thing ever. I keep trying to teach him the song about the little kid who just wants to get his front teeth for Christmas but he's not having it. You have to see this. Stay right here."

And with that, she takes off around the corner toward the annex. As soon as she's out of sight, I hightail it into the sanctuary even though service hasn't started yet and sit in the pew in the back. I think I can see the back of Karen's head on the front row. Fortunately, the acolytes begin their march down the aisle to light candles and signal the beginning of service before more time passes.

When the pastor enters the pulpit, I am struck with feelings of both lust and remorse at the same time. So this is the Rev. Simmons I've been hearing about. I'm going to guess he's just at or over six feet tall with milk chocolate-colored skin, a nice, clean, low fade and a body that looks as though he regularly goes to the gym. Every time he says a word with a long "e" sound, I even see dimples. I instinctively close my legs to feel them press together in the place where they join. Then my thoughts are interrupted by the vibration of my cell phone. I take it out of my purse and examine the envelope at the top of the screen. It's a text message from Steve the street salesman:

Are you ready to let me take you out?

I immediately type back: No.

Steve: Come on. You can meet me for a drink.

Me: I quit drinking.

Steve: Since when?

Me: Yesterday.

Steve: That sounds like a damn joke.

Me: Better late than never. And please don't call or text this number again.

Then I power off my phone and turn my attention back to the church.

I spend much of the service trying to ignore the preacher's good looks and alternating between listening to the choir and my own thoughts. When they sing the song, "I Love the Lord" I become teary eyed and begin my own conversation with God. Instead of bowing my head and closing my eyes, I just fix my gaze on a hymn book in the pew in front of me and think real loud, hoping he can hear me. Or better yet, that he will choose to listen.

First of all, Lord, I really hope you are not so upset with me that you would ignore my prayers. I am sorry for all the stupid shit—I mean, mistakes I've made over the past several years. In spite of those things, I've never stopped loving you. I hope you know that. I even keep the picture of Jesus on the cross with the crown on his head and the thorn going through his hip with the thunderstorm brewing behind it in the living room, so it is the first picture people see when they walk into my house. Mama always told me to make sure I put you first, and if I did, everything else would fall into place. Well, shit hasn't been—excuse me, things haven't been going quite right for me so I must be doing something wrong.

My eyes become hot and watery so I look up at the ceiling lights because I read somewhere that looking at something up high will prevent your tears from falling, but it's not working for me so I just blink hard a few times and then just close them.

This is what I'd like to know: Why am I here? Did you give me any real talents? If so, then could you please reveal them to me so I can make some real money? I'm tired of struggling but I am not lazy and work really hard just to stay afloat. Sometimes it feels like you gave Karen and Patricia all the brains in our family and didn't have any left over to pass out to me. You and I both know that Karen takes hers for granted— she's smart but at the same time, she's not. And Mama always taught me that pussy—I'm sorry, Lord, sex--isn't something I should just hand out so I try real hard to make my potential mates work for it but now in Atlanta, something is wrong. I think they're mostly gay and don't have much use for women anymore. And there are so many women who are just giving it out easy that I might as well join the leagues of them because it you can't beat them you should just join them right? Because men aren't trying to be providers and take care of us anymore, Lord. I feel alone, like I have to fight out here in this world all by myself. All I want is to make fifty thousand dollars a year and have a good man to protect me at night and keep the rent paid and fuck me good without bringing me any diseases. And speaking of that, Lord, how am I supposed to find somebody to love me now that I have bumps scattered all over my coochie? Real life isn't like the commercials on TV where people have this shit and love it—rowing canoes on white water rapids and whatnot. I know I brought this on myself and I'm coming to you and asking for you to fix it. I was embarrassed as hell when I ran into Douglas in the pharmacy yesterday. Why did you have to send him to fill my prescriptions? What if he could have been my husband? I would have told him eventually, but I didn't need him knowing about my little problem right off the bat.

I lift my head for a second to think about what else I need to tell God and the lady next to me touches my shoulder. When I open my eyes, she hands me a tissue. I decide I'm finished with this conversation with God right now so I wipe the water off of my face and say "Amen" out loud with the preacher and the rest of the congregation. I decide right then and there that I will spend as much time as I need to get myself together as a celibate woman. I briefly wonder if I should go home and screw tonight and begin my vows tomorrow, much like having a big feast before fasting for several days. Good sense kicks in right behind it, and I decide I'm going to have to give the good-girl version of me an honest try.

Service is over before I think I'm done singing with the choir. Karen actually spots me before I have a chance to wave her down. She asks me if I want to sit on the benches in the garden with her to wait for the traffic to pass. I agree. She looks pretty. And her hair is done.

"Feeling any better?" she asks while pulling on one of her curls.

"Yes. It still burns and itches, but not as bad as it did at first."

"I wasn't talking about that."

"Oh. Are you asking about the job?"

"Yes."

"I'm actually okay. The break has done me some good by giving me a chance to actually study for my licensure exam."

"I'm happy to hear that."

"Karen?"

"Yes?"

"I'm sorry."

"For what?"

"Everything."

Then I lean over in the pew and cry on my big sister's shoulder. And I am so happy that she lets me.

* * *

When my home phone rings, I look at the caller ID before picking it up. Right after I put the phone to my ear, I close the practice exam book that I'm studying and sit and wait in silence for Aunt Camilla to talk.

"Hello? Are you there, Contessa?"

I wonder why she would ask me that when I know she just heard the phone pick up. I almost respond by saying something ugly, but I remember I just made God a bunch of promises in church a few hours ago and I decide against it. "Yes, I'm here."

"Your sister doesn't want to talk to me."

"I don't either." That wasn't supposed to come out. "I'm sorry for saying that."

"No, I deserved to hear it."

I don't argue with her.

"Okay, listen. I didn't call you for me. I'm calling because I'm worried about your mother."

"She seems to be doing okay to me."

"She's not okay. She's miserable because her girls haven't been coming around much."

"That's not true. I just went to visit her yesterday. And just this morning in church, Karen told me she would be dropping her Sunday dinner plate off to her before evening."

"But it's my fault."

"What's your fault?"

"Everything. The reason we've had to keep so many secrets. The way you girls heard the news."

"About Patricia, you mean?"

"Yes. About Patricia."

"So let me ask you something, Auntie."

"I gave her to your mama because I couldn't even identify her father, much less identify myself as a mother to her. I did what I thought was best."

"That's not what I was going to ask you."

"Well, what is it?"

"Why was it suddenly so important for all of this to come out now? We're all adults. Whose bright idea was it to disrupt our lives with this bullshit in 2014?"

"You can watch your fast-ass mouth with me. I'm still your auntie."

"Sorry for cursing."

"At first I had to ask Emily the same thing, but it didn't take long for me to understand."

She's talking very slowly and she's taking too long to get to the point. "Understand what?"

"You can't keep a man to save your life, Tessa, and even though nobody says it, you're on the verge of being down right loose."

"Wait a minute."

"No, you asked, so you wait a minute. You think you're entitled to shit without working for it, which is sad, because you waste a lot of talent by being so lazy. Karen was fortunate enough to get a successful career, but is a dumb blonde if we've ever seen one, but not because she was born stupid but because she doesn't have enough self-confidence to trust her own common sense and intuition. And Patricia could—"

"You mean your daughter Patricia."

"I love Patricia dearly. I gave birth to her. But she really is Emily's daughter. You don't know half the sacrifices she made to raise her while I was out doing God knows what with God knows who."

"Doing stuff like what?"

"That's beside the point."

"But just give me an example. Sex? Drugs? Violence?"

"All of the above."

"For real?"

"For real."

"What kinds of drugs?"

"I tried a little bit of everything, but cocaine is what got me in the most trouble."

Shit. I've smoked a lot of weed, but I've never done any cocaine. "How do you take that? Up your nose?"

"Yep."

"And so what about the sex and the violence?"

"We are getting way off subject, Tessa. But let's just put it this way. I slept with a lot of men, some of them abusive, in a short period of time."

"But wasn't it just you who just called me a whore?"

"No, that's not how I said it. But yes, that's what's I meant."

"So you're saying it takes one to know one."

"You'd better watch your damn mouth right now."

"Sorry."

"Anyway, I was going to say that Patricia would like herself if she only took the time to get to know herself. She's had her own identity mixed up with her husband's for years now. To be honest, I'm glad he's gone."

"I thought I was the only person who felt that way!"

"You're not. But that's not the point, either. The fact of the matter is the three of you have been so busy trying not to be like Emily that you've missed everything she was trying to teach you."

"And what was that, exactly?"

"You would ask me that. She can explain it better than I can. Ask her. But I do know this: She has made it clear, on more than one occasion, she feels she's failed you because she never allowed you to get to know the woman she really is underneath that façade."

"When you say 'you,' are you talking specifically about me? Because I don't know if I'm the one who should be hearing this."

"Just shut up and listen. She was too busy trying to put on a hell of a show in order to stay married to Frog and be a strong example for her girls to follow that she turned you off with her bullshit and cold demeanor. And I haven't wanted to admit it because I wasn't ready to accept my part in this story, but she's probably been right all along."

"So telling us that Patricia really wasn't her birth child was supposed to fix all this?"

"Yes and no. She wanted Patricia to know how much she wanted and loved her. She wanted you three to understand that unconditional love for your sisters isn't about whether or not you agree or disagree with each other's lifestyles. It's about loving each other in spite of your shortcomings. But most of all, she thought that if she could communicate to each of you how much she loves you, that you could start doing a better job of loving yourselves."

"Mama has always said she doesn't care what people think about her, including us."

"And that's right, for the most part. It's true she has never given a fuck about the opinions of the general public, but she lied when she said she didn't care about your opinions. Wait, I don't know if I said that right. Let me try it again. She didn't understand, until recently, just how much your opinion of her does matter. And she loves her grown daughters enough to try and correct their distorted perceptions of her so they can finally see themselves. All daughters are extensions of their mothers in some way or another, you know. Even if they can't see it or don't want to be."

I'm stunned and speechless for the first time in a long time. I need some time to process what I'm hearing. Fortunately, she continues talking so I don't have to.

"I was supposed to help her communicate this to you in a much more tactful way, but I clearly fucked that up at the cookout. I'm getting ready to quit drinking, you know."

"Again?" I ask. Then I go ahead and apologize before she can tell me I'm being disrespectful and I need to watch my damn mouth.

When I hang up the phone from talking to my auntie, I don't even bother to replay the contents of the conversation in my head. The only thing that matters to me at the moment involves something that Mr. Brown said to me during my one-on-one visit with him yesterday. It struck a nerve, but I forgot about it until just now when Camilla read me my rights. Suddenly, it seems very important. So I unpack my laptop computer, pull up the internet site where you register for the teaching test-preparation courses, and sign up for the next available class. Then I Google the phrase "entitlement issues and self-esteem" and read voraciously any article that explains what a person can do to address them.

* * *

"Your watch must be slow. I told you to be here at 5:00," I tell Karen as soon as she walks in the door.

"You'll have to give me a pass today. I was involved in an accident on my way here."

"Oh my God," I say while inspecting her from head to toe. "Are you okay?"

"I'm fine. It was minor. I didn't even get a scratch on my bumper."

"Where were you?"

"Exiting off of I-285. There's not much to tell. He was driving so slowly that I didn't even see him when I was getting over and I clipped his bumper. You know the people on 285 can't drive. Sometimes I feel like I'm the only person out there who knows how to steer a car."

I'm not going to go there with her today.

"I'm only a few minutes late, right?" she asks. "What kind of meeting is this? And isn't that Patricia's car outside?"

"Yes, it is. Come on in and have a seat on my sofa." I open my door wide, ignoring her other question.

"Hey, Karen," Patricia calls out from the kitchen. "She won't explain anything to me either. She just called and told me to get my skinny ass here on time. Unquote."

"What smells so good?" Karen asks.

"Some recipe she got out of *Better Homes* magazine," I answer.

"No it's not! This is my very own recipe. I've been making fondue for longer than you've been alive," Patricia answers. "The first one is cheese. What you're smelling is garlic bread in the oven and you're absolutely going to love it. I usually put beer in it but I wanted you to be able to have some, Karen."

"Thank you, Pat. What's behind door number two?"

"Chocolate fondue."

"Damn!" I holler while snapping my fingers. "I knew I forgot something. Can we eat it without the fruit? I'm sorry."

"What did you forget? This?" Karen asks while pulling a bag of strawberries and sliced apples out of a tote bag I hadn't even noticed she was carrying. "We knew not to depend on you to provide anything except a space for us to meet," she jokes.

"Praise the Lord," sings Patricia from the kitchen.

I don't say anything but it's a good thing they know me well; otherwise we would be licking chocolate fondue off those frozen strawberry popsicles in my freezer because I sure as hell forgot to get to the store.

"So what's the big announcement?" asks Karen.

"There is no big announcement."

"You didn't call us over to share food you didn't even cook, I know," Patricia says as she enters the room.

"Of course not. She didn't even want to go buy the fruit." That was Karen's big mouth.

"How do you afford to buy groceries at all?" Patricia asks smartly.

"Your man buys them for me."

"I'm going home," says Karen.

"No you are not. Not that this is any of your business, but I get a real good student loan check. I'm still in school, remember? Now sit back down. I called you here because we need to talk, seriously. We're getting ready to have an intervention."

"Uh oh. She's been watching Iyanla Vanzant on the Oprah network again," says Patricia.

"No, I'm serious. I had a conversation with Aunt Camilla and I think there are a few things that you should hear her out on."

"You can stop right there. I didn't come here to listen to you serve as Camilla's proxy. If I wanted to talk to her then I would have gone to her damn house instead of yours."

Karen and I stop talking and look at Patricia. Neither of us can believe what she said. In fact, there is no sound in the room until I plop the silver fondue bowls down on top of my coffee table and light the burner underneath them.

"Patricia, look me in my face and tell me that you would rather have been raised by Aunt Camilla when she was a whorish, wild teenager who did drugs."

Pat doesn't answer. I turn my attention to Karen. "And you."

"Please don't say it. I already know I'm the dumbest doctor in the history of planet Earth who was hard up and desperate enough to have unprotected sex on her first date with a con artist whom she hardly knows and gets knocked up and that I should probably have my medical license revoked because I can't possibly be of sound enough mind to advise a patient on anything."

"Yes, this is true. But that's not what I was going to say," I tell her.

"Well, what did I miss?"

"Nothing, except the whole damn point. People make mistakes, Karen."

"Is that what I brought my good fondue pots over here to hear?"

"Yes."

"I thought we tried this already in counseling, which, by the way, you ruined for the three of us."

"There's no need for you to bring up the past, Karen. That was so last week. But, for the record, that therapy session was a waste of time and money. I can do a better job of telling you two what to do and how to think." I can't help but smile as I say that.

"Why haven't you said anything about yourself?"

"Yeah, why are we the subject and purpose of this intervention?" Patricia says.

"What is there to say about me?" I ask, sincerely.

"I won't even go there," says Patricia.

"Are the pills I gave you helping you to manage your outbreak?" Karen asks, as if a light bulb just went off in her head, without intending any harm.

I could curse her right now. But instead, I tell her that yes, they are helping. Then I ask her how she's going to explain to her unborn child how she managed to give the baby a crook for a father who could possibly be sentenced to jail by the time he or she is born.

"I already told you I'm not sure what I'm going to do about this baby," Karen says while picking at a piece of lint on her blouse.

"And I already told you you're having it," says Patricia, sternly. "There isn't a day that goes by I don't regret the abortion Gary talked me into having before we were married. You're not going to make your big sister's mistake, and if that means I have to strap you to a bed and push prenatal vitamins down your throat every day, then so be it."

"Speaking of that, Patricia, do you think your decision was more justifiable than the one Aunt Camilla made?"

"What? That's totally different."

"What's so different about it? I mean, neither one of you were prepared to become mothers. She did what she felt was best, just as I'm sure you did at the time."

Pat's face begins to turn an odd shade of green. Something in between olive and booger.

"I don't mean to hurt your feelings," I quickly add. "I'm just saying. I don't think anybody in life has it easy. We all get stuck in some mud at one point or another and then we spin our wheels as hard as we can, just trying to get out of it and back onto course. Eventually, we figure the shit out as best we can and we find a way to survive it, just as all strong black women do."

Karen and Patricia look thoughtful for a minute.

"I don't know if our sister-girl definition of a 'strong black woman' is what I aim to be anymore," says Karen.

"And what exactly do you mean by that?" I ask.

Karen quickly pauses before answering. "It almost feels like, by trying to achieve that status, you voluntarily commit to stretching yourself beyond normal human limits in ways that don't even make sense. Everybody else develops unfair expectations of you. For example, you can't cry when you're afraid, or you can't even be afraid for that matter. Or you have to try to figure out how to feed a house full of kids with only a fifty dollar paycheck, or learn to survive abuse or neglect without acknowledging its pain or its impact on your life, or maybe, like me, stay in a piss poor relationship where you're supposed to contribute enough love and money for the both of you. Do I need to go on?"

"I feel you," says Patricia, while chewing on an apple and rotating her ankles in a circle.

"You don't see other women trying to take on all that responsibility," Karen continues. "Only us who are hell bent on being so-called strong black women. And folks say we have attitudes. We probably do. Shit, we're tired."

"Amen," says Patricia while waving her hand in the air. "I agree."

"I don't," I say. "Our people did it all the time, and we're better and stronger because of it."

They all turn to look at me.

"What in the hell are you talking about?" asks Karen.

"Didn't you see the movie *Twelve Years a Slave*?" I ask. "Thank God our ancestors had enough grit and resolve to live through that shit. That's when strong black women were invented, and if they hadn't been, we wouldn't even be here sitting on this sofa as their living descendants."

Karen says, "I don't watch movies like that because they make me mad at white people for at least a few days and I cannot afford to have an attitude with all of them on my job come Monday mornings, but I do read and I did study my history. They had grit and resolve for sure, but at what cost was it developed? And how long should you have to operate under that type of mental pressure?"

I don't have an answer for her, but I'm trying to think of one as I imagine Patsy, from the movie, being tied to that post.

Patricia continues. "We shouldn't have to try to do the impossible every day to prove a point. And just because Jesus could feed five thousand people with five loaves of bread and two fish doesn't mean we can."

Well. Since she put it that way.

"You know, I don't think movie stars get such a bad deal out of life," Karen says wistfully, as though she's considering changing professions and moving across the country to Hollywood.

"You should check out TMZ sometimes," I advise Karen. "They have it worse than us."

Patricia dips a piece of garlic bread into the cheese fondue before filling her mouth with it. I pick up a sliced apple and dunk it in the chocolate.

"Hell yeah," I add, just to break the silence. "They're the most fragile people on the planet and half of them don't know the difference between their own home and a rehab facility."

"You could use one yourself, couldn't you?" asks Karen.

"Use what?" I ask, knowing full well what it is that she's referring to.

"Something to help you cut back on your own drug use."

"You must be crazy. I don't do drugs. I smoke marijuana, and there's a clear damn difference. You should know it's now legal in the state of Colorado, since you read so damn much," I say through a mouthful of fruit and chocolate. "This intervention is over," I announce as soon as I swallow.

I turn on my TV to lighten the mood as we continue to munch on the delicious fondue. We're all staring at a *Scandal* rerun on BET, but none of us are paying attention to the actions of Olivia Pope and associates. We're too busy trying to think up solutions to help us manage our own scandalous affairs.

Later that evening, when my sisters leave, I smoke up every last bit of weed I can find in my house. I am determined to quit this nasty habit, starting tomorrow. But for a second, I do contemplate the idea of packing up all my shit and moving to a blue state, where my pleasures are less likely to be banned and considered illegal, just in case I ever decide to have a voluntary relapse.

Patricia

Unexpected Guest

I ALMOST DROP A DISH back into the sudsy water in the kitchen sink when I think I hear the doorbell ring. The music coming from my Bose system is playing the new Matt Marshak jazz album and at first I think it may be one of those weird sharp or flat keys in the song. The second ring, however, seems much louder than the first and scares the hell out of me.

I sling the suds off of my fingers, head toward the door and peek through the blinds. When I see Gary standing on the other side, I contemplate pretending I'm not at home. But then I remember the music is playing so close to the door that he's probably already heard it. So I decide not to fake anything and yell, "Hold on" while I grab the key to unlock it.

Standing sort of slumped over with faded jeans and a Howard sweatshirt, he looks much shorter than I remember. And maybe slightly more gray in the head. "What's up, Gary?" I ask, standing in the middle of the doorway so he can't get into the house.

"Hi, Patricia. Sorry for not calling. I just was wondering, if we, could, um, talk for a minute."

I make a point of exhaling very loudly while I extend the door to him and clear the entry way. Not caring whether or not it falls on him, I let it go and slide across the wood floors in my socks over to the sofa in the living room. He follows.

"You mind if I have a seat?"

"Not at all."

He fidgets with his fingers and pretends to be interested in the television even though it's on mute. "What you watching?"

I look up at the TV and notice a movie is playing. I have no idea what it is, nor do I recognize any actors. I wonder what channel this is and why the TV is on in the first place. This is one of the reasons my electricity bill is so high. I must have gotten this habit—leaving everything on in the house—from Gary. I am taking so long to respond to his question that I decide to go on and ignore it. My attention returns to him and his new gray hair. I don't try to hide my stare.

"Talk to me," I say, and surprise myself with the authority that is imbedded within my voice.

"I miss you," Gary blurts out.

At first, I do not respond. I don't know what I should say. I don't know if I miss him.

Silence.

He stares at air above my head. I redirect my gaze to the floor.

"Listen, I know I hurt you during this marriage. We hurt each other, really."

"What the fuck do you mean by that? Did you come here to tell me what I can do better?"

"No, no, I wasn't saying that at all. Why do you even have to go there? See? That's what I mean, Pat. You're always so defensive with me."

"I have to be."

"Why would you say that?" he asks and then frowns. "When did we stop playing for the same team?"

"When you started finding fault in everything I did." I pause for a second to see if I want to add anything else to that statement. I decide that, yes, I do. "Probably when you started fucking outside of our marriage."

"Why do you have to do all of this cursing? Do you like it? Are you just saying whatever? Because I think we both know that's not true, Pat."

I turn to him and stare some more. He's graying on the stubble on his chin. He really needs to be shaved. And, now that I really look at him, I think that he's gained weight.

"You act as if you haven't really liked me in years," he continues. "You would look at me like everything I did would get on your nerves. I just felt like I couldn't make you happy anymore."

"Did you make your project whores happy? Probably not, if they had to work half as hard as I did to get your dick hard." I immediately regret saying that. He looks deflated. "I'm sorry," I add. I look down at my thighs. If I don't watch it, they'll soon be fat. I'm not having any more damn surgery. I make up my mind right now to take a run around the block when Gary leaves.

"I want to come home."

"You can't," I surprise myself and say.

He's silent for a full minute.

"What will it take, Pat? I know we can fix this." He moves over on the sofa toward me and places his hand on my knee. They feel rougher than I remember.

"I do love you, Gary. I'm sure that I always will."

He stares at me, waiting me to follow that with another thought. I don't.

"I've found us a counselor to start seeing. Trent from work told me about him, said he fixed him and Veronica when they were on the verge of breaking up a few years ago. I already made us an appointment for next Monday."

"That's New Year's Eve."

"Oh. I meant the Monday after that."

"Gary, Karen is moving in at the end of January. With the baby."

"What baby?" His eyes are big now.

"The baby in her stomach."

"Karen? Karen? The almighty pediatrician? The same Karen who can't do wrong, let your mama and your sister tell it?"

"She's not a pediatrician. She's a gynecologist. But, yes, the same one."

"When did she get a man?"

I'm not sure how to answer this one. "She has a friend."

"A friend that shoots a baby up her ass? Wait a minute. I know Karen didn't go out like that for real. She used to prescribe you your pills if I'm not mistaken. She must have gotten real desperate and went and found a sperm donor from one of those clinics, huh?"

I don't answer that.

"And since when are the two of you close enough for you to let her to move into our house? Didn't she forget your birthday again this year? And does she still introduce you to her pediatrician friends as her half-sister?"

I decide not to correct him about the pediatrician part this time. "You know what, Gary? I appreciate you reminding me of just how fucked up you are. I was starting to forget why I wanted out of our damn marriage in the first place."

"What are you talking about? I'm just being honest. You and I both know you've never had much of a family. That's why I'm trying to keep us together—you and I are a family for each other. We need each other."

"Let me tell you something, Gary. I have a damn family. A living mother and not one, but two whole sisters. They might be dysfunctional and we might not have been close for a long time, but all of that is getting ready to change. They are my family more than you are. And If I'm not mistaken, you have a baby of your own to worry about so never mind Karen and her business."

"Pat, you don't have to try to prove any points to me. I'm not the enemy here. I just want to love you and get back to the way we used to be."

"Bullshit!" I holler. "The way things used to be means you want a damn dummy who believes your lies. You want help taking care of your son when you see him on the weekends. You want fried chicken when you get home and a house that smells like lemons and bleach. You want clean laundry and starched shirts. You want fish and grits in the morning for breakfast and somebody to run all your stupid ass errands for you. You want a maid and a mop who has low self-esteem and won't ask you any questions about your comings or goings, just as happy to have a warm, breathing man in the house who is capable of paying the bills and rubbing between her thighs every now and then. And I am not a damn low-self-esteem ass mop. At least not anymore."

He sits back down. "Tell me what it is you want, Patty."

I try to think.

"Tell me what it is so that I can give it to you."

"I want a real friend. I'd like for my husband, my mate, whatever—to actually care about who I am and what I like. Do you know what my favorite color is? My favorite foods? Do you know the last movie that I sat home and watched, as usual, by myself, because you refuse to take me to the theater because you say the seats are too dirty?"

He looks stumped.

"Red. Authentic Italian eggplant parmesan. *Olympus Has Fallen.* Before that, *Catch Me If You Can.* And just last week, *Django.*"

"I don't mind taking you to the movies, Patty."

"Well why in the hell does it take all this for you to offer? Wait. Don't answer that. It's not just the movies, Gary. It's us. Me. You don't know me anymore. And you stopped trying."

"I can try. If you want to."

We're both quiet for a moment. "Do you?" he looks over at me and asks.

"I don't know," is the most honest answer that I can give.

I stand up and walk over to the door. I sort of wonder where I'm suddenly getting these balls from. Gary looks like he's wondering the same thing. I open it just a bit and turn around and look at him.

"Baby," he whispers, standing up. He joins me at the door and slips his arms around my waist. If I didn't know any better, I would think I saw tears in his eyes. I'm almost teary, too, but in a different sort of way.

"What?" I answer.

"I'm sorry."

"What exactly are you apologizing for, may I ask?"

"For hurting you. You deserved better."

And just think, Patricia. All this time I've been waiting to hear this from him, certain it would make me feel better. But it doesn't. So I just nod and open the door wider for him to leave.

As soon as Gary disappears from my doorstep I feel horny. I wish I had a Mr. Goodnight to call, but I don't.

My jackrabbit is on the shelf in my closet. It's easily visible, now that Gary's stacks and stacks of clothes have been removed. I take it down from the shelf and immediately notice how cold it feels in my hands.

It takes too long for the water to warm up in my sink (I'm wondering how long it will take me to finally stop thinking I only have one sink in the bathroom instead of two, but for now I'll keep using the one on the left because it feels right) so I turn on the hot water in the tub. It's ready almost immediately. One day, I would love to ask a plumber how that works.

I place the jelly-filled penis under the hot water for twenty-five or thirty seconds before pulling it out and towel drying the base. I pay special attention to the base and control panel to make sure they don't get wet. Right here on the bathroom floor, I lift my house dress and pull off my cotton panties. My thighs still feel tight from the surgery as I slide down, very gently, onto the purple phallus.

At first, JR doesn't respond to the commands of the vibration and rotation buttons. It takes a second or two for the white pearl beads in the base to begin humming and moving in a clockwise motion. I don't want to close my eyes, so I try to find an object to concentrate on. I decide on a shoe that I can see poking out of my closet. And because I'm gaining momentum on this ride, I decide to flip the switch to the opposite side of the remote to cause the toy to begin a counter-clockwise rotation. I'm thinking that this is beginning to work, but that I may be missing some stimulation. So I balance myself on both knees while I pull the shirt off and over my head, then unsnap my bra.

My left hand is stroking the base of JR much like I used to do Gary, probably out of habit, but the difference is that the toy's stem is much firmer. My right hand is now playing with my breasts, teasing, stroking my nipples. I take my eyes off the black slippers that they've been focused on and close them so I can lie to myself and envision my lawn man. And it's working. I feel myself lifting my ass off the ground to rotate and catch the thrusts of JR.

I swing my hips once, twice, then a third time before JR slows down. At first I thought I gripped it too hard with my pussy muscles, so I relax them. But as soon as I do, the rabbit comes to a complete stop. Goddamn batteries!

When I stand up, my knees feel tight, my thighs hurt worse, and this purple plastic is still being held in place, firmly inside me. I pull it out more quickly than I know I should, stomp into my bedroom and throw it, as hard as I can, under my bed, before flopping on top of my mattress and opening my legs for my own hands. Then I remember the K-Y warming liquid I keep in my night-stand drawer and sit up in order to reach over and retrieve it.

It's been a while, but the feeling is much better than I remember. Caressing the top of my clitoris feels much more pleasurable than the bottom, so I keep my fingers high, just over my pussy bone. Before I know it, I'm grinding to the rhythm of my own hands, and my fingers are sloppy and slippery. Without thinking, I slide one, then two fingers inside of my entrance and give myself some gentle pressure, aiming toward by belly button. I come so hard within ten seconds that I cry out to the lawn man and beg him not to stop.

When my legs stop shaking, I roll over onto my side and hug my big body pillow. It's far too cold and much too soft for me to imagine it's Gary, but I'm perfectly alright with that because I'm satisfied. I didn't realize how exhausted I felt until right this minute, but before I doze off to sleep, I make myself a mental note to buy Sharon some KY liquid and a gift card for the sex toy store next time I'm out running my errands. Hell, I might even write the purchase off as a charitable donation this year when I file my taxes.

* * *

Later in the day, I'm fluffing up the sofa pillows where Gary's ass flattened them out and am waiting for Karen to answer her cell phone. She picks up on the fourth ring, just before I was getting ready to hang up.
"Do you want to come and live with me for a little while?" I blurt out.
Radio silence on the other end.
"Never mind, Karen. It was a stupid idea. I just thought that with your lease expiring and the baby coming up, you could use some help and some room without committing to—"
"You would let me come live with you?" she interrupts.
"Yes."
More silence.
"What about Gary? How are y'all going to mend your marriage with a third—and fourth—wheel in the house?"
"I'm not sure how much mending I'll be in the mood to do for a while, Karen. And I really wouldn't mind having the company."
"Girl, I would love to come stay for a while. Oh, thank you, God, for answering prayers! You don't know how much this means to me, sister!"
Hearing her call me sister feels different. Nice. Like I'm a part of a real family. I don't dare say this out loud, but instead, ask, "So when you coming?"
"How's February? Is that too early? Can I come on the first?"
I smile. And when I hang up the phone, I open the letter I've been holding in my hands, take a moment to appreciate the invitation to membership from the Golden Dove Society, and then place it in the trash can.

* * *

"Get your ass in this car and ride with me to go get Mama. I can't lift her up by myself!" I call out to Tessa. Even though her kitchen window is up and her head is poking out of it to look at me in my car, I honk the horn. She looks pissed but doesn't dare say anything. Thirty seconds later, she bounces outside, locks both doors, and jumps in the passenger seat of my car with bare feet. She catches me looking down and pulls some flip flops out of that gigantic purse before I get a chance to ask about her shoes.

"When did you start wearing makeup?" asks Tessa.

"It's only a little eyeliner." I look up at my eyes in the rearview mirror to see if it's really that noticeable. "And you should try some lipstick to cover up those black lips."

She ignores my comment. "Did I tell you I got a job?"

"No, but that's wonderful news. Congratulations. Where is it?"

"Riverbend Elementary. I'm going to be a teacher's aide for a kindergarten class."

"You like kids that much?"

"Hell, I don't know, but we're about to find out."

"I hope you can keep your seductive hands off of those children's principal."

"She's pretty, but I think I'll pass," she says, teasingly. "And speaking of pretty, you're looking kind of hot yourself lately. You're losing weight all over, not just in your hips and butt. And your teeth are so white they could glow in the dark."

"I have shed a few pounds in the last couple weeks. It's just about healthy living and lowering your stress levels." I ignore her comment about my teeth.

"You been brushing with baking soda?"

"Not quite."

"Well, whatever you're doing is certainly working."

"Thank you. I feel good. And you know, I haven't been brave enough to wear a bikini in years, but I'm planning to give it a try in a few weeks when I go on my cruise."

"Excuse me, Miss skinny-minny moneybag with no husband who's living the lifestyle of the rich and famous. It must be nice being you."

I pause to think about that for a second before responding. "Actually, I think it is."

Emily

The Trouble with Red Lipstick

"I THOUGHT YOU SAID you bought some of that non-alcoholic Moscato! I don't see anything except some expired milk and a can of relish in your refrigerator!" Karen calls out from the kitchen.

"What? I don't think they make non-alcoholic Moscato. I said I bought some sparkling grape juice. Look in the freezer," Tessa yells back. "Matter of fact, pull it out before it busts open." Karen curses under her breath while she walks into the living room to get her glass. I know how she feels. I didn't have the desire to drink until I got pregnant. And, hell, nobody really needs to drink the liquor until the children actually arrive. But nobody tells you that when you're pregnant.

"Sister, I'm so glad you're letting me tag along on this trip! Whoo hoo! It's springtime and this weather is lovely! I've never been on a boat, before, you know. I can't wait to put on my bathing suit. How many single men you think will show up?" That's Tessa.

"You need to be thanking me since I'm the one who paid your way," says Karen.

I hear a bunch of shuffling and clinking sounds coming from the kitchen. I'm enjoying listening to my girls talk more than this television. I wish I could reach it to turn it off. It's too damn loud.

"Ooh, I think I feel something!" Karen says, frozen like a statue in between the door of the living room and kitchen. Patricia walks over and places a hand gently on Karen's small, round, growing belly. She smiles. I do, too.

One by one, they each go back to the bedroom, to the car, through the kitchen to fill up a glass, giggle through the living room, sit down for a second to watch the Lifetime movie they've left me parked in front of. The first time Tessa walks past close enough for me to touch her, I grab her leg. "What you need, Mama?"

I form my hand into the shape of a cup and bring it to my mouth.

"Pat, pour Mama a glass of cranberry juice while you're standing in the kitchen!" She calls out. "And she likes a lot of ice. The kind that's crushed!"

I shake my head back and forth no. Then I point to the pink wine in her glass.

"Mama, this is wine."

Now I know they must think they are my mama, instead of it being the other damn way around. "Give me some of that," comes out of my mouth much more clearly than I expected it to.

"Mama doesn't need any alcohol, Tessa. She doesn't know what she's asking you for." Who asked her to butt in?

"I'm fixing her some juice and a snack to take with her medicine anyway," Karen continues. "Pat, you go on and see if you can find that suntan oil before we forget to pack it in there. It costs too much to buy that stuff from those expensive stores on the boat."

The doctor, my very own educated fool, made that tacky statement. The one who I know I just heard say "shit" because her pregnant ass can't have a glass herself. I watch her take the glass Patricia just poured for me and places it in my hand before shuffling back off to her car and bringing in yet another bag. This one is small and pink with white polka dots.

Tessa comes and plops down next to me on the sofa. The color of her lips has evened out since I last saw her. She watches a woman on television follow her husband after work to go meet his girlfriend for a few minutes before she announces to the room that she's seen this movie before. When she looks over at me for permission to change the channel, I point back to the glass in her hand. She nods her head and looks around to make sure Karen and Pat are somewhere occupied before pouring her wine on top of my cranberry juice and ice. I immediately begin drinking the contents of the glass. It reminds me of the berry-flavored wine coolers that I used to enjoy before my stroke.

As soon as I'm finished, I drive my wheelchair into the bathroom. I love Patricia's house because the bathrooms and kitchen are as big as most folks' bedrooms. I wonder how she's going to pay for it now with no husband. I sit on the toilet for a while and poke my left toe into the plush floor mat. I hear the girls giggling again. I say a silent prayer before getting up. I must be taking too long because somebody bangs on the door and hollers out, "Mama, you okay?"

"Uh huh," I yell back.

I look in the mirror to reapply my red lipstick and am pleased with my appearance. On my way back to the living room, I notice Patricia's door is open just down the hall. Out of curiosity, I ride over there to see what that big yellow and black suitcase is doing open on the floor. While in her room, I look around for signs of a man. Not a shirt or big shoe or hat or condom in sight. I reach down in my right pocket for the piece of paper that I prepared for this very moment but my fingers don't grab anything except lint. I almost hurt myself by trying to reach my right arm across all this fat and over to my left side in search of the paper, hoping that it was in the left pocket, only to realize that these pants don't have a left pocket. It's just a seam that looks like one. How impractical. I'm wondering if drinking that wine wasn't such a good idea after all when I see Karen saunter on over to the bathroom I just came out of.

As if on cue, Karen yells "Mama! Is this your paper folded up in here on the floor?"

I can't get the damn wheelchair turned around fast enough to answer her.

"What is it?" she continues. "Your medications or some instructions? Did your doctor send you home with a note?"

As much as I would like to jump up and grab the paper from her hands, I can't. This is the problem with being handicapped. I've been sold out.

"Mama, this is a letter."

I nod.

"It has my name at the top."

"Why the hell would you write a letter to Karen and not to anybody else?" asks Tessa.

"That's your mama, Tess, so watch your mouth," says Patricia.

"She's your mama, too, Patricia, but that doesn't change the fact that OUR mama CANNOT write!"

"That's what you think," says Patricia.

"Give me that paper." Tessa snatches it out of Karen's pudgy little fingers. "This is Auntie Cam's handwriting."

"How do you know?"

"Because she's dyslexic and all her b's look like d's."

"You have got to be kidding me. I never stood a damn chance," says Patricia.

"Mama, is this something that belongs to Auntie?"

They all look at me. I just blink.

"Read the letter," demands Tessa.

"Dear Girls," Karen begins. "Wait. I need to sit down."

"You just noticed your damn period was missing and you're already acting like you're nine months pregnant," says Tessa. That's my baby.

"Shut up," says Karen as she walks back out toward the living room. Patricia gives me a push to help me navigate around a corner in the hallway.

I can't understand why my heart is beating quickly and I feel anxiety around my own children. I wish I could melt down into the blue leather of this wheelchair they bought me for Christmas and become invisible. Karen continues to read:

"First of all, let me say that I love you. I know I didn't say that enough when you were young. At the time, I really didn't know how important it was to say it. I'm sorry about that."

When Karen pauses to look up at me, I make a quick decision and hope I don't regret it later. I plant both of my hands onto the armrest of my wheelchair and say a fast prayer that I can do this without falling. After counting silently to three in my head, I slowly stand up. Karen is sitting close enough to me that I can take the paper from her hands. I take my reading glasses off the neck of my shirt, unfold them, and push them high up on my nose. They slide down anyway. I clear my throat and begin reading to my children, hoping they can understand my words.

"I want you to know that Frog and I were in love when we married. He was my childhood sweetheart, my first love, my best friend, my everything. And I don't have a single regret about that, or about having our children. Having and raising you have been my greatest accomplishments in life. Each of you."

I stop and look at Patricia. She's looking down at her hands, playing with a silver bracelet around her wrist.

"But when our marriage took a turn for the worse, I got scared as hell. I know it might be hard for you to understand, but I was taught never to separate from a man who works and puts a roof over your head, even if he cheats, does drugs or whoops your butt. I wanted you to see me as being strong because inside I always felt so weak and powerless, and like I always had the weight of the world on my shoulders.

"I know I was mean and demanding when I should have treated you with more kindness, but I felt unloved and unwanted myself. I was empty. Can't you see? How does an artist sculpt without clay? How should a cook prepare a meal without a pot and groceries? I hope you get the point. You do your best, but after a while, you begin to feel as though you're drowning and nobody out there will throw you a raft.

"It wasn't until this past year after my stroke happened and I couldn't speak that I realized what a gift it is to have your own voice, and by that, I don't just mean being able to talk. I mean being authentic, one hundred percent human. Round and not square. The three of you never really got to know me as a woman. You only saw me on stage. I was too stupid and afraid of looking frail to give you the tender parts and I've been in a lot of pain now that I realize it was me, all along, who kept me from you."

The next word comes out all wrong. "Di di di da." Dammit. I had been doing so well. I take a moment to just run my tongue across my teeth.

"It's okay, Mama," says Karen. "Take a break. Sip this water."

I don't want to sip any water so I don't take the cup she offers. Instead, I imagine my lips wrapping around the letters like the therapists instructed me to do and try again.

My heart is racing. This is next to impossible. But I continue to read this letter to my children. The words come out more clearly this time.

"Did you know my first time wearing red in public was when I attended Frog's funeral? Had you noticed? My father had told me it was a color reserved only for whores and prostitutes. My mother beat me until I bled when she caught me experimenting with rouge fingernail polish when I was a teenager."

"Is she crying?" One of them asks. I don't know who.

I hadn't even realized my cheeks were wet. I wipe my face with the back of my hand.

"Oh, Mama." That was Tessa. "Here," she says as she hands me a paper towel that had been wrapped around her wine glass. It's already wet from condensation.

I want to read more but it's hard for me for two reasons. The first is because Camilla wrote most of this and her b's really do look like d's. It's confusing. The second is because my heart is so full. Each time I try to read the next word on the page, I stutter.

"It was my first act of defiance, and I hadn't even realized what I had been trying to resist. But I owe an apology to all of you. I know that one of the hardest things to do in life is build something sturdy without having a blueprint to follow."

Just about every other word or two is coming out a little garbled, but I keep going anyway.

"I am not sorry for wanting to stay in Derbyshire instead of living with you because you are all still young women who need to have lives of your own and not have your mother get in your way. I'm afraid I've done enough of that, already."

"Mama, you don't have to do this. I love you," Karen says as she throws her arms around my neck.

I put the paper down. The words on the page sound cornier and rehearsed when I read them out loud than they do on paper. I don't need it to say what I want to say.

"I love you, too," comes out of my mouth perfectly.

Nobody else says anything so I keep talking to Karen, who is the one who looks the most interested.

"You aren't the first woman to get pregnant under some less-than-favorable circumstances, and you will not be the last. Hell, I think almost all women have had a similar experience at some point in their lives. Welcome to America."

She smiles and nods her head. I turn my body so I can face Tessa.

"Tessa, I like the fact that you have standards, but I don't want you to be so hard on people that you end up alone. Nobody has everything. Not even you. So stop expecting perfection from folks. I don't want you to be lonely. You are really too classy and smart to act as ghetto as you do. I did not raise you to be like that."

"Okay, Mama. I know."

"And another thing. Please stop looking for love in the crotch of men's pants. You'll never find it there."

"Aw, man. Are you sure?" she asks, teasingly.

I take the paper towel she gave me, ball it up, and throw it at her. She is her daddy's child.

Patricia is still playing with her jewelry, so I follow her eyes down to her hands and start talking to the charm on her bracelet.

"Patricia, I am very proud of you, just the way you are right now at this very minute. You might not be biologically mine, but I love you just the same. I have always loved you. And so has your other mother. I don't care if you get back with Gary or not, just as long as you are happy. You don't have to have a husband to prove anything to anybody. You are already a first-class act."

She looks up at me. For the first time, I realize she has my eyes. Maybe it's true what they say about children looking like whoever feeds them. I want to keep talking before I lose the nerve. I'm not pronouncing these words perfectly, but the girls seem to understand everything I'm saying.

"Please, baby, know that it's okay to forgive people, too. Doing that doesn't make you weak, as long as you keep your own voice! Believe me."

Tessa snatches the paper off my lap and reads the remainder of the letter out loud.

"I forgive y'all for not inviting me on the damn trip to the Bahamas. You can stop tip-toeing around it now and just make sure you bring me back something pretty. And now that you know all my heart's secrets, can you please start taking me to the hair salon every two or three weeks? Have I earned that yet? I still like to look pretty. There are some handsome widowers who come to visit on Sundays, and I hate for them to see me not looking my best.

"P.S. I almost forgot. Please ask the nurses at Derbyshire Manor to consider moving me to the East Wing. There is a woman across the hallway from me named Alice who is entirely too nosy."

Tessa picks up the same piece of paper towel that we've been throwing back and forth and touches my mouth with it. "Open up, Mama," she says. "You have lipstick on your teeth."

That's the only trouble with red lipstick. You can be so convinced you're looking fabulous while wearing it only to find out that if you smiled too wide or cried too hard then it got smudged across your teeth and left you looking more like a clown than a vixen or a maverick. I open my mouth and lean my head back, allowing my youngest daughter to wipe it off.

Karen, upon watching us, begins to cry for the second time. Tessa cries for the first. I cry for the one hundredth.

Patricia gets up off the floor, goes into the kitchen, and picks up the telephone. After a few seconds, I hear her saying hi to Camilla. She stays in the kitchen, talking on that telephone, for a very long time.

* * *

The scenery I observe during our drive to the Atlanta airport is different from what I remember. They've built up so much around Camp Creek that it hardly feels like the same place where deer would jump out in front of your car and smash up your windshield if you drove over 55 mph. There seems to be a brand new neighborhood on every corner and none of them look cheap. When Camilla pulls up to the familiar orange and tan airport, I can hardly believe the changes. There's even a sign that says you have to get on Interstate 75 in order to get to an International Terminal.

Patricia is first to hop out of the car. She's wearing some tight jeans and a white button-down shirt with some cowboy boots and a cowboy hat with a red bandana tied around it. I wonder if she got confused and thought she was going to a rodeo in the Midwest instead of a Carnival Cruise to the Bahamas, but I don't ask. When she opens up the front passenger door and bends down to hug me, I peck her on the lips.

Tessa is wearing a beautiful dress that has purple and blue swirls everywhere. She looks good in it but it's too tight and shows too much cleavage. I understand they're going to the Caribbean but I can't help but wonder if she won't freeze to death on the airplane first. She reaches over the seat and squeezes my shoulder before hopping out of the car. When she passes my window, I thump her on the butt and watch it jiggle.

Karen is fumbling with tickets and takes forever to look up and bid me and Camilla farewell, but when she does, I take a second just to admire her beauty. Pregnancy has put a glow on her face like nobody would imagine, and thank God she finally took out those hideous weaves, slapped a perm in her head, and got it cut into a bob. The red pocketbook slung over her shoulder is huge and beautiful. She hugs me so tight my breasts hurt, but I don't dare pull away from her until she lets go first.

Dear Reader,

I hope you've enjoyed reading this book as much as I've enjoyed writing it for you.

While *The Trouble with Red Lipstick* is completely fiction, I keep hearing that many of the situations and conversations that occur in this book ring true for many of its readers. After all, mother-daughter relationships can be so complex (loud sigh). Feel free to leave a book review wherever you purchased it or drop me a line at my website thekjdixonexperience.com and tell me if you agree.

I look forward to hearing from you soon.

Sincerely yours,

K.J. Dixon

More Great Reads from Booktrope

Running Secrets **by Arleen Williams** (Women's Contemporary Fiction) Flight attendant Chris Stevens is bent on self-destruction until she meets Gemi Kemmal, an Ethiopian home healthcare provider. Together the women learn that racial identity is a choice, self expression is a right, and family is a personal construct.

Who Killed 'Tom Jones'? **by Gale Martin** (Women's Contemporary Fiction) When a leading contestant in a Tom Jones Tribute Festival is murdered, a smart but lonely twenty-something is determined to catch the killer and find lasting love.

Double Album **by Mary Rowen** (Women's Fiction Collection) This genre-defining collection explores the complex–and often maddening–influence of music in the lives of two very different women. Includes the novels *Leaving the Beach* and *Living by Ear*.

A Thirty-Something Girl **by Lisa M. Gott** (Women's Fiction) A Thirty-Something Girl is a story about the power of human resilience, the importance of friendships, and the magic of true love.

Would you like to read more books like these?
Subscribe to **runawaygoodness.com**, get a free ebook for signing up, and never pay full price for an ebook again.

Discover more books and learn about our
new approach to publishing at **booktrope.com**.

Made in the USA
Charleston, SC
20 November 2015